Dearly
Unbeloved

By Sophie Snow

Dearly Unbeloved

SOPHIE SNOW

For the days I couldn't get out of bed. For the days I still can't.

For the scars, and the tears, and the nights I hoped I wouldn't wake up the next morning.

For the sixteen-year-old who fought to survive, even though she really didn't want to. And the thirty-year-old who's still fighting, but is so grateful she's still around.

This one's for me.

Author's Note

Dearly Unbeloved is a work of fiction and is not intended to be used as an educational tool. The sexual acts described in Dearly Unbeloved are not intended to be used as a guide. Please always do plenty of research and have clear discussions of consent before trying anything new.

In Dearly Unbeloved, Rose struggles with depression and self-harm. We're used to seeing self-harm in the form of physical scars, but there are many ways to self-harm that are not only not as obvious, but aren't seen as a concern until it's too late. Things like over-exercising, over-working, substance abuse, isolating yourself, and more. Self-harm can take many forms, and it can be difficult to see the behavior for what it is while you're in it.

If you, or someone you know, is struggling with mental health, please seek support. You can find a list of mental health helplines by country at www.findahelpline.com

Content Warnings

Dearly Unbeloved is an adult novel that features explicit content and some topics that may be triggering for some readers. The following is a list of topics featured in Dearly Unbeloved:

Alcohol, antidepressants, anxiety, body insecurity, body shaming, depression, difficult parental relationships, discussions of infertility (side characters,) divorce, explicit language, explicit sexual content (bondage, collaring, face sitting, fingering, leashing, nipple play, oral sex, pillow humping, praise, public sex, sex toys, spanking, tribbing, vaginal penetration,) explosion, family pressure, fatphobia, hospitals, injury, medication, narcissistic parent, nightmares, no contact family, overstimulation, pregnancy (side characters,) racism, racist micro-aggressions, self harm, therapy, vomiting, weed.

You can read about these content warnings in more detail at www.sophiesnowbooks.com.

Previously in Seattle...

Although all of the books in the Spicy in Seattle series can be read as standalones, you'll meet the characters from the previous books in Dearly Unbeloved, and I thought it might be helpful for us all to have a catch up!

In **Legally Binding**, we met **Maggie Burlington**, the people-pleasing personal assistant to business lawyer **Cal Michaelson**. After six years of working together, Maggie and Cal run into each other at a sex club, and start to see each other in a whole new light. Maggie and Cal spend Legally Binding navigating their feelings for each other, their 28 year age gap, and their own personal issues—most importantly, Maggie's parents, who have essentially used her as free labor and their personal bank to run their cafe. As you'd expect with a romance book, they figure it out and live happily ever after!

As part of their happily ever after, Maggie and Cal get married! Which brings us to…

False Confidence, which starts with a bang as Maggie's best friend, **Jazz Cannon**, and Cal's son, **Liam Michaelson**

(who's been obsessed with Jazz since the second he laid eyes on her), hook up at the wedding. But Jazz hasn't had an orgasm in ten years, and fakes it. A few months later, after they hook up and Jazz fakes it again, Liam finds out she can't come and offers to help her get there. *Such* a gentleman. It turns out, Jazz's inability to orgasm has everything to do with how out of touch with her own feelings she is, thanks to the pressure her parents have put on her and her siblings. Liam helps her open up, and orgasm, and, after a lot of ups and downs, they get their happy ending. Everyone's happy ending looks a little different, and Jazz and Liam's looks like a Halloween party that's actually a surprise wedding, two months after they start dating—Rose and Sierra aren't the only ones with an unconventional wedding!

I love to sprinkle in little hints or future books, and you'll find plenty here for book four in the Spicy in Seattle series, Xander and Kami's book. And while I've got you, here's a little tease for their book: the title is both a Taylor Swift song title, and an object...

Enjoy!

CHAPTER ONE

Rose

I'm going to kill my roommate.

My knuckles are white, gripping the papers I went out of my way to have printed—because who has a printer at home anymore—ahead of my job review. Sure, I could've just shown up with the stats I painstakingly put together, outlining my time at SEALAB on my laptop or tablet, but I'm trying to look as professional as possible.

It's hard to do that with Sierra's scribbles all over the back of the paper. She's infuriating. How many times have I asked her nicely (ish) not to write the answers to the stupid radio quiz she's obsessed with on my shit? And how many times has she blatantly ignored me and grabbed whatever paper was closest? This is the last thing I need right now.

I rub the ink helplessly with my thumb. God forbid Sierra have the foresight to grab an erasable pen from the penholder on the kitchen counter.

"Rose? Are you ready?" Lisa, my boss, is smiling at me from her office doorway.

Lisa's office is… homey. Like the kind of soft, comfy

living room I thought only existed in sitcoms growing up, because my parents wouldn't know homey if it slapped them in the face. She has a scuffed oak desk with a white leather office chair, but she sits on the squishy gray sectional. I look between the couch and her desk.

"I like to keep reviews informal," Lisa says, patting the seat beside her. "We're just catching up."

I perch on the edge of the couch, awkwardly crossing my legs at the ankles. *Informal*. I didn't prepare for informal. "That sounds perfect." The lie is like lead on my tongue.

It's been a little over a year and a half since I dropped out of med school, crushing my parents' dreams of having a doctor for a daughter. In school, I always preferred the practical work, and after an internship at SEALAB, an innovative lab focused on researching low-cost solutions for infectious diseases, I fell in love with the work and the atmosphere. I've never been a people person, and the lab is the perfect place for me to put my head down and work on my own.

I don't have the fancy title my parents have been dreaming of since I first showed an interest in science when I was three, but I've never been more professionally content. And at least I'm not wasting the double major in biology and chemistry I spent four years exhausting myself over.

"I can't believe you've been with us for eighteen months already! Time really flies, doesn't it? How are you finding things?" Lisa asks, and I take a deep breath as I smooth the papers over my lap, scribbled side down.

The job is great. The money is… fine. It could be worse, but Seattle isn't a cheap city, and I'm desperate to get a place of my own. I love my apartment, but the company is less than ideal. My parents kicked me out when I left med school, and I thought I'd struck gold when my sister told me her assistant, Sierra, was looking for a roommate. In reality, it's been fucking awful. Sierra is impossible to live with, and I need to get out.

But for that, I need a raise, which means I need a promotion. And I just so happen to know that one of the team supervisors is leaving Seattle next year. Though her job hasn't officially been posted, everyone is talking about it. I may not be the chattiest, but I listen.

SEALAB favors internal candidates, and based on when she's leaving, it looks like they'll be hiring to fill her job in around three months. Which means if I want the job—and god, I want it—I have to put my best foot forward now.

Lisa listens as I talk her through my first eighteen months, the highs, the lows, and the steps I've taken to work past them. The proof is in the stats: I've excelled at SEALAB. I know I'm the most efficient person on the team. I know I'm the most dedicated. I regularly work unpaid overtime without being asked, and I'm always the first one in the lab. If anyone needs someone to step in and cover them, I'm there. When new people join the team, I spend time with them, giving them tips and tricks. I even stay late every time the team has after-work drinks planned, so they can leave early. Of course, I could always do more, but my results speak for themselves.

"Wow, Rose. What a year and a half you've had," she

says with a wide smile. Lisa has to be around my mom's age, but her smile is a lot softer. Probably because my mom is surrounded by sycophants who act like getting older is the worst thing in the world, so she's spent a small fortune to make sure she doesn't look a day over forty.

My mom is beautiful, and I love her, but sometimes I wish I'd gotten to know my parents before their business took off. Back when they were just Alex and Lilia Cannon, living in a rundown two-bedroom house in Marysville comfortably, but not excessively. But it's easy to think that way when you've grown up as privileged as I have—I've never wanted for anything. My parents might not have given out much love, but I've had a more comfortable life than most.

"Thanks, Lisa. I've really enjoyed all the projects we've worked on," I say, setting the papers down on my lap again. "I've learned a lot and really pushed myself."

"I can tell. You're a real asset to the team, and it hasn't gone unnoticed. We appreciate all the hard work you've put in."

Her smile is warm and genuine, pushing me to sit up straighter, and untangling some of the *what if I'm not good enough?* knots in my chest. Of course I'm good enough. I'm Rose Charlotte Cannon, and my parents might not have hugged me growing up, but they taught me to succeed. I've got this.

"I've been happy to do it," I reply, projecting as much confidence as I can.

"Glad to hear it. Now, usually in reviews, this is when we talk about things you'd like to work on over the next year. You included a lot of that in your recap, and I think everything you're working toward is achievable. It sounds like you have a good idea of how to get there, but let me know if you need help with anything. Is there anything else you'd like to work toward? I know we talked about us helping you get your master's if that was something you wanted to do. Generally, that's a benefit we reserve for two years of service, but given how dedicated you've been this year, we can look at bringing that forward if it's something you'd like to do."

Oh. I wasn't expecting that. Getting my master's is the next logical step in my education, but I don't know if I'm ready to put myself through school again. I still wake up in a panic some days, thinking I've forgotten an assignment.

My hesitation must show, because understanding dawns on Lisa's face. "There's no rush to decide," she assures me. "I just want you to know you have the option."

"Thank you. I'll definitely think about it." I clear my throat. "Actually, there is something I wanted to talk about working toward."

Lisa gestures for me to go on, her expression nothing short of encouraging, but the mention of going back to school has derailed me.

I take a deep breath. "I heard Kayleigh is going home to England next year and there's going to be a supervisor position available. I'd love to be considered."

The change on Lisa's face is minute, but her brows lift a fraction, her eyes just slightly widening in surprise. It's gone as soon as I notice it, but it's enough for my stomach to sink.

"That is something we're going to be looking at over the next couple of months. Though I must admit, I'm surprised you're interested." She doesn't sound put off by the idea, at least.

"I hoped my work over the past year would show how dedicated I am." I hug the papers to my chest. "I really love working here."

"Oh, Rose. No one would doubt your dedication. You put in more hours than anyone else, even when you don't need to. But there's more to being in a supervisory position than the work side of things."

I try not to show how confused I am, but my eyebrows pull together of their own accord. "Like what?"

Lisa's lips twitch, and I get the feeling she's trying not to laugh. She leans forward with a reassuring smile. "We're a close-knit team here. As far as research labs go, we're pretty small and, although we pride ourselves on our work, it's also important to us to have a comfortable and friendly culture. Most labs I've worked at over the years have been brutal, just work, work, work. It's soul crushing."

"Right. I've never felt uncomfortable here." A new worry hits me at full force. "Oh no. Am *I* making people uncomfortable?"

"No, not at all," Lisa replies quickly. Thank god. "But you're not immersed in the team. I don't think anyone here knows anything about you beyond your name and how hard you work."

"And that's a problem?" I'm here to work. Why does anyone need to know anything beyond how good I am at my job?

"It's not a problem, per se. But it is important for the team to feel like they know their supervisors. Although you know nothing is mandatory, we do look for supervisors to come to our team lunches and drinks, and when we do family days. You're so focused when you're working, and you eat lunch alone, so no one ever gets the chance to get to know you," Lisa explains, and, while she's not wrong, I hadn't realized I was supposed to be socializing here.

"I thought it was more important to stay focused and get my work done," I reply slowly.

"Of course we want everyone to get their work done, but there is a social aspect to the job, too, especially in a supervisor position. You've been here for over a year, and I know the team is curious about who you are outside of work. We like celebrating together—big life events, like Angie getting engaged last year. Things like that, you know?"

Any hope of getting this promotion fades as her words sink in. I'm a hard worker, I'm good at doing what I'm told and going above and beyond in a work capacity. But I'm not good with people, and it's not like I've got anything like Angie's engagement to share anyway.

My older siblings got all the social skills in our family; there were none left by the time I came along. My brother, Xander, is the picture of charisma, a miniature version of our dad—but less of a dick. My sister, Jazz, is an extrovert to the extreme. She thrives on being around people and can strike up a conversation with anyone, anywhere. And then there's me.

I tried to mimic other people in school, watching them form friendships and connections, and I did a good job of faking it, but it's never come naturally to me. And the older I get, the more exhausting I find it.

Could I pretend long enough to get promoted? Maybe. What comes after, though? I don't want to come to work every day and tire myself out by putting on a mask. But if that's what it takes, maybe I'll have to.

"The social side of things has never been my strong suit," I admit, and Lisa nods, seemingly unsurprised.

"I understand. And it can be hard to push yourself out of your comfort zone with things like that, but it would be nice to get to know you, Rose."

"Right. That's definitely something I can work on."

I wish I was doing something wrong professionally. Not working fast enough? Work faster. Not doing enough? Show up earlier. Not doing things perfectly? Do better. Fixing a glaring personality issue that I've had since birth is significantly trickier. But I'm not a quitter. And I don't actually have to change anything; I just have to lie my ass off.

I paste a forced smile on my face, and while Lisa doesn't look particularly optimistic, she looks somewhat reassured.

"Perfect. Well, I look forward to getting to know you better. We're doing drinks after work on Friday if you'd be interested?"

Shit. "Oh, um, I'm actually going to Vegas this weekend, so I'm taking leave on Friday," I say, cursing Jazz for booking a girls' weekend, and for forcing me to come.

"That sounds fun. You'll need to tell us all about it when you get back!" Lisa replies, leading me toward the door. *Why does that sound like a threat?* "Maybe next—are those the answers to this morning's *Monika and Cleo In the Morning* quiz?"

I still as I realize I'm accidentally holding the papers answer-side out. So much for professional. But Lisa looks more excited than disappointed. "They are," I confirm. Sierra is obsessed with the morning show and listens to it every day while she's getting ready for work, but I don't pay much attention, so I'm screwed if Lisa asks me about it. "But they're not mine." Lisa's face falls. Fuck. Why couldn't I just pretend?

I mentally kick myself, and that's the only thing to blame for what slips out of my mouth next: "They're my fiancée's. She loves Monika and Cleo."

Lisa stops in her tracks, her face lighting up. "You're engaged? Oh, congratulations, Rose! We had no idea." Well, they wouldn't, considering it's a boldfaced lie. This is *not* the kind of pretending I had in mind. Shit.

"Sorry," I offer with a feigned guilty look. "We've been keeping it quiet. Our families are both big wedding families, but we want something small. An elopement." *Why the fuck did I say that?*

Lisa's eyes widen. "Oh my god, is that why you're going to Vegas this weekend?" I don't know what in the world possesses me to nod, but I feel my head rising and falling before I can stop it. "That's so exciting!"

Lisa leans against the doorframe and, like it or not, I'm in the lie now. "So, tell me all about her. What's her name?"

"Sierra," I answer before I can bite the word back. "Her name is Sierra Hayashi, and she's... amazing."

The lie tastes like acid on my tongue.

CHAPTER TWO

Sierra

Quit touching my stuff. Surely you have enough of your own considering it's taking over the apartment. – R

KYO

You've been thirty for two months, SiSi. You have less than a year left. I love how optimistic you are, but it might be time to just accept you're not getting the money.

Guilt and frustration curdle in my stomach. I sit back, kicking my legs up on the couch as I consider my reply.

A year's a year. Have a little faith, Kyo. ;)

My brother replies with an eye roll emoji, but he quickly follows it up with a message that tugs on my heart.

You know how much I love you, right? I really appreciate you trying so hard to do this for us, but if you can't make it happen, it's okay.

I know, I love you too. And it's going to happen.

If anyone can do it, you can.

I toss my phone on the couch and rub my face, groaning. What a clusterfuck.

My brother and I never met our maternal grandparents —they died when our mom was still in college—but that hasn't stopped them from stressing us from beyond the grave. We knew we had an inheritance to look forward to growing up, but our parents never explained the strings attached until Kyo and I were teenagers: we couldn't claim a penny until we turned thirty, and we had to be married before they would release the inheritance. If we hit thirty-one unwed, the money will be split between a list of charities of my grandparents' choosing.

As teenagers, we barely thought about it. We had plenty of time. But then he fell in love with two people, and as progressive as Washington is, he can't marry both of them. No amount of money in the world would have made him choose between Rylan and Lina, and he didn't seem upset by the lack of inheritance.

Until Lina got sick. She's better now, but the treatment took any chance of them conceiving naturally away. IVF is their only option, and their insurance won't cover it. If I get my inheritance, I can give them the money they need. Not getting it isn't an option.

But finding a wife in the next nine months, when I've failed for the past three years, is looking unlikely. I've met people, I've dated, and I've called every relationship off after three months. Because the more I let people in, the higher the risk of them hurting me. I keep trying, but I haven't met anyone worth getting hurt over yet.

It wouldn't be unreasonable to say I have commitment issues.

I look around the apartment and sigh. Rose is going to lose it when she gets home. I had a shitty day at work, so I stopped by my favorite flower shop on the way home and bought three bunches of fresh flowers and two plants. Considering her name, you'd think my roommate would be a little more foliage-friendly, but she hates all things green.

"They're supposed to be outside. You can keep one. Get rid of the rest," she said when she came home our first week living together and spotted the vases all around the apartment. Did I have too many? Maybe, but I couldn't have cared less if she liked them or not. I still don't, but when I refused to get rid of them, she did it for me. I came home from work the next day to find every vase empty except one —the smallest—and the rest of the flowers in the trash. There was a purple Post-it Note on the remaining vase, with Rose's perfect handwriting:

I told you to get rid of them - R

And that was the moment I realized that Rose and I would never be friends. At this point, we barely tolerate each other. The second I get my inheritance and give Kyo half, I'll be using the rest to get my own place far, far away from Rose Cannon.

Our apartment is big by Seattle standards, airy and bright, and the perfect environment for plants to flourish. Despite what Rose thinks, I try not to push her. It would be stupid to keep buying things I know she's going to throw away, so I keep my plants in my room, and stick to one flower arrangement at a time… mostly.

Not today, clearly. She can take it up with her sister if she has a problem with it—I don't want to deal with the fight today, and it's Jazz's fault I'm so tired.

Rose and I met through her sister. Jazz is the executive assistant to Cal Michaelson, the top business lawyer in the Pacific Northwest. He's also her father-in-law and her best friend's husband, but they work well together, considering they're family. I'm Jazz's assistant, and although I love my job, she's not the easiest person to work for. She's as organized as a rummage sale and, usually, we're in sync enough that it doesn't cause problems, but I've been off my game since I turned thirty and realized just how close my deadline is.

Everything I tried to do today was set back by something Jazz had forgotten to do, and by the time the end of the day came around, I was so ready to get out of the office.

I should get up, put the flowers in vases, and move the plants—and the brownies and three bags of weed gummies I bought—into my room, but I hear the jingle of Rose's keys in the door before I get the chance. Great.

She walks into the living room, and I brace myself. Her long blonde hair is thrown up in a high pony, perfectly neat considering she's spent the whole day working in a lab. Rose and Jazz are polar opposites in personality, but they share their mom's golden-hazel eyes. Rose is tall and lithe, with permanently rosy cheeks to match heart-shaped lips that spend most of their time scowling around me.

Objectively speaking, Rose Cannon is the most beautiful woman I've ever laid eyes on. It's a shame she's so fucking insufferable.

Her eyes land on the kitchen island, taking in the mess I've left behind. But instead of snapping like she usually does, she just sighs and tosses a pile of papers on the island. They come close to knocking my brownies over, but some-one, somewhere, is looking out for me.

"Stop writing your stupid quiz answers on my shit," she mutters, but there's no heat in her words. Something's rattled her. Something that isn't me, for once. I might care enough to be worried—again, if she wasn't so fucking insufferable.

But she is, and I don't care that something's bothering her. I should just take it as a win. Only one pissy comment, instead of the usual twenty-five the second she gets home, should be a relief. Especially after the day I've had. I should keep my mouth shut and take it... but I'm predisposed to snap back at this point.

"It's not a stupid quiz just because you're shit at it,

Cannon." I fully expect her to shoot daggers at me. But she doesn't. She just lifts a shoulder indifferently.

"Doing well on a pop culture quiz about celebrities and gossip I don't care about isn't exactly high on my priority list," is all she says as she opens the fridge and grabs a bottle of rosé.

She gets a glass from the cabinet and pauses in front of the island. With an inhale, she slowly pushes a pink pothos plant to the side without a word and sets the wine and the glass down.

I feel my face pull into a tight frown. "Did someone die?" I ask, standing up and hovering by the couch.

Rose raises a perfectly arched brow, unscrewing the bottle top and pulling her glass toward her. "No."

"Did you fuck up and accidentally facilitate the spread of some deadly disease?" Truthfully, I don't really understand what she does at work, but I expect that would count as a terrible day.

"No."

"Did your coworkers finally call you out for your glowing personality?" I say sarcastically, and her stony expression slips. Bingo.

A split second later, she's back to the pretentious ice queen I know and hate, just in time for her to stop the wine from overflowing. She sets the bottle down and rolls her eyes.

"Maybe I just don't want to talk to you. Oh wait, it definitely is that." She puts the half-full bottle back in the fridge and bumps it closed with her hip. "Clean this shit up," she says, and then she's gone.

"A delight, as always," I mutter under my breath as I hear her bedroom door close.

Despite Rose's one-bunch rule, I kept my vase collection when we moved in together. I like to switch them out, depending on the flowers. There's a thick layer of dust on most of them, since whoever designed this apartment thought the aesthetics of open shelving were more important than the practicality of doors, so I grab a few and set them in the sink to wash.

Usually, since I only get one bunch at a time, I buy them pre-made, but I went all out today, buying bunches of individual flowers so I could make the arrangements myself: snap dragons, lilacs, carnations, sweet peas, roses, and a bunch of mixed greenery to fill out the displays.

I hear the whirr of Rose's treadmill from her room seconds before her workout playlist blares through the apartment. Our building has a gym, but she never uses it. She runs outside before work and on her treadmill after work. Forty-five-minute runs, twice a day, every day, even on major holidays. At least her playlist is good, and I find myself humming along as I trim stems and carefully arrange the flowers.

Maybe I shouldn't have been so snippy. She's clearly had a bad day, and, as much as I'd rather not breathe the same air as her, I don't have to be an asshole. I'm not like this with anyone else. Rose just brings out the worst in me.

CHAPTER THREE

Rose

_The living room is a common space. That means I
get to put my stuff there too. I'm so sorry
for your loss. - S_

Thank god for my sister's best friend. Maggie is the most organized person I know, and knowing she's coming on this trip is the only reason I stopped protesting when Jazz told me my presence was required.

A little over four hours before our flight is due to take off, right on schedule for pick up, there's a knock at the front door. _Thank you, Maggie._

I wouldn't usually take a full day off work for an evening flight, but it took Jazz so long to confirm the flight time that it was just easier. And it's been nice to have the day to make sure I have everything ready.

It would've been nicer if Sierra hadn't also taken the day off, but I've kept out of her way. I have no idea why she chose today of all days, but her boss, Maggie's husband, Cal, pushes his employees to take Fridays off when they're not too busy. From what I can tell, he mostly does it so he can take the day off to hang out with Maggie without feeling guilty.

I open the apartment door to let them in, and Jazz skips through the doorway, Maggie following behind.

"Hey. Just let me grab my bag—I'm all packed."

"Of course you are," Jazz says with a snort, shaking her head. "I bet you were packed days ago."

"For the last time, it's normal to pack in advance," Maggie says, with an air of exasperation that tells me it's not the first time they've had this conversation this week. How Maggie and Jazz's friendship has survived for so long, I'll never understand. I love my sister, but she's complete and utter chaos. Maybe they balance each other out.

I run into my room to pick up my bag, running my gaze over everything to make sure it's in order before we leave. When I make it back to the living room, Jazz and Maggie are still bickering.

"It doesn't matter when you pack as long as you make it for last call at the airport," Jazz counters, and Maggie just sighs. "I bet Sierra's still throwing the last few things in her bag."

"I finished an hour ago, actually," Sierra says, and I spin around. She's standing at her bedroom door with a purple patterned duffel slung over her shoulder.

"Where are you going?" I ask, not surprised she hasn't told me. It's not like we keep each other apprised of our comings and goings, and I never told her I was going to

Vegas this weekend. I would've texted her from the airport so she didn't wonder if I'd died or something, but it's not like we're friends. Besides, she works with Jazz, so she probably knows all about the Vegas trip.

Sierra narrows her eyes at my bag. "Where are *you* going?"

"I asked first."

Sierra opens her mouth, presumably to snap back, but Jazz's voice cuts across us both:

"What the fuck are you talking about? We're going to Vegas."

Her words must sink into Sierra at the same moment they do me, because we both look at Jazz, then back at each other. "She's coming?" we say in perfect unison.

"We're all going!" Jazz claps her hands excitedly. "It's a girls' trip!"

I pull Jazz aside. "What the hell, Jazz? Why didn't you tell me Sierra was coming?" I ask under my breath.

"Because you wouldn't have come," she says with a shameless shrug. "And she wouldn't have come if I'd told her you were coming. This way, everyone's going."

"Why is she coming, anyway? I'm your sister. She's just your assistant." Not that my being Jazz's sister means much. We probably spend less time together than she and Sierra do. We're not close, and I was surprised by the invite in the first place.

Jazz holds up a hand, her brows drawn together. "Uh, we don't say 'just an assistant.' Cal married his assistant, remember?"

Technically, Maggie quit her job as Cal's assistant before they got together officially, but that's not important.

"You're already married, and your husband is weirdly obsessed with you. Were you planning on leaving him to run off—"

"You know I can hear you, right?" Sierra interrupts, and I have to wonder what makes her think I give a fuck if she overhears. This is going to be a long weekend.

Though Sierra and I were technically assigned adjoining seats, Cal upgraded us all to first class, so we spent the two-and-a-half-hour flight from Seattle to Vegas separated by a half-inch sheet of plastic.

Thankfully, Jazz had the foresight not to make us share a room. She and Maggie are sharing a suite, and Sierra and I have our own rooms on the same floor. I desperately needed time to myself to decompress before we head out tonight.

I planned for Jazz. I planned for Maggie. But Sierra? I can't pretend I wasn't looking forward to a whole weekend without having to deal with her. At least there's no expectation to stay sober this weekend.

My closet isn't exactly packed with Vegas-appropriate attire. I rummaged right to the back, looking through the box of clothes I haven't touched since college, but I was far from a partygoer, so it was mostly old workout clothes and sweaters with holes that I never got around to getting fixed.

After work last week, I went to the mall, walked into the

store with the most people my age milling around, and purchased three outfits exactly as they were on the mannequins. What's the point in trying to figure out what looks good when some professional has already done it?

I pull the shiny satin black skirt over my hips and half tuck in the loose button-down covered in silver sequins, exactly how it was styled in the store. The skirt is shorter than I usually wear, but if you can't risk showing your ass off in Vegas, where can you?

Knee-high black boots that I might actually wear on a regular basis complete the ensemble, and I check myself out in the mirror. My makeup is darker and smokier than I usually do it, but I'm useless with my hair. It falls down my back, in loose, slightly frizzy waves—not wavy enough to look intentional, but I've never met a curling iron I can use successfully. I sigh and grab the black clutch I bought to match all three outfits. I'll do.

The hotel is so quiet up here that you wouldn't know we were on The Strip. I get lucky with the elevators and head down to the lobby where Jazz told us to meet. I'm only a few minutes early, but naturally, I'm the first one here.

I hover by a giant, waxy plant and wait. After a moment, the soft click of heels sounds on the marble floor, and I look up. My breath catches in my throat, but I'm not happy about it.

For all her flaws, and my god, she has a lot, Sierra is… unfortunately gorgeous. Frankly, it's incredibly inconvenient.

Her long black hair is slicked back and pin-straight. I know she straightens it, I just have no idea how she gets it to look so nice. She has deep brown eyes, so dark they're almost black, wide and framed with thick lashes. Her ability to line them with a perfect cat eye every time pisses me off, but fuck, it suits her.

She's wearing a skin-tight black two-piece that shows off every curve, and a bronzed leg peeks through a thigh-high slit going up one side of her skirt. I might spend a good ninety percent of my time pissed off at her, but I have eyes. And those eyes enjoy Sierra, even if the rest of me would prefer never to see her again.

She looks me up and down and raises her brows. "Wow. This look almost makes it seem like you don't have a giant stick up your ass, Rosie."

"Charming as always. You know, I'm surprised you were able to find any clothes to pack, considering they all seem to be in that giant pile of laundry in the middle of your room," I volley back.

"It was hard, but I managed," Sierra replies sarcastically. "Oh, I borrowed your laundry detergent, by the way. Sorry." The sly smile on her lips tells me she's not sorry at all, and I take a deep breath, trying not to let her get a rise out of me.

We're less than ten minutes from liquor. In a half hour, I'll be buzzed enough to forget about Sierra and how socially awkward I am, so I can find someone equally tipsy on the—inevitably sticky—dance floor. With how busy work's been keeping me lately, I've been in a bit of a dry spell.

Seattle has a lot of amazing queer and lesbian bars and clubs, but I'm better online than in person, and trying to find women who are interested in hooking up on apps is harder than it sounds.

I looked up the club we're going to tonight, and it seems to be pretty queer-friendly. And sure, a girls' trip with my sister isn't an ideal place to meet women, but Jazz won't care if I disappear for a while. We don't all have obsessed spouses to go home to every night. Some of us are forced to go home to the worst fucking roommates.

Not tonight, though. Thank god.

CHAPTER FOUR

Sierra

What part of one bouquet at a time don't you get?
If I wanted to live in a garden, I would. - R

She's pissing me off, and she's nowhere near me. I recognize that it's not rational, but every single thing she does gets under my skin. It's impossible to relax and enjoy myself when she's around.

She laughs at something Jazz says, and I think about the passive-aggressive neon pink sticky note she stuck on the fridge last week, reminding me to finish the open carton of oat milk before opening another one. She takes a sip of her espresso martini, and I think about her complaining that my shoes by the door are ever so slightly out of the perfect line she demands. She leans on the bar with a flirty smile and puts her hand on the arm of a gorgeous redhead, and I... I just don't like it.

I throw back the dregs of my tequila sour and tap the tablet fixed to the table to order another. This is arguably the most dangerous club I've ever been in, since it's so easy to order repeat drinks, but our flight home tomorrow isn't until the evening, so what the hell.

A trip to Vegas isn't exactly my dream getaway. I like the odd party, but I'm not a shots and flashing lights kind of girl. A night at home with a gummy and a bottle of wine is more my thing.

But I love hanging out with Jazz and Maggie. Most people aren't close enough to their boss—and their boss's boss, I suppose—that they get invited on girls' trips and to family dinners, and, as someone who isn't used to having friends, it's taken a little getting used to.

I usually skip things when I know Rose is going, and I know Jazz has noticed. Which is definitely why she didn't tell me Rose was coming on this trip. There's not a snowball's chance in hell I'd have come.

I might loathe Rose, but I know how much Jazz has been trying to build a relationship with her over the past couple of years, since their parents kicked Rose out. I'm not trying to come between that.

The past couple of days haven't been so bad, though—loathing aside. Rose and I have avoided each other as much as possible, something we're both pretty good at after living together for a year. I've taken it easy on the alcohol, all too aware that we're going back to work the day after tomorrow—but watching Rose flirt across the club has chipped away at my willpower.

A server arrives with my tequila sour, and I drain it instantly. They raise an eyebrow, and I can't tell if they're impressed or concerned.

"Thirsty?"

"Something like that." I look out at the dance floor, spying a flash of Jazz's fiery hair as she spins around with Maggie. "I'm going to dance," I say, my blood already feeling a little fizzy from the shock of the tequila.

The server just chuckles and plucks the empty glass from my hand. "Enjoy."

Jazz squeals when she spots me wading onto the dance floor. She grabs me, twirling me, and then pulling me into a bone-crushing hug.

"SiSi! You're here!" she shouts with a wide grin. Oh, she's so wasted.

"I'm here," I reply, laughing and letting the pounding beat guide my body. Maggie wraps her arms around me from behind and tugs me away from Jazz, the three of us dancing and singing along to the music. We might dance for hours, for all I know.

At some point, Maggie disappears and returns to press plastic cups into our hands, and I don't even ask what's in it before I drink—straight whiskey.

I swallow it down, spluttering. "Holy shit, Maggie."

"I remember when you used to drink fruity little cocktails. Cal changed you," Jazz groans, swiping her hand over her mouth and smudging her lipstick.

"*Cal.*" Maggie sighs in a way that can only be described as dreamy.

I try not to laugh, but there's too much liquor in my system to hold it back. I'm punished immediately—my throat is still burning from the whiskey, and I choke on the laugh. Jazz whacks me on the back, but Maggie checked out the second she mentioned Cal's name and doesn't notice.

"I think I'm going to call him. You want to come with and call Liam?" she asks Jazz, who throws her hands up, sloshing the last dribble of whiskey in her cup all over herself.

"It's girls' night!" I protest. "No boys allowed."

The song transitions into a throwback I remember from high school, one I know Jazz loves, but she doesn't notice. "I hate to be that person when I'm here having fun with my girls, but I miss Liam." She doesn't say it so much as whine it, gripping my forearm like a vise.

I carefully detach her fingers. It's hard to be mad at them when I love them and their husbands. Besides, they've done well to make it this far, and I won't be sorry to leave the club and not have to see Rose anymore. "Let's go back to the hotel, and you can call your men."

Jazz's hazel eyes, so similar to Rose's, light up. "Are you thinking what I'm thinking?" She raises an eyebrow, and I shrug. "Phone sex."

Nope. Not drunk enough for this.

"Believe it or not, I, a lesbian, was not thinking about having phone sex with your husband."

"He's really good at it."

"I believe you."

"Yeah, I don't need to hear about Liam's phone sex skills. Let's go," Maggie says with a shudder.

Jazz purses her lips. "What about Rose?"

I nod toward the bar, where she's still standing with the redhead. It's not that I've been keeping tabs on her, I've just been… conscious of her location. "She's fine. She's with someone." She's wearing a white sparkly dress tonight, with long sleeves and a ruffled hem. It has a deep V-neck that stops right above her belly button, and I hate how good she looks in it.

Before I have time to blink, Jazz is dragging us over to her. "Rosie!" she shouts loudly enough that at least a dozen people look in our direction. Including Rose, who seems surprisingly laid back—until she sees who Jazz is dragging behind her, anyway. She spies me, and her lips settle into a thin line.

"We're going back to the hotel so I can have phone sex with Liam," Jazz says matter-of-factly, and entirely too loudly.

"Great," Rose replies, looking a little nauseated. "I'm going to hang out here with Allie,"—she nods to the redhead—"but I'll see you in the morning."

Jazz turns to look at me, eyes narrowed. "You should stay, too."

"No," Rose and I both say in unison. So rare for us to be on the same page—I should take a picture.

"Stay. Enjoy yourself," Jazz insists. "Do you have any hot friends?" she asks Allie.

"I can do better than that," Allie replies with a laugh. "Hey, Court. Get over here."

An identical redhead sidles up beside her. Twins. Shit, I might be too drunk for this.

"This is my twin, Courtney. Court, this is…" She trails off, looking at me expectantly.

"Sierra," I say. "Hi."

"Hi, Sierra. You look like my kind of fun." Courtney grins at me. She's gorgeous—they both are—but I really would rather head back to the hotel. "Let's get some shots."

I look up and see fire on Rose's face. She's pissed I'm even considering staying, and that's good enough for me. I smile back at Courtney. "Shots sound perfect."

CHAPTER FIVE

Rose

*I'm so sorry, Rosie! I must have missed the part
where I have to listen to what you say! - S*

W hy is the wind screaming? And so warm, and close to my face and... I force my eyes open and realize I'm smooshed against the pillow. It's not the wind; my own breath is just so fucking loud.

Everything hurts. A crushing ache spreads from the very top of my skull, shooting down my body as I peel myself away from the pillow, groaning. My mouth feels like it's full of dust and tastes like bad decisions. I sit up, my arm flopping uselessly to the side, hitting something that feels suspiciously like hair. I'm alert enough for it to scare me, but too hungover to do anything but shriek, flail, and immediately see stars because I moved too quickly.

"What the fuck?"

For the first time, Sierra's voice actually calms me

down. At least she's not a stranger who's likely to murder me.

"Why are you in my room?" Her voice is scratchy and deep.

"This is my room." Although the rooms in the hotel are more or less identical, I can tell this is mine because the floor isn't covered in clothes.

When I wrench my head around to look at Sierra, her black hair is a knotted mess. But that's not what knocks the breath from my chest. She's lying face down on top of the covers, wearing nothing but black underwear. I drop my chin, looking down at myself. Unlike Sierra, I'm tucked under the thin hotel blanket, but I'm also sans clothing.

"Sierra."

"What?"

"Why are we basically naked?"

Sierra turns her head and cracks her eyes. Fake lashes I didn't even notice her wearing last night are barely hanging on. I hold the blanket tight to my chest as she runs her gaze over me, her expression pained, like she's trying to wrack her memory.

"We probably were so wasted last night that we just stripped off and climbed into bed. It's no big deal," she says dismissively.

"You don't think we—"

"Definitely not." Her voice is firmer. She sits up, folding her arms across her chest. I try not to look, but how did I not know about the tattoo covering her sternum? A detailed black snake winds its way down her skin, wrapped around a thorny rose. It starts between her breasts and stops right above her belly button. "If we had, I'd be able to tell. I'm always calmer the day after a good orgasm."

I raise a brow. Or I try to, anyway. My eyes are so fucking dry that even the tiniest movement hurts like hell. What was I thinking, falling asleep with my contacts in?

"Nice to know no matter what you think of me, you believe I'd give you a good orgasm," I reply sarcastically.

"I mean, if you didn't, I'd have done it myself. I don't care about your feelings enough to fake it."

"Of course you don't."

Since she's lying on top of the covers, I grab a pillow to shield myself before trying to stand up. But before both of my feet are solidly on the ground, Sierra grabs my hand and tugs me back down.

"Ouch. What the—"

"What the fuck is that?"

She's gripping my left hand firmly, and when I look down, my stomach drops. A plain silver band with a clear, glittering oval stone is hanging out on my ring finger, where it definitely doesn't belong.

I swear Sierra is moving in slow motion as she drops her left hand from her chest and holds it beside mine. Her ring is gold and more ornate, with a rich purple pear-shaped stone surrounded by a halo of tiny dark blue, sparkling stones.

Sierra snatches her hand back. "Shit. I'm going to be sick."

She rushes to the bathroom, and I perch on the edge of the bed as I listen to her retching. The nice thing to do would be to keep an eye on her or offer to hold her hair back, but she doesn't sound like she's choking or anything. She'll survive.

I take a closer look at the ring. It looks expensive—more expensive than I'd expect for a potential drunken wedding. Fuck. I don't do this kind of thing. Hell, no one actually does this kind of thing. There's no way it's real. I don't remember anything after Jazz and Maggie left last night, but there's not a chance in the world Sierra and I got married. Not for real, anyway.

My head spins as I cross the room and push open the curtains, inspecting the stone in the sunlight. It shines suspiciously diamond-like, and something tells me I probably don't want to check my credit card statement anytime soon.

Sierra steps out of the bathroom wearing a robe—my robe—and wiping the sleeve over her mouth. She stops short, taking me in, and I realize I'm still only wearing underwear. My dress from last night is folded neatly on the chair by the window. Sierra's is crumpled by the side of the bed she was sleeping on. Both of them are covered in glitter, and if something scratchy touches my skin right now, I'm going to die.

I walk past Sierra and open the closet, my fingers closing around my favorite sleep shirt. It's usually a comfort to feel the soft cotton falling over my body, but I'm pretty sure there's nothing in the world that I'd find comforting at this point. I close the closet door and lean against it, clearing my throat.

"It's not legal, right? Like, you can't just *get married.* There are processes and stuff you have to follow. You can't just show up the night of and do the damn thing."

Sierra crosses her arms and glares at me. "Why are you looking at me like I should know that? I have no idea."

"You work at a law firm. And didn't you go to law school?"

"I flunked out of law school! Which is why I'm an assistant to the assistant of a *business* lawyer. In Washington. Believe it or not, Nevada marital law doesn't come up much."

I cover my face with my hands. She's so goddamn loud. "Could you maybe shout a little louder?" I mutter and hold up a hand when I hear her sharp intake of breath, presumably readying for another rant. "We have to stay calm so we can figure this out."

"Given what Vegas is known for, I think it's safe to assume that you can just get married on a whim here," she says, more quietly, after a moment. "Whether that means it's legal, I don't know. I assume if it was, we'd have paperwork or something."

She looks around, presumably for the paperwork, but aside from my dress on the chair, hers on the floor, and our shoes in a pile by the door, there's nothing out of order.

With a sigh, I yank open the closet again and crouch down to type the code into the safe.

Sierra hovers behind me. "I know you like things in their proper place, but do you really think you'd go to the effort of putting something in the safe when you were blackout drunk?"

The safe beeps and swings open and, sure enough, even blackout drunk, I'm still me. Me enough to make sure important documents go in the safe—not me enough to make sure I don't get fucking married in Vegas, apparently.

I grab the folder and hand it to Sierra, not sure I could actually read with my dry-ass contacts in. I can make out the giant pink letters on the outside of the wallet of documents, though:

Congratulations Mrs. & Mrs.!

Sierra blows out a long breath. "Well, at least they're inclusive, I suppose."

"Sierra," I groan.

She ignores my exasperation and flips the wallet open. A purple poker chip flies out and rolls across the carpet, stopping when it hits my foot. I bend down, the room spinning, and pick it up as she scans what appears to be an information sheet.

"It says here that our official marriage certificate will be mailed to us within ten business days, but there's a temporary one in here until then." She leafs through the papers and pulls out the temporary certificate, listing two brides: *Sierra Kimiko Hayashi and Rose Charlotte Cannon, married on August 21st, at Dearly Beloved Chapel in Las Vegas, Nevada.*

Shit.

Sierra sits on the bed, dropping the paperwork on the nightstand and pressing her palms into her eyes.

I sit on the other side, trying to force the wave of panic threatening me to recede. Panic isn't going to get us anywhere. I unclench my palm, inspecting the poker chip.

Dearly Beloved is printed across the center in a pretty silver script, and there's a magnet stuck on the back. As far as tacky Vegas wedding favors go, I can think of worse, I suppose.

Sierra eyes it, and I drop it into her palm. She reads it and laughs, the sound mirthless. "More like dearly *un*beloved. How the fuck did this happen?"

"I'm pretty sure 'shots sound perfect' might have something to do with it."

She whirls on me, her eyes narrowed. "Are you seriously blaming *me* for this? I didn't force you to drink, and I didn't force you to sign the fucking marriage license. This is as much on you as it is on me." She laughs, the sound humorless and sharp. "I guess Little Miss Perfect can fuck up like the rest of us mere mortals. Who knew?"

Her words sting, but I can't let her see that. Mask firmly in place, I roll my eyes—ouch—and ignore her comment. "Pass me my phone so I can figure out how we can undo this."

Sierra grabs my phone from the nightstand and all but tosses it at me. It's clinging on for dear life, but eight percent should be enough charge to find what I need to. This has to be a common issue here.

Sure enough, one quick Google search later, and I have the details for a nearby twenty-four-hour annulment service. For five hundred dollars, we just have to show up and wait to be seen, and someone will put an end to this whole ordeal for us.

Sierra goes to her room and we both get dressed quickly, determined to get out of the hotel before we're spotted by Jazz or Maggie. If all goes to plan, my sister never needs to know that I accidentally married her assistant. Because if Jazz finds out, everyone will find out. She's a pro at keeping her own secrets, but no one else's are safe.

I meet Sierra in the lobby, and we drop our bags at the front desk, in case we're not back for checkout. We still have a couple of hours, but I have no idea how long this is going to take.

I use the paperwork to shield my eyes from the blazing sun as we walk ten minutes in silence to the annulment office. It's bigger than I expected, and there's a short line waiting at the desk when we step inside. Thankfully, the line moves quickly, and a smiling elderly woman greets us when we're up.

"Welcome in. How can we help today?"

I clear my throat. "We're looking to get an annulment," I say quietly, like it's embarrassing. Which it is, but presumably everyone is here for the same reason.

The woman—Cherry, according to her name tag—points to a sign sitting in a plastic frame on the counter. "Do you have everything listed here?"

Temporary marriage license, ID of both parties, evidence to prove a reason for annulment... "What counts as evidence?" Sierra asks.

"Well, that depends on your reason for annulling. Intoxication is a common one—"

"Yeah, that's us."

"Do you have a receipt or credit card statement to show you were in a bar or club prior to the wedding?" the woman asks, and I breathe a sigh of relief. I keep all my receipts, just in case.

I nod, and she smiles widely. "Excellent. Here's the paperwork you'll need to fill in before they see you. You'll have plenty of time—we're a little busy today." She hands a clipboard and a pen over to Sierra. "Your number's at the top of the page. They'll call you when it's your turn. Just head up the corridor. The waiting room is the last room on the left."

We thank her and head up the corridor. The navy carpet is worn and patchy in places, and there's a faint smell of tobacco, but it's not as seedy as I expected from the website.

Sierra pushes the waiting room door open and stops so suddenly that I walk straight into her.

"What the hell are you—" I look over her shoulder, and the words die in my throat. There have to be a hundred people in here.

We're a little busy today. I'd hate to see what really busy looks like to Cherry. Jesus.

I follow Sierra, and we find two seats in a corner. There's a screen above the door showing the next number to be called: 13.

"What number are we?" I ask, and Sierra holds the clip-board up: 68.

CHAPTER SIX

Sierra

They've taken eleven couples in an hour. At this rate, we're going to be here for at least four more hours, and we need to be at the airport in six.

Rose filled in the paperwork while I texted the group chat with Jazz and Maggie to make excuses for our absence at breakfast. As far as they're concerned, Rose and I had such a good night with the twins—whose names I can't even remember—that we're seeing them for brunch, and we'll meet up at the airport.

Neither of us charged our phones last night, so we have to reserve what little battery we have. Which means sitting in silence.

Ordinarily, people watching in a room full of people who got drunk and married on a Sunday night in Vegas, and now regret it, would be fun. It's less fun when we are those people.

The irony of the fact that just a couple of days ago, I was promising Kyo that I still had time to find a wife to get my stupid inheritance, and now I'm waiting to get divorced. Or annulled. Whatever.

I snort to myself, and Rose's head snaps in my direction. "What about this could possibly be funny?"

If I wasn't so exhausted, so hungover, I might have a witty comeback, but I don't. Instead, I tell her the truth. "My mom's parents left me a really big inheritance, but I have to be married to claim it. If I'm not married by thirty-one, I lose it. Kyo lost his, and I have nine months to get married to claim mine. I've been trying to find a wife for three years with no luck, yet here we are." I don't mean to sound as bitter as I do, but god, what are the odds?

Rose raises her brows. "Seriously? What happened when Kyo lost his?"

"It was donated to charity. I don't know which, but based on how my mom talks about my grandparents, I probably don't want to know. Let's just say if they were alive, they'd have written my mom out of the will the second she married a Japanese man." And I hate to think how they'd have reacted to two biracial, queer grandkids.

Rose scrunches up her nose like she always does when she hears something she doesn't like, except she's wearing her glasses, and the movement causes them to slip down her nose. If it wasn't Rose, I'd think it was cute. She huffs and sits back in her chair.

"They sound awful," she says, shaking her head. We're quiet for a moment before she continues. "Do you want to hear something else funny?"

"What about this could *possibly* be funny, Rosie?" I repeat sarcastically, and she scowls at me.

"You know how I had my review with my boss earlier this week?"

"Yeah."

"There's a promotion opportunity coming up. I want it, and although my boss is happy with my performance, she's concerned that I'm not a team player."

"You're not a team player. You hate working with others," I point out, and she doesn't argue.

"Apparently, the team wants to get to know me. They want me to be sociable. So I figured I'd just pretend and lie my way through it. But my boss saw the quiz answers you wrote on my papers, and I panicked and said you were my fiancée, and that the reason we were coming to Vegas was to elope."

I clap a hand over my mouth, trying to hold back the laugh and failing miserably. She didn't laugh at me and my inheritance-issues—it's shitty of me to laugh at her thing, but I can't help myself. "Shit, you really manifested this, huh?"

"Shut up," she groans, but there's no heat in it. We might not like each other, but, for once, we're both in the same sinking boat.

"Far be it from me to pay you a compliment, Cannon, but you being introverted isn't a personality flaw," I say, and she eyes me with suspicion. "Don't get me wrong, you have many, but that's not one of them. It's just who you are, and that's... fine, I guess. Sure, you could maybe stand to be more sociable, but anyone trying to get you to change that much, your boss included, is a red flag."

Her suspicion fades, confusion replacing it, like she

can't understand me saying something semi-nice to her. Which, given the past year, is understandable. She sighs. "That's easy for you to say when your boss is Cal Michaelson."

I can't argue with that. I've had awful bosses before, and I know how lucky I am to be where I am now.

Rose drums her nails on the clipboard, like she can't bear to sit still. She flips open the wallet and pulls out the papers from the chapel. Neither of us looked beyond the information sheet and the temporary certificate, but there are a bunch of travel coupons, and even a flyer for a divorce attorney. Lovely.

"What's that?" I ask as Rose's fingers close around a white envelope.

She shrugs and opens it, pulling out a glossy photo and laying it flat on the clipboard. It's a little blurry, like it was taken on an old disposable camera. Rose and I are standing, facing each other, holding hands beneath a purple neon sign that says Dearly Beloved, but half the letters aren't lit up, so it looks more like *ear love*. We both have stupid, drunken smiles on our faces, and I'm not sure I've ever actually seen Rose look so light.

"We look…" I trail off because I'm a second away from complimenting the picture.

"Wasted," Rose finishes for me. Right. I must still be a little drunk.

"Mhmm. Funny that we were both wearing white last night."

"Yeah," Rose agrees, clearing her throat and sliding the picture back inside the envelope.

We both look up as the number twenty-five is called, and I groan. "Only forty-three to go."

Rose sighs, shuffling the papers in her lap into a pile and hugging them to her chest. "What would you spend the money on? Your inheritance, I mean."

I start at the sudden change of subject. It's not like Rose to small talk. But I suppose it'll help time pass faster. "Kyo and his partners want to have kids, but Lina needs IVF, and her insurance won't cover it."

"That sucks," Rose says, shaking her head. Her eyes are glued to the screen, the numbers moving at a snail's pace. "So, how long do you have to be married for before you get the inheritance?"

"Three months."

Rose hums, and I narrow my eyes as I watch her expression move from contemplative to resolved. What is she—

"Then let's stay married."

I sip gingerly at the shitty diner coffee just for something to do with my hands. The too-bright fluorescents reflect off the tarnished metal tabletop, stinging my eyes.

Rose is pushing flambéed strawberries around her plate with her fork, looking a lot like she's trying to keep the contents of her stomach inside. Why she ordered pancakes is beyond me—I ordered plain toast and unseasoned hash browns, and those have been hard enough to choke down after whatever we had to drink last night.

We picked the place right across the street from the annulment office, and it's the dictionary definition of dingy. Everything is a little tarnished, the menus are sticky, and the napkin holder has what looks like a dent from a fist in it. There are a couple of guys working behind the counter who would make me cross the street if I saw them out at night, fucking around. I watch as one of them licks his thumb and wipes a smudge on a glass before sitting it on top of a precarious tower of glasses. Gross.

Rose finally pushes her plate away, and I waste no time. *"Let's get out of here and eat before we talk,"* she said, like she didn't just drop a fucking bomb on me. I've been waiting as patiently as I can, but who does something like that?

My wife, apparently. Jesus.

"Can we talk now?" I ask, and she takes a long draw through her straw, wrinkling her nose. That's what she gets for getting soda at this time of the morning.

She swallows and pushes the glass away, too. "Yeah. I mean, it just makes sense. We're already married, we live together. What's the harm in just staying that way until you get the money?"

I can't believe she, of all people, is suggesting this. Uptight, never put a toe out of line, Rose Cannon. "There is the issue of us loathing each other," I point out, and she shrugs.

"My parents barely tolerate each other most days."

I've spent enough time around Lilia and Alexander Cannon to know what she's talking about, but it's not the same. "I think getting married specifically to claim an inheritance probably constitutes fraud."

"That's not why we got married, it's why we're staying married. Besides, no one has to know. As far as anyone around us will be concerned, our hatred of each other has just been to cover up our true feelings, and we could no longer fight them. Or something like that. We can figure out the logistics before we have to tell our families," Rose says, like it's somehow the most reasonable thing in the world. Who is she?

I rub my eyes with my fingers, and they come away flecked with black and silver glitter, because I did a bad job of taking off last night's makeup while rushing out the door for a fucking annulment.

"I can't understand why you'd offer to do this. You know your parents will be furious you eloped, and it's completely out of character. What's in this for you?"

"I'm not against pissing my parents off. I never got to do the teenage rebellion thing, and now Jazz has settled down, maybe it's my turn to stress them out a little. As for what's in it for me..." She clasps her hands on the table in front of her, squaring her shoulders and straightening her jaw so she's looking ever so slightly down on me. There's the Rose I've unfortunately come to know so well. "I'll be your wife, so you get your inheritance, and you'll be my wife for all the social events I need to go to get my promotion at work. You're better with people than I am. People seem to like you—not me, to be clear, but people."

"Wow. Thank you?" I snort, rolling my eyes. It might be the nicest thing she's ever said to me.

"If all goes to plan, in three months, you should get your inheritance money, and I'll get my promotion. The promotion comes with a raise, and we'll both be able to afford to get divorced, move out, and only see each other when Jazz insists—and she might insist less if we claim it was a bad breakup or something."

I can't go as far as saying it's a flawless plan—it's actually batshit crazy—but it might work. With a few amendments. "We can't claim it was a bad breakup. I'm not willing to lose Jazz, Cal, or my job over this. If things end badly, they're obviously going to choose you. You're family, and I'm just a friend."

"Technically, you're family now, too. You're Jazz's sister-in-law," Rose points out.

Shit. "She's going to kill me. When she asked me if I would be your roommate, I don't think she had us getting drunk and married in Vegas in mind."

"She married Liam after they'd been dating for two months. She's also Jazz. I don't really think she has any kind of moral high ground here. Look, the way I see it, this is the last thing either of us wanted, but we might as well take advantage of a shitty situation."

I pick at the crust of my toast, my ring sparkling in the harsh lighting. It's a really pretty ring—both of our rings are much nicer than I'd expect, considering we bought them at 1 a.m. at a pawn shop, according to my mobile banking app. It seems I also spent a decent chunk of my savings on it, and it's too pretty for me to sell, so I guess I'm going to need that inheritance after all.

"Alright," I agree, finally. "I guess we're staying married."

There's a resounding crash as the tower of glasses tumbles to the ground behind the counter, smashing to smithereens.

Now, that's an omen if I've ever seen one.

CHAPTER SEVEN

Sierra

The drawer by the door labeled "shoes" is for your shoes, by the way. I labeled it just for you. No need to leave them in the middle of the floor. - R

P.S. 91 days until we get divorced

My head is still pounding when I walk into work on Tuesday morning. Between the lingering effects of the alcohol and my complicated new marital status, my mind is in knots. Jazz has been needling me all morning, asking if I'm sick and holding her hand up to my forehead to check for a fever, because I've been quieter than usual. But quiet is better than blurting out that I married her sister over the weekend.

Rose and I decided to wait until this coming weekend to tell everyone. Maggie and Cal are hosting family dinner at their place, and it'll be easier to just rip the Band-Aid off and tell everyone at once. And her parents are more likely to be civil in company. But that means four whole days of work without breathing a word of it to Jazz.

I have to tell my parents, and I know they're going to want to meet Rose. For the first time, I'm glad they live so far away. Kyo's partner, Rylan, is an engineer, so they move around the West Coast every couple of years. When they moved to Sacramento earlier this year, my parents decided to move with them. They're both semi-retired (my dad does some freelance web design, and my mom volunteers for a children's charity) and with Lina's health problems, they wanted to be close to her.

Sacramento is a twelve-hour drive, and I don't like flying, which is a perfect excuse not to introduce them to my wife. *Wife.* Jesus fucking Christ, how did we end up here?

But at least we don't have to worry about our families for a few days. In the meantime, though, there is one person I need to tell—because if I don't tell someone, I'm going to explode. Besides, I really need to make sure what we're doing isn't going to land either of us in prison, since it's technically fraud.

I knock lightly on Cal's office door. "It's open," he calls in his thick Irish accent. He looks up from his desk when I walk in, a wide smile on his face. "Hey. How was Vegas?"

"It was good. I'm still a little hungover," I admit, dropping into the chair opposite him. The soft, worn leather hugs my body, and I could so easily curl up and take a nap. Cal probably wouldn't mind, but that's not why I'm here.

Michaelson and Hicks is the top business and corporate law firm in the state, and it couldn't be in a better spot. The building isn't huge, but Cal has the penthouse office, and the floor-to-ceiling glass windows let in the gorgeous late-summer light.

"I can imagine. Maggie said you and Rose were struggling on the flight home. You know, if you need the day—"

"I'll be fine," I promise, leaning my head on my hands, and wondering how to approach this with him.

Cal eyes me suspiciously. "Everything alright?"

"Yep. Mhmm. Definitely alright... I'd like to hire you," I blurt out. "For legal advice," I clarify, but it does nothing to clear up the confusion on his face.

"Sierra, we're friends. You can just ask me for legal advice."

I shake my head. "Nope. Because if I ask you, you're going to want to tell Maggie, and you're going to end up feeling like either a bad friend if you do, or a bad husband if you don't. If I hire you, you're legally required to keep my secrets."

Cal raises his brows. "That's sneaky. I like it. I'm pretty expensive, you know."

I roll my eyes and pull a five-dollar bill from inside my phone case. "How about five dollars, and I'll buy you lunch?" I slide the bill across the desk and Cal pockets it.

"Five dollars, and I'll buy *you* lunch, because I feel so guilty for accepting your money," he counters.

What a Cal thing to say. I laugh and lean back in the chair. "Perfect. Although, I think I'm getting the better deal here."

"I have a million things on my to-do list today, and I don't want to do any of them, so you're giving me an excuse not to," he replies with a shrug. "What can I help with?"

"Do you remember last year when I asked you to look over the terms of my inheritance?" I figured there was no harm in asking Cal to see if he could find a loophole. He couldn't, and, though he offered to reach out to an old friend who specializes in inheritance law, he said it was pretty airtight. "I understand that I have to be married, and I'll receive the inheritance after three months, but what happens if I get divorced after those three months? Can they take it back?"

Surprise lights Cal's face. "Not that I can remember, but I'd need to double-check the terms again. Do you have a copy?"

I pull it up on my phone and pass it over. Cal scans it. "There's nothing in here to say you have to stay married once you have the money. The only issue that might come up in a situation like that would be if someone else claimed you'd committed fraud by getting married just for the purpose of the inheritance, but since there's no one expecting the money if you don't get it, I don't think there's much of a risk there."

I breathe a long sigh of relief. "Good. That's... good, yeah."

"Any other questions?"

"Yeah, um, hypothetically, if an employee had a poten-tial conflict of interest with a direct manager—like Jazz being your daughter-in-law, for example—they would need to report that ASAP, right? Or the employee who didn't report it could get in trouble."

"Yes…" Cal draws the word out, his brows meeting in the middle. "Why?"

I take a deep breath, practicing the words in my head before I say them out loud for the first time. "Rose and I got married on Sunday."

It's almost comical how wide Cal's eyes get. He opens his mouth and closes it about four times without saying anything.

"So, yeah… Jazz is my sister-in-law now. If you could pass that on to HR, but also not tell Jazz, that would be great."

"What the… You and Rose got married for your inheritance?" Cal asks, leaning forward. Shit, I forgot what a gossip he is. Still, he legally can't tell anyone.

"No, we got married because we were blackout drunk in Vegas. We're *staying* married for the inheritance."

"But you two hate each other."

"Yes, well, alcohol."

"Shit." Cal rubs his jaw. "I can't tell Maggie about this. You told me this knowing I can't tell Maggie. What the fuck, Sierra?"

I wince. "Sorry. It's only for a few days, if it helps. We're going to tell everyone at family dinner on Friday. Which gives you plenty of time to practice acting surprised."

"This is… I have so many questions. Christ. So what, you're going to stay married for three months, then get divorced?"

"That's the plan. Oh, and no one else can know about the inheritance part. I'm already worried Jazz is going to kill me for getting drunk and marrying her baby sister. I don't need to make it worse."

"What if Maggie figures it out? Can I tell her then?"

"How the hell would she figure it out?"

Cal chuckles, something like relief shining on his face. "What?"

"You know I love you, but there's no way you and Rose are going to be able to act like you like each other enough for Maggie not to figure out something is up."

I groan, leaning my elbows on the desk and letting my head fall into my hands. He's right. Rose and I have barely spoken since we left the diner, because we have no idea how to speak without fighting. We're so fucked.

What the hell have we gotten ourselves into?

"*Baywatch?*"

"*Lord of the Rings?*"

"Where the hell are you getting that? It's clearly *The Little Mermaid.*"

"*Titanic!*" I shout above my bickering family.

"Sierra got it," Kyo says, and everyone groans.

My mom crosses her arms. "You two are always too in sync for these things."

"Or I'm just really good at charades," I counter, tilting my laptop screen so the glare of my bedside lamp stops reflecting off of it.

"You're good at everything, Sierra," my dad assures me. It's a lie, but one I appreciate.

Since my family moved to California, we've tried to keep in touch as much as possible: texting, calling, video call game nights. At all times, there are a dozen different conversations going on between my parents, Kyo, Lina, Rylan, and me. Which means there have been at least a hundred opportunities for me to mention I got married.

All five of them are on the call for a change, and I can't put it off any longer. It's now or never.

"So, I have some big news. And it might come as a bit of a shock."

My parents exchange a concerned look.

My mom leans in toward the camera. "The last time you had big news, you told us you were a lesbian. Are you *not* a lesbian? Because you know we'll support you no matter what, SiSi, but I think your dad's flag tattoo is probably too big to cover."

I almost laugh. My parents really are the most supportive parents in existence. Not only did my dad tattoo a watercolor lesbian flag on his shoulder when I came out, he tattooed the polyamorous flag on the other arm for Kyo, Lina, and Rylan.

"I'm still a lesbian. That's not going to change," I assure them. "Actually, speaking of lesbians, you know my room-mate, Rose?"

"Of course we do. You complain about her constantly," Rylan chimes in. "I feel like I know her personally at this stage."

"Right. Well, about that... As it turns out, our dislike of

each other might not have been as strong as we thought it was." God, it sounds so stupid when I say it like that.

Lina gasps, whacking Kyo on the arm. "I told you they had feelings for each other!"

"You and Rose are dating?" my dad asks, and it's a testament to how great my parents are that he looks happy to hear that his daughter might be dating the person she's been ranting about for a year straight.

Now let's see if that happiness extends to the ring on my finger.

"We're not dating, per se…" I hold up my hand, flashing my ring, and their jaws drop. "Surprise! We got married!"

My mom squeals and claps her hand to her mouth. I think I hear something like "oh my god" muffled behind her hand.

Dad recovers first, clearing his throat. "Congratulations, SiSi. That's…Well, like you said, it's a bit of a shock. Are you happy?"

Are you happy?

It's what my parents ask whenever we do something they don't understand: when I came home with an eyebrow piercing (that I took out a week later,) when I quit law school, when Kyo and Lina canceled their wedding because they didn't want to marry each other if they couldn't marry Rylan, too. As long as we're not hurting ourselves or anyone else, they don't care what we do if it makes us happy.

"Yeah, Dad. I'm happy. Rose and I are both happy." The lie makes me nauseous, like I'm spitting on something sacred—my parents' trust.

But it's enough for my mom, Lina, and Rylan's shock to morph into excitement as they congratulate me. Kyo's the only one who looks suspicious, and I wish I could say I'm surprised.

By the time my family's finished quizzing me on all things Rose and our wedding, and my mom has asked no less than ten times when they get to meet her, it's almost midnight, and we're all yawning. We say our goodbyes and goodnights, but my relief is short-lived when we finally hang up.

Almost immediately, my phone lights up with a video call from Kyo. I lie down before answering it, propping my phone up on my pillow.

"Are you hiding in the bathroom?" I ask, peering at the wall of duck paintings on the wall behind him. My mom loves a theme.

"Yes. What the fuck, Sierra? Tell me you didn't marry your roommate for money?"

"I didn't marry my roommate for money," I reply instantly. "I didn't! We got drunk, and you know how it is."

He glares at me. "Not really."

Kyo and I have always looked more like twins than siblings, favoring our dad so strongly that people often seem surprised that our mom isn't Japanese, too. Side by side with her, we look nothing alike—until we show any emotion, that is. Our mom never learned to hide a single emotion from her face, and Kyo and I are exactly the same. Everyone talks about how we have her smile, but we have her frowns, her fury, her frustration, and her resting bitch face, too.

There's no point in lying to him—even if he didn't know about the inheritance stipulation, he's always been able to see right through me. My parents are probably under the impression that I've given up on the inheritance, and I've never told them, or Lina and Rylan, that my plan was to give Kyo the money for IVF.

"We woke up married, and we both saw a benefit to staying that way for a little while. I get the money, Rose gets a promotion—it's a long story—and no one ever needs to know. Be serious. Who's going to be surprised when they hear we're getting divorced in three months? No harm, no foul."

Kyo looks skeptical. "I feel like you're making that sound a lot simpler than it is. You're going to have to spend a lot more time together to convince people you're married. Why not just be honest about it? You know Mom and Dad wouldn't care."

"It's not our family that's the problem. Rose's parents are a nightmare, and I don't want Jazz to think I'm taking advantage of Rose by using her to get the money."

"Isn't that what you're doing, though?" Kyo asks, and I glare at him.

"Ouch. I mean, technically, but she's using me, too. We're both benefiting here. It's all good, Kyo."

"Okay," he says, looking less than convinced. "You know I love you, and I appreciate you doing this for me. Just be careful."

"I love you, too. Quit worrying, Ky. What's the worst that could happen?"

CHAPTER EIGHT

Rose

I know you hate plants, but I think a certain plant could do wonders to calm you the fuck down, if you know what I mean. - S
P.S. 88 days

I spin my ring around the ring finger on my right hand. Walking in with a diamond on my left hand felt like flashing a neon sign. I've noticed Sierra wears hers on a dainty gold chain around her neck, but I hate how jewelry feels around my neck. I hate how jewelry feels in general—I begrudgingly wear my smart watch because I like tracking my steps—but the ring isn't so bad.

Everyone made it to family dinner at Maggie and Cal's place this week: my parents, Jazz and Liam, Liam's moms, Eliza and Danisha, and Xan.

Sierra and I—god, I hate that we've become a duo—strategically picked the spot at the table closest to Eliza and Danisha, and furthest from my parents. I love my parents, I do, but Liam truly hit the parental jackpot. I know Eliza and Danisha will at least pretend to be happy for us, and Sierra said Cal took it relatively well when she told him.

My parents will be pissed off, I know that. Xan will probably just be confused. Jazz is the wildcard. Not that she isn't always the wildcard, but I'm not usually on the other side of it. She's side-eyed Sierra and me multiple times already, probably wondering why we're willingly sitting beside each other. We're waiting until everyone's finished eating to drop our news. It seemed like the best thing to do, but now I can barely choke down Cal's mushroom ravioli, and it's my favorite.

There's a lull in the conversation, and Jazz and Liam exchange a look before she clears her throat. "So I have some news. I went to the doctor last week and—"

"Oh my god, you're finally pregnant?" my mom interrupts, and Jazz visibly flinches. It's not a secret that she and Liam are desperate to be parents, and it's not a secret that they're trying, but Jazz was diagnosed with PCOS last year, so it's not as simple as just trying.

"No," Jazz replies through gritted teeth. My mom knows better than to ask. She just doesn't give a shit. But Jazz takes a deep breath and forces her lips into a tight smile. "I'm sure this will come as a huge shock to everyone, but I was officially diagnosed with ADHD!"

There's silence around the table because it comes as a shock to literally no one.

Maggie leans across the table toward Jazz. "Is this a 'yay, you finally got an answer' or an 'oh no, we're so sorry to hear that' situation?"

"The first one."

"Yay!"

Congratulations erupt around the table from everyone except my parents. They don't look upset, just like they're not sure how to act. To say my parents' relationship with Jazz has been rocky is an understatement. It all came to a head when they kicked me out for dropping out of med school, and Jazz called them out on how they treated us all growing up. At first, it seemed like things were getting better. They stopped passing quite so many judgmental comments and pretended to be happy when Jazz and Liam surprised everyone by getting married at their Halloween party just two months after they started dating officially. But as time's gone on, it feels like they've gotten comfortable slipping back into their old ways.

Jazz is telling Xan about the medication her doctor recommended when my mom interrupts. "What are your doctors saying about you not getting pregnant? You've been trying for months."

"Mom, I don't think everyone at the table wants to hear about that."

My mom waves a hand, and Jazz's shoulders slump. No one does dismissive like Lilia Cannon. "Will this new medication cause problems with you getting pregnant? Are you not doing what the doctors are recommending? You need to be sleeping and eating right, and exercising, but not too much..."

I can see Jazz getting more and more upset as my mom talks, but it's Liam I'm keeping an eye on. His usually sunny disposition all but disappears around my parents when they're on their best behavior, and Mom is far from on her best behavior tonight.

She shakes her head and grabs her purse, rummaging for her phone. "Maybe you need more testing done. I'll get you the name of my doctor. Make sure you mention you're my daughter. This shouldn't be so difficult, Jazz—you're a Cannon."

"She's a Michaelson, actually." Liam sounds perfectly calm, but he doesn't look it. He glares at my mom, his expression stony. You could cut the tension at the table with a knife.

Liam and his parents are pissed. Jazz is dejected. My mom seems confused about the issue. My dad looks ready to jump in and defend her if Liam says anything else. Maggie's on edge because any kind of family conflict stresses her, and Xan just looks exhausted, because we've been dealing with this shit for so long.

And I have the perfect thing to take the heat off Jazz.

The nice thing to do would be to warn Sierra, but I don't see any way to do that without making things more awkward.

I clear my throat, and everyone looks at me. "Sierra and I got married last weekend."

Jaws drop, and hands are slapped to mouths, but the silence is deafening. It's Cal who finally breaks it, clapping his hands and making Maggie jump beside him.

"That's lovely news, girls. Such a surprise, really, could never have guessed, but I'm happy for you. Aren't we happy for them, love?" He nudges Maggie, but she just narrows her eyes at him.

"Did you know about this?"

Sierra mutters something that sounds suspiciously like, "Fucking hell, Cal," under her breath before speaking up. "I had to tell Cal, since Jazz is now my sister-in-law, and that could be a conflict of interest at work. Legally, he wasn't allowed to tell you."

"I think we've strayed away from what's important here," Xan says, disbelief on his face. "What the hell? You two hate each other."

Sierra and I exchange a glance, and I try not to look like I loathe her. Based on her answering grimace, I'm not sure I succeeded. "Well, you know what they say. There's a fine line between love and hate."

"Yeah, and you were firmly on the hate side, like last week." Xan scrunches his face up, like he just can't comprehend it. And really, who can blame him? This was a bad idea. We should've told everyone individually.

"Hate's a strong word," Sierra says, grabbing my hand and threading our fingers together. It's awkward and clumsy, but I'm hoping everyone is too stuck on the shock of our announcement to notice.

"You came to work a few weeks ago and ranted for almost an hour about how you couldn't understand Rose and I coming from the same DNA because she, I'm quoting here, 'doesn't have a likable bone in her body,'" Jazz says.

Ouch. It's not the worst thing either of us has said about the other in the year we've been living together, but it still stings. I want nothing more than to pull my hand away, except maybe to leave, but I can't.

"That was then, and this is now," Sierra replies, like it's the most simple thing in the world.

"When did you even have time to get married in Vegas? We were with you all weekend except when we left you doing shots with those red-headed twins," Maggie says.

"Well," Sierra begins, "that's actually what made us figure out how strongly we felt about each other. You know, we were about to leave with the twins, and we realized we didn't want to go home with them because..."

She looks at me, eyebrows raised and dark eyes panicked.

"Because we were already home, with each other," I finish lamely. God, I might be sick.

"Aww," Liam says, the only one at the table who doesn't look like he's been clubbed over the head. "I've been rooting for you guys to have a hate-to-love, roommates-to-lovers arc since day one." He gasps. "*Roomhate* to love. I think this is great."

"Not everything is a romance book, Liam," Maggie says.

He raises an eyebrow. "Okay, miss boss-employee, age gap—"

Jazz nudges him until he closes his mouth. Once Maggie and Liam start quibbling, it can go on for a while. Jazz shakes her head, sitting back and sighing up at the ceiling. "This just feels like it's come out of nowhere."

I know it's not a real marriage, and I know we blind-sided everyone, so I can't explain why the reaction of the people we care most about stings. It shouldn't feel as personal as it does.

"It's not nowhere," Sierra says. She sounds a little tired, like maybe she wants to get out of here as much as I do. "Don't you remember the day I met Rose? I told you then I thought she was beautiful."

"I believe your exact words were 'she's pretty hot,' actually. And I told you to stay away from my baby sister."

I frown at Sierra. I didn't know that they'd spoken about me at all. That day is kind of a blur for me. I showed up at the office to beg Jazz to let me stay with her since my parents had just kicked me out. Truthfully, I barely remember meeting Sierra.

"You did tell me to stay away from her, that's true. But you married your best friend's stepson." Sierra shrugs, and Jazz snorts.

"It's hard to argue with that."

"Liam's right. You guys are perfect together. We're happy for you," Danisha says, and, slowly but surely, congratulations are muttered around the table. I can't say they seem genuine, but it's better than silence.

"Well," Maggie says, with a truly baffled smile. "I'd say this calls for…" She glances at Jazz.

"Hard liquor?" Jazz asks at the exact moment Maggie says, "A toast?"

"I'll grab some champagne." Cal jumps up quickly, like he's been waiting for an excuse to leave the table.

My parents are suspiciously silent. In fact, I haven't heard a peep out of them since I broke the news. "Mom, Dad, you guys have been pretty quiet."

My dad sighs, his lips pressed together in a thin line. In theory, Xan is his double, but there's a softness to my brother that I've never seen on my dad's face. "I don't really have anything to say, Rose."

"Well, I have plenty to say!" my mom interjects, because of course she does. "How could you do this to us, Rose? We tolerated Jazz's wedding *thing* because she's always been a bit, well, you know…"

Liam looks like he's about to boil over, but Jazz places a hand on his chest and shakes her head.

"But now this? You've taken away our last chance to see one of our children have an actual wedding!"

None of us has a chance to respond before she stands up, clutches her hand to her forehead, and leaves the room. My dad follows her, and the familiar sinking feeling of disappointing my parents rears its head. It's been a while.

It shouldn't matter—it *doesn't* matter. This isn't real. There's no need for the sudden, screaming urge to apologize and promise to do better that overtakes me. But old habits never really die. They lie dormant, ready to wrap their claws around you and suck you back into whatever dark cloud you were so happy to finally escape.

"Did they forget about me? I could have a wedding," Xan grumbles.

"To who? I'm pretty sure the last time you went on a date, you were in college, and we all know you're in love with Kami," Jazz replies with a snort, easing a little of the tension around the table. Kami has been Xander's best friend for as long as they've both been alive, and he is, without a doubt, in love with her. She has the sweetest four-year-old daughter, Lexi, and a god-awful husband.

Sierra nudges me lightly with her shoulder. "Hey. Are you

okay?" she asks quietly, and I'm not sure which is worse: my parents acting exactly like they always do, or her acting differently. She actually looks concerned, though it's probably more because of how my parents have been with Jazz tonight.

"I'm fine," I snap, and the concern melts off her face. Beside her, Eliza and Danisha exchange a look. Fuck. Newlyweds don't snap at each other like that. "I'm sorry, I'm just stressed. I should go talk to them," I add on.

"You want me to come with?" Sierra asks, but Xan answers before I can.

"We've got it. No need for anyone else to have to deal with any more Cannon bullshit today," he says, pushing away from the table.

Jazz gives Liam a kiss before standing up, and I'm not sure what possesses me to copy her, but I lean in and kiss Sierra's cheek without thinking about it. It's softer than I expected. She widens her eyes, but quickly schools her expression into neutrality.

"I'm here if you need me," she says, playing along without flinching. Shit, she's better at this than me.

We find my parents sitting in Maggie and Cal's living room, both silent. My mom is clearly upset, and my dad is clearly pissed, but it's not like they've ever gone out of their way to comfort each other. Why start now?

"What more could you possibly have to throw at us?" My mom sniffles, and I'm not entirely convinced her dramatics aren't forced.

Xan drops onto the couch opposite them. "Don't you think you're being a little unreasonable, Mom? It's understandable to be upset that you didn't see Rose get married, but it's not like she planned to exclude you specifically."

"Exactly," I say as Jazz and I sit beside him. "Honestly, it was a spur-of-the-moment thing, and you know me, I don't like a fuss, so it worked out perfectly. It's not that we didn't want you there."

She's actually pouting, and it would be hilarious if it wasn't directed at me. "You know, sometimes it feels like I can't do anything right. Am I just the worst mom in the world or something?"

Past Rose would have jumped in immediately to reassure her. She's probably expecting it, considering she loves to throw out the same thing anytime we don't all immediately bend over backwards to accommodate her feelings over our own. After so many times, it no longer hits quite so hard.

Xan sighs. "No one is calling you a bad mom."

She sniffles, wiping away a nonexistent tear. Jesus. I hope I didn't inherit her acting skills, or I'll never be able to pull off this sham of a marriage.

"It's like the three of you are a team, and we're not important in your lives. After everything we've done for you."

"The three of us are supposed to be a team," Jazz says, and I can tell her patience is wearing thin. "That's the whole point of siblings. You should find it comforting that no matter what happens, we're all here for each other. Do you have any idea how lucky we are to have that? Liam never had that, and Maggie doesn't talk to her siblings anymore.

The three of us will always have each other, even when we don't have you."

I look up at her, surprised, and notice Xan doing the same. We've never been close, and, though things have been better over the past year, I didn't realize she felt so strongly about us.

"It would be nice to feel included in your lives more," Mom says.

"We can do that, right?" Jazz asks me and Xan, and we both murmur our agreement. It's not like I have much going on in my life that's worth sharing. I'll be sure to let them know about the divorce, I guess.

"And for the record, when I get married, I want a big wedding," Xan says, I assume to reassure my mom, but she scoffs.

"When are you supposed to meet someone? All you do is work, and when you're not working, the only person you spend time with is already married!" She sits back, looking like a kid on Christmas Day who's had their presents snatched away. "I suppose we should just give up. It would be nice for one of you to have a real wedding or give us grandchildren, but I guess we're asking for too much."

It's the final straw for Jazz. She sucks in a breath, but says nothing as she stands up and leaves the room.

"Mom," Xan chides, pinching his brow as whatever progress we made crumbles into dust.

"What? I'm not allowed to share my feelings now?"

I shake my head. How the hell is she so clueless? "You have to stop pushing Jazz about kids. Do you have any idea how hard this is on her? She's desperate to be a mom."

"And I'm desperate to be a grandmother. It's hard for me too!"

She can't seriously be that dense.

"Leave it, Lilia," my dad says, though I'm fairly sure it's just because he's fed up with the conversation and doesn't want to listen to her complaining anymore.

I rub my face, pressing my palms into my eyes. Fuck my mascara—let it smudge.

A soft knock catches our attention. Maggie is standing in the doorway, a furious-looking Cal right behind her.

"Alexander, Lilia, we called a car to take you back to Marysville. It's outside," Maggie says, and my parents exchange a surprised look.

My dad jumps up. "Oh, sorry, we didn't realize everyone was leaving." My mom trails him to the door.

"They're not," Maggie responds firmly. "But you made Jazz cry—again—so you're no longer welcome in our home."

My parents stop in their tracks. "Maggie! How da—"

"No," Cal interrupts, and my mom snaps her lips closed. "It was Jazz's choice to invite you, which is why I've kept my mouth shut tonight while you've acted so poorly toward your children, all of whom I care about very deeply, but you will not speak to my wife like that."

It's easy to forget what Cal does for a living day to day since he's so gentle and easygoing. Very little rattles him and, when it does, I can see why his record of winning court cases is so good.

My parents disappear out the front door without so much as a glance back toward me or Xan. Maggie closes the door behind them and leans against it with a groan. "What a fucking night. But that," she says, pointing at Cal, "was really hot." She steps forward into his arms and he chuckles, kissing the top of her head.

I've dated here and there, both casual and long-term, but I've never been with anyone where affection has felt as natural as it seems to be for Maggie and Cal, or Jazz and Liam.

Maggie peers at us over Cal's shoulders. "We made the guest rooms up earlier in case you wanted to stay. Eliza and Danisha are making cocktails."

"If I ever say no to one of their cocktails, something is seriously wrong," Xan says, and he seems lighter already now that our parents are gone. "I'll stay. Are you and Sierra staying?"

"Oh. Uh…" I've gotten so used to my parents having an issue with everything we do that I actually forgot what started all this for a moment. Sierra. My wife. Shit. If we stay, we'll have to share a room. But if Xan is staying, it would be weird if we didn't. I should probably ask her before agreeing, but I don't do well on the spot. "Yeah, sure, that sounds good. Is Jazz okay?"

"She will be. She's upstairs with Liam in their room if you want to check on her."

I glance at Xan, and he looks as uncertain as I feel. We're not those kinds of siblings. We don't talk to each other about our feelings, and the one time I tried to help take the heat off Jazz, all I did was escalate things so badly that she's upstairs crying. I'm probably the last person she wants to see.

"She's in good hands with Liam," I say, crossing my arms over my chest.

"Yeah, we'll leave them to it," Xan adds, sounding almost relieved. He can't be any more comfortable with the idea of trying to talk about our parents than I am.

It's not like they'll ever change, and it's not like it'll ever not hurt. There's no point in rehashing it all.

CHAPTER NINE

Sierra

*Do you really need three different candles on the
bathroom counter? - R
P.S. 88 days too many*

I won't take my family for granted ever again. The
Cannons never fail to surprise me, even though I've
heard Jazz ranting about her parents more times than I
can count. At least she has good in-laws.

Maggie and Cal's house seems big when you consider
that it's just the two of them living here, but most family
dinners seem to end with Eliza and Danisha's cocktails and
everyone sleeping over. I've stayed here many times, but
this is the first time I'm sharing a room here with Rose. The
first time I'm sharing a room with Rose, period, if you don't
count the night we got married, which I don't, considering
neither of us remembers it.

She trudges up the stairs, her shoulders weighed down
with the stress of the night. Did I expect her parents to take

the news well? No, but I didn't expect them to take it out on all of their children. Kyo and I are so lucky to have the parents we do.

As the owner of an interior design company, it's no surprise that Maggie has impeccably designed every inch of their home, and the attic bedroom she assigned us is no exception. It's dark and cozy, with soft taupe walls and deep violet accents. The bed is massive, taking up most of the back wall.

I groan as I sit on the plush mattress, close my eyes, and let my body fall back, sinking into the pillowy cloud. I feel the bed sink and turn my head, opening my eyes. Rose is perched on the edge, spinning her ring around her finger. She does it almost constantly.

Her face is hidden by her smooth curtain of blonde hair, but her body betrays how she's feeling—she's hunched over, the muscles in her neck taut. If this was real, I would check on her, comfort her. But it's not real. We're not even friends. I'm not an asshole—I don't want her to be upset— but it's not like she'd care if *I* was upset. It's all so fucking confusing.

We both look up as footsteps sound on the stairs, and a second later, Cal knocks softly at the door. "Everyone decent?"

"Yeah," I call back, and he steps into the room, a thick comforter over his arm.

"I couldn't find a way to get you a second bed without Maggie being suspicious, but I figured separate blankets were at least something."

My heart falls into my stomach as Rose gets up and

takes it from him, setting it on the bed. What the fuck are we doing? We're lying to everyone we care about. We're asking Cal to lie to his wife. I don't like Rose's parents, but it was still shitty to blindside them like this, and all it did was make things worse for Jazz and Xan. None of this is fair of us. It's for a good cause, sure, but they don't know that.

"Thanks, Cal," Rose says softly. She sounds completely done.

He eyes her with concern. "I know you're not really a hugger, but you look like you could use a hug."

I expect her to immediately decline. I've never seen Rose initiate casual affection, and she grumbles whenever Jazz hugs her. She's quiet for a moment before answering, "A hug would be nice, actually." Her voice cracks, and I have to look away as Cal pulls her into a fatherly embrace.

I'm not used to seeing this side of Rose. I know her well enough to know she would never willingly be vulnerable in front of someone she hates, which means she's so exhausted she can't even fight it right now. There's a dull pain deep in my chest like heartburn.

I look back at Rose and Cal just in time to watch Rose release a deep breath, a little of the tension falling away from her body. "Thank you," she murmurs, looking at the floor. "I'm really glad Jazz has you."

"You have me, too, Rose. I'm not going to say anything about your parents because... well, frankly, I have nothing nice to say, but you're family. You'll always have a place with us. Both of you," he adds, nodding to me, and all it does is make me feel more guilty. "Alright, you two, get some sleep, and I'll see you in the morning. If you need anything, you know where we are."

He claps the doorway as he leaves, and it's such a *dad* thing to do that I can't help but smile. Until I think about the fact that Rose's dad probably never did that. It's hard to imagine him even offering her a hug.

I clear my throat. "I'll get ready first."

Rose nods but says nothing as I disappear into the en suite.

Maggie is so organized that she keeps an overnight bag for everyone who regularly spends the night. She restocks them often, adding in things she thinks we'll like and things to make us more comfortable. There's a new headband in my bag, the kind to keep your hair out of your face while you do your skincare, printed with an adorable floral pattern. It's the kind of thing she can't have just stumbled across—she probably noticed that I keep a similar style in my bathroom at home and went looking for one to keep here. That's just who she is.

Once, not long after I started working at Michaelson and Hicks, I commented that I felt guilty for everything Maggie did. On that particular day, she sent Cal to work with a box of pistachio macarons for me, with a handwritten note saying she'd seen them and thought of me since she knows I like pistachio lattes. But Cal told me that Maggie just loves taking care of people, and that couldn't be a more accurate description of her. I try to be thoughtful, to remember the little things about people, but it doesn't come so naturally to me.

I finish up and leave the bathroom to Rose, making the

bed while she gets ready. She's always cold, even in the dead of summer, so I put the thicker comforter on her side and climb under the soft blanket Cal brought us. It's still perfectly toasty, but considering Rose sleeps with two extra blankets at home, she'd probably be freezing under this.

She leaves the en suite, her hair in a single braid over her shoulder, and gets into the bed. Without a word, we turn our backs to each other and switch off the bedside lamps, plunging the room into darkness.

There's no "goodnight" or "sleep well," because we never wish each other those things at home. But tonight, it feels awkward. Maybe because there's less than a foot of space between us, or maybe because of the rings on our fingers. Even if the sentiment is fake, the impact is not.

I huff a sigh and turn around. "Rose? Are you awake?" I whisper.

"It's been twenty seconds since we turned the lights out. How the hell would I be asleep already?" she bites back, and it's almost a relief to hear her snapping at me like old times.

"Can we talk?"

She sighs and spins around so we're face-to-face. I blink. I didn't consider how close we'd be like this. There's a crack of light shining through a small gap in the curtains, lighting up her hazel eyes so I can see each individual fleck of green and gold. I can also very clearly see the impatience on her face.

"You wanted to talk. Talk," she says, gesturing at me to hurry me up. Right.

"I think we made a mistake," I say, and she raises an

eyebrow, clearly asking for me to elaborate. "With this whole staying married thing. We don't like each other, so it's not us who are going to be hurt when this is over. But I don't want to hurt anyone else, either."

Rose draws her bottom lip between her teeth. "I do feel bad about Cal lying to Maggie. But short of telling everyone the truth—which I don't think we should do, because my parents are the kind of people who would report you for inheritance fraud—I don't see how we can take it back now." She sighs, the muscle between her brows popping out. "This is so messy." She sounds almost accusatory, and I feel my hackles going up.

"It was your idea for us to stay married," I hiss.

"And you agreed. I don't recall forcing you." She glares daggers at me.

"Typical. God forbid you admit that maybe you had a shitty idea."

"I was trying to help *you*—"

"Don't pretend, Rose. This is as much for your benefit as it is for mine. I can find another wife to get my inheritance, but good luck trying to explain why you lied to your boss."

Her nostrils flare, the moonlight catching the fire in her eyes. "Why the hell are we even arguing about this? We've committed to it now. The fact that you didn't think about the consequences and now feel guilty isn't my problem."

She doesn't give me a chance to respond, just turns her back on me and tugs the covers up to her chin. My heart pounds furiously in my chest, angry because she's being fucking stubborn. But also because she's right. I thought about Jazz being pissed and how it would impact me, but I didn't consider how this was going to affect anyone else.

And she's right about something else: we've committed to the lie now. I just have to grin and bear the fact that, when this is all said and done, some of my favorite people might not want to be in my life anymore.

CHAPTER TEN

Rose

Do you really need that stick up your ass? - S
P.S. 87 days (but who's counting?)

"**W**hat are you wearing?"

I look down at myself, wondering what I could possibly be doing wrong with this outfit. Black slacks, a white shirt, a black blazer. "This is what I always wear to work."

Sierra is wearing an ankle-length white floral dress with a caramel-colored shirt over top, tied in a bow at the bust. "You're not going to work, Cannon. You're going to a picnic."

"A *work* picnic."

Sierra pinches her brow. "Oh my god. You can't wear that. You're supposed to be showing people you have a life outside of work."

I consider myself and, though I won't admit she's right out loud, she might just be. "Fine, whatever. You can pick what I wear. Make me look like you or whatever you need to do to make me seem likable."

The corner of her lips lifts in a shit-eating smirk. "Are you saying I'm likable?"

"No, I'm saying you *look* likable. The problem starts when you open your mouth."

She shrugs. "Eh. It's compliment-adjacent. I'll take it."

"You really should raise your standards," I mutter under my breath as I follow her into my room.

"Yeah, no shit," she replies as she yanks my closet doors open. "I've been thinking the same thing ever since I woke up married to you."

I bite my tongue. If I don't, we're going to be snapping at each other all day, and I don't think that's entirely typical of newlyweds.

"Lose the blazer and the pants," Sierra says, rummaging through my closet. I wince as a shirt falls off a hanger. She looks over her shoulder at me and snaps her fingers. "Now, Cannon. You're the one who's pissy if you're not twenty minutes early."

Gritting my teeth, I shrug out of my blazer, step out of my slacks, and fold them. I turn around to place them on the end of my bed—hopefully I won't have to steam them before work on Monday.

"Huh."

I spin around, and Sierra is squinting at me. More specifically... "Are you staring at my ass?"

She shrugs, nonplussed. "You just didn't strike me as a pink satin kind of girl."

"They're coral," I correct, and her nostrils flare as she sucks in a breath. She throws a bundle of fabric at me.

"Put those on."

She's picked out a pair of beige, high-waisted pants, a thin brown belt, and a navy V-neck sweater. It's a nice combination, only a little more casual than I usually wear to work.

"This isn't what I expected," I admit as I put them on, tucking my shirt and the sweater into the pants before I belt them.

Sierra hums, grabbing for me and roughly rolling up my sweater sleeves so the cuffs of my shirt stick out. She unbuttons them so they're looser around my wrists, then reaches for the buttons by my collar. Her fingers graze my skin as she unbuttons them, and we both still for a moment. Have we ever willingly been so close to each other? Not including the drunken mistake we made last weekend. She steps back, the sudden distance sending a chill over me. There's a sharp pain in my chest, the kind I get when I don't breathe properly on a run.

She turns us both so she can look me over in my full-length mirror and tuts. "You'll do."

A glowing review.

"I can't see how this is more likable. I still look like me."

"Well, yeah. There's no point in making you look like someone else. If you're too different, it won't be believable. This is more approachable than a pantsuit."

"Fine," I begrudgingly agree. I flick my gaze between

us. We're somewhat matchy. "Do you think our being married looks believable?" I ask, toying with my ring.

Sierra snorts and turns away. "Us *looking* married is not the problem here. The acting is the problem. We somehow need to make it through a three-hour picnic without biting each other's heads off."

I follow her out of the room, grabbing my purse from the barstool at the kitchen island. "At least I'll be so focused on trying to be sociable and personable that I probably won't have any energy left to make my true feelings about you known."

Sierra sits on the bench by the door to tug her shoes on, and I lean against the wall, sliding my feet into the brown boots she passes my way.

"I'm going to say it one more time and then I'll leave it," she says, buckling her wedges and looking up at me. "While I personally think your personality is, well, awful, you shouldn't have to change it to please people at work. You can be social without changing everything about your-self. You're twenty-seven, not sixteen, trying to fit in with scary high school girls."

I hate that I have to do this, and I hate that she's the only person who knows about it. The downside of being so intro-verted is that I just don't have friends, and I'm not close enough to any of my family. Even if I was, it's not like I could talk to Jazz without her putting two and two together about me and Sierra.

I have no desire to talk shit out with Sierra, and she doesn't know what she's talking about, anyway. She finds people easy to get along with—not me, but other people.

"Thanks for the advice I didn't ask for," I say, and she rolls her eyes.

It's not until we're climbing into her car that I fully process what she said. "By the way, I'm only twenty-six. That seems like something my wife should know." A year of living together, and almost everything I could tell you about Sierra is shit that pisses me off, or things I've absorbed through Jazz. I only learned her middle name was Kimiko when I read it on our marriage paperwork. I don't know her favorite color, where she grew up, what she wants from her future—none of the things spouses are supposed to know about each other. And I'm almost certain she doesn't know any of those things about me.

Sierra pulls out of the parking lot, shaking her head. "We are so fucked."

CHAPTER ELEVEN

Rose

Thirteen basic facts you should know about your partner!

I scan the list, swiping through it on my phone. We really should've talked about this before introducing our relationship to other people.

"What's your favorite food?" I ask Sierra. We still have a few minutes of the drive left, and I'm not going to waste them.

"Italian food. But real Italian food, with fresh tomatoes and basil and lots of pepper. And yours is Chinese food—specifically the chili garlic tofu from the takeout place a couple blocks from our apartment."

I side-eye her. "How did you know that?"

"I pay attention. What's next?"

"Any allergies? I'm allergic to—"

"Bananas, I know. None for me."

I'm not even sure my dad knows I'm allergic to bananas. What the fuck?

"Favorite sport?"

Sierra hums, considering. "Women's ice hockey. I like to see them fight." She sounds downright dreamy just thinking about it. "Yours?"

"I don't really like watching sports, but I like running." Watching other people do things has never been exciting to me. All it does is make me wonder if I could do it, and if I could do it better.

I scroll down the list and snort. "Favorite flower?"

Sierra is obsessed with the things. I swear it feels like we're living in a flower shop sometimes. I did put my foot down on only having one vase at a time, but she seems to have forgotten about that over the past couple of weeks.

"It *was* roses, but you've kind of ruined that for me. What with your thorny demeanor and all," she replies dryly. "But from a semi-fake marriage point of view, that'll be my answer if anyone asks. Not that anyone is going to ask."

"I don't have a favorite flower."

Sierra pulls into a parking space on the street outside Lisa's house and turns to face me. "Yeah, no shit."

We both look up at Lisa's house. From the outside, it's perfectly unassuming, all-American. But there's so much riding on this fucking picnic. Too much. If we can't convince a group of relative strangers that we're happily in love, we might as well give up and admit everything to our families.

"You ready for this?" Sierra asks, because she knows as well as I do that she's not the issue here. I nod, and she unclips her seatbelt. "Then let's do this—*wife*," she adds, sarcastically, scrambling out of the car before I can protest.

I jog along the sidewalk to catch up. "Don't call me

that," I grumble as she loops her arm through mine. It feels unnatural, walking up to Lisa's front door, so close together.

"It's technically true," Sierra points out. "And if we're going to sell this, you might want to look a little less disgusted at the thought of spending time with me."

She knocks on the door and pastes a perfectly neutral smile on her face as we wait for Lisa to answer. It's not too over the top, to the point it feels fake, and it doesn't feel forced. I try my best to emulate it, hoping it doesn't show how out of my depth I am.

The door swings open and Lisa beams at us. "Rose! I'm so glad you came. And you must be Sierra. It's great to finally meet you. I'm Lisa."

Sierra takes her offered hand and shakes it. "You too! Rose talks about you all so much that I swear I feel like I already know you. I can't wait to meet everyone."

Fuck. She really is a natural liar.

Lisa leads us into the house, through the bright, airy hallway and into the kitchen, where a bunch of my colleagues are standing around with plastic cups in their hands. The conversation hushes immediately when we walk in, like no one actually believed I'd show. I would feel worse if I didn't know myself.

Thankfully, Lisa is in hostess mode, and she introduces everyone without me having to do more than wave and say, "Hello."

Sierra nudges me gently. "Honey,"—what the fuck?— "the donuts."

She nods to the paper bag I'm holding. Right. "We brought donuts," I say, passing the bag to Lisa, awkwardly.

"They're from our favorite donut place. We go, like, every Saturday morning. Well, when Rosie can get me out of bed early enough! I'm not a morning person," she says with a self-deprecating eye roll. It's actually kind of impressive how comfortable she seems in a room full of strangers, lying through her teeth—not about not being a morning person. That part is true.

"We're not either," Jenna, one of the other lab techs, pipes up. "There's this breakfast place downtown, though, and it's totally worth getting up early for."

And just like that, the whole group starts talking about their favorite Seattle cafés and restaurants, like Sierra didn't lead them toward the conversation. It's fascinating to watch.

And it's an easy conversation for me to keep up with because, though I might not be the most sociable person in the world, I like coffee and treats. I'm able to chime in with recommendations and talk about some of the places I've been recently without too much of a struggle—and every time I do, Sierra manages to twist what I've said into something more couple-y.

"There's a coffee place by my sister's house that has amazing brownies," I say, and she immediately adds, "Oh my god, they're so good. We went with Rose's sister and her husband a few weeks ago, and all ordered different flavors so we could do a brownie flight. Amazing!"

As we move to the yard, where Lisa has tables and picnic blankets set up alongside a buffet, the conversation turns to eating while traveling.

"And speaking of traveling, I believe congratulations are in order. Vegas, right?" Collin, one of the senior lab techs, says, smiling at us. At work, Collin scares the shit out of me. Here, standing and lying to his face? Somehow worse.

"Thank you," I reply, hoping like hell my cheeks aren't burning as much as they feel like they are.

"It was the perfect weekend," Sierra adds, squeezing my arm. The cool band of her ring bites into my skin, but it's clearly intentional, because everyone immediately zeroes in on it.

"Oh wow, that's gorgeous! Let's see it up close—yours too, Rose!"

We both hold out our hands, and I try not to cringe as everyone touches mine, turning it here, there, and everywhere, so the diamond on my finger catches the light.

"You have to tell us everything," Jenna says, leading us to one of the picnic tables. "How did you meet? When did you get engaged? What was the wedding like?"

Sierra leans on the table, resting her head on her hand. "I'm actually Rose's sister's assistant, and she introduced us when Rose was looking for a new roommate. We moved in together a few weeks later."

"Aww, how sweet. Was it love at first sight?"

Sierra chuckles, batting her eyelashes and flashing a bashful smile. Who the fuck is she? "More like love at first *fight*," she says. "We didn't get along at first, did we, honey?"

I swallow. Deep breaths. If Sierra can do this, I sure as hell can. "You could say there were some adjustment issues when we first moved in together," I admit, winding my arm around her shoulders and hoping it looks smooth. Sierra snuggles into my side, and she smells pretty good. Like sugared violets. I need to find out what shampoo she uses—there are like twenty empty bottles in the bathroom at home.

"But the more time we spent together, the more we realized how much we have in common," I continue. Sierra looks up at me with a sweet smile, but I've spent enough time around her to notice that it doesn't reach her eyes. "Once we noticed that, there was no going back. I knew she was going to be my wife someday."

"You guys are adorable." I barely notice who said it. It's been twenty minutes and I'm already exhausted. Sierra must see it in my eyes, because she looks away and changes the subject.

"Kayleigh, Rose tells me you're from England? My brother's partner, Rylan, is from Brighton. Where are you from?"

I sit back and let her take the reins, wondering how the hell I'm supposed to maintain this for the next three months. It doesn't feel so bad here when Sierra is directing the conversation. Nothing seems to rattle her.

Until Richard, an asshole technician who works in the same lab as me, appears, that is. I hate him. He's loud and makes jokes that aren't appropriate for the twenty-first century, let alone a workplace. And I completely forgot to warn Sierra.

"Where are you from, Sierra?" Richard asks. From anyone else, the question would feel like polite small talk. But I can tell Sierra recognizes where this is going without me needing to warn her by her slow intake of breath.

"I was born in Washington, but my dad's Canadian, so we lived in Toronto for a good part of my childhood," she replies. She sounds breezy, even if her hold on my waist tightens.

"Right, right. But where are you really from?"

There it is. I open my mouth, but Sierra squeezes my waist, so I bite my tongue.

"Specifically, I was born in Yakima. My parents lived there for a few years before they had me."

Richard frowns. "Oh, yeah, but I meant—"

"We all know what you meant, Richard," I snap before I can stop myself, and several surprised faces turn my way. I take a sharp breath. "Either ask outright, or let it go."

Sierra looks a little stunned at my outburst, but she recovers quickly. "Rosie can be a little protective of me sometimes. I assume you were wondering about my ethnicity?"

Richard's face is bright red, and I expect he's not used to being called on his bullshit—by a woman, no less. "Yes," he practically mumbles.

"My dad's second-generation Japanese Canadian. His parents moved from Nagoya to Calgary in the '50s. My mom's from Washington, but her family is German and Dutch." Sierra's answer sounds rehearsed. How many times has she been asked the same thing, the same way? I know she loves talking about her heritage, but it has to feel really shitty when people constantly dance around it like that.

And based on the unhappy looks Richard is getting, I'm not the only one who's noticed it. Lisa clears her throat, dropping onto the bench opposite us.

"Have you visited Japan? I've always wanted to go. It looks incredible."

"It is," Sierra says, her face lighting up. "We went a few times when I was a kid, but it's been a while. I'm not big on flying, and it's a big trip. Still, I'd like to take Rosie someday. I always dreamed of getting to take my wife to visit the places my grandparents talked about."

She has a wistful expression on her face when she talks about it, and I imagine her taking her wife one day—her actual wife, not me. For the second time today, I feel a sharp pain in my chest.

CHAPTER TWELVE

Sierra

You realize the sink isn't a storage space for your dirty dishes, right? – R
P.S. 81 days

"**S**hit," I groan. I knew this was coming. Jazz has been suspiciously quiet about me and Rose in the week since family dinner. And by that, I mean, she hasn't brought it up once. And I certainly haven't volunteered anything.

I drop my phone on the kitchen island and hop down from the stool. "Do you want this?"

Rose looks over from the coffee machine and arches a brow at my avocado toast. "What did you do to it?"

"You got me. I'm giving up on the inheritance, and I took out a life insurance policy on you instead. I mashed poison into the avocado," I reply, rolling my eyes. "I didn't do anything to it. Jazz just sprung on me that she's picking me up in ten minutes so she can take me to breakfast—presumably to grill me about us—and I need to finish getting ready. Eat it or don't. I don't care."

Ten minutes later, when I'm rushing out the door, the plate is empty.

"So." Jazz narrows her eyes at me over her iced latte.

"So," I echo.

"I have a question."

"Shoot."

"What the fuck are you doing, Sierra?" Jazz asks, slamming her latte down on the table so hard that some of the lavender whipped cream falls off. "Look, I'm no stranger to a drunken mistake, but *getting married?*"

"You and Liam got married after two months of dating," I point out.

Jazz glares at me. "'Dating' being the optimal part of that sentence. There's also something to be said for the fact that Liam and I didn't hate each other approximately two hours before said wedding. I was with you, remember?"

It's hard to argue with that. In Vegas, hungover in the diner, this all seemed so much more manageable. I didn't consider how hard it would be to actually lie to people I care about—how guilty I'd feel. And it feels really fucking unfair that I'm the one feeling guilty when it was Rose's idea to stay married. She doesn't seem remotely fazed by any of this.

"I understand that this seems a little out of the blue," I say, finally, and Jazz rolls her eyes.

"Seriously? Did you practice that? What the fuck, Sierra?"

I throw my hands up with a frustrated groan, almost upending my coffee. "What do you want me to say? I'm not going to apologize for marrying someone I... care about. I know the circumstances aren't ideal, but since when did love happen conveniently?"

It doesn't sound remotely convincing to my ears, but Jazz's expression softens.

"How did it happen?"

"What?"

"How did you go from hating each other to being in love in the blink of an eye? I mean, I assume it's been building a while, but it didn't seem like that when you were both pissed that the other was coming to Vegas."

Right. This is something Rose and I should probably have discussed ahead of time—*the story*. Liam got Jazz hooked on romance books, and the two of them love a love story. Lying comes naturally to me, something I should probably unpack, but storytelling has never been my forte. I only just scraped a B- in my college creative writing class.

They say the best stories are rooted in truth, but there's zero truth to our nonexistent love story, so I'm on my own here. I clear my throat.

"Well, it's like you said: it's been building for a while. We spend so much time together, not intentionally, but we live together, you know. And I guess it started to change when…" I wrack my brain, trying to think of something that might trigger our feelings to change, and almost clap my hands when something comes to mind. "Do you remember when I had that really bad flu a couple of months ago?"

"I remember. You sounded so rough that I started mentally planning your funeral," Jazz says nonchalantly.

"That's… What?"

She just shrugs.

"Anyway. Rose looked after me. She made me soup." She begrudgingly brought the soup I ordered from the front door to my bedroom and was kind enough to fill up my water bottle maybe twice.

"Rose cooked for you? I've never seen Rose cook in my life," Jazz replies skeptically. And fairly. Neither Rose nor I spend much time in the kitchen. Mostly we reheat shit. Which is just as well because when I do cook, I'm messy, and I think I'd probably cause her an aneurysm.

"I didn't say she cooked," I correct. "She picked up soup from somewhere and reheated it, but the gesture was nice. And she kept an eye on me to make sure I was okay."

"And then what?"

"When I was better, we went out, and I bought her

dinner to say thank you." We went to the grocery store together because my car was in the shop, and I paid for her pre-made salad because she forgot her purse.

"And then?"

Jesus. Does she want a full timeline?

I raise my brows. "I don't think you want more details than that, considering Rose is your little sister."

She wrinkles her nose at the implication. "Gross. No, thank you. I'm not going to pretend I get it, because I don't, but thank you for telling me that."

We're quiet as our food arrives, and with one bite of her strawberry pancakes, Jazz momentarily forgets I'm sitting across from her. I dig into my avocado breakfast stack— admittedly nicer than the toast I make at home—and enjoy the quiet, until Jazz drops her fork on her plate and sighs.

"We're friends, so I'm going to ask you something as a friend and not a big sister who's concerned about her sister's wellbeing."

I gesture for her to go on with my fork.

"What happens in three months?"

My lungs burn as I inhale the avocado and sriracha. Shit. I take a big gulp of my coffee and a deep breath, trying not to meet my demise in a fucking diner. What the hell does Jazz mean by that?

"What are you talking about? Three months?" I ask, hoping I look suitably oblivious.

"Come on, Sierra. I've known you for years now. I know your pattern."

I don't have to pretend to look oblivious as I answer. "My pattern?"

"Amy, Molly, Zhi, Sydney…" She ticks off her fingers as she recites the names of the women I've dated in the three and a half years she's known me. "Am I missing anyone?"

She's missing Toni and Mariana, but I somehow don't think it's necessary to mention them.

"What's your point?" I ask wearily, though I already know where she's going with this.

"My point is that you meet someone, you date for three months, and then you break up with them, no matter how much you like them. With seemingly no exceptions. I thought Molly and Zhi might actually last longer than three months, considering how much you liked them, but nope. Three months on the dot, you ended things."

I had no idea she was so observant. Shit.

I could tell her that I have a strict three-month limit on relationships because the easiest way not to get hurt is not to give people the chance to hurt you. I could tell her that I usually have the same rule for friends, but she somehow weaseled her way into being the exception to the rule. I could tell her where it all started, because god knows I've never really opened up to her. I could tell her that none of it matters, because Rose and I have a three-month agreement, anyway.

But I don't tell her any of those things.

"What can I say? Three months is long enough for me to know if I want to be with someone long-term or not. Why prolong things if I know it's not going to last?"

"And Rose is the person you've decided it's going to last with?" she asks.

I nod, feeling more and more guilty with every lie I tell her straight to her face.

Jazz hums. "I suppose it makes sense that you'd be so picky. Your parents are stupid in love. Kyo too. Marriage must be pretty important to you, considering how long your parents have been happily married."

"It is."

Why do I sound defensive? Thankfully, Jazz keeps talking, like she didn't notice my sharp tone.

"Between you and me, I'm really happy that it's your family Rose married into. She's always seemed so lonely, and you know what our parents are like. It was so healing for me to be accepted by the Michaelsons—Maggie, too—and feel like a part of a real family for a change."

I push a piece of arugula around my plate with my fork, squirming uncomfortably.

"How did your parents take it? Were they excited?" Jazz asks, but I don't look up. I can't look up.

"Yeah, they were really excited. They can't wait to meet Rose."

"That's sweet. She deserves a good family to look up to —and you both deserve a marriage like your parents, Sierra. Don't get me wrong, I'm still a little baffled and blindsided, but I'm happy for you both."

I thank her, then hide behind my almost empty coffee cup, dragging out the last mouthful.

All I've ever wanted is a relationship like my parents have. Marriage is a sacred thing between them, and I know Kyo struggles with the fact he'll never get to marry both people he loves. Yet here I am, trampling all over something so important to them. They would be ashamed of me if they found out. They're going to be devastated when Rose and I get divorced.

I know I'm not entirely blameless here, but fuck Rose for putting me in this position. Fuck her for being so unbothered by it all.

What I need is a break—from Rose, from the guilt, from all of it. What I need is to spend my Friday night in a bar, and to leave with someone who's going to make me forget all about Rose Cannon.

CHAPTER THIRTEEN

Sierra

I look myself over in the mirror, smoothing my hands over the tight, burgundy leather-style pants. They're not my usual style, but they were on clearance and I've never met a bargain I could pass up—even when my closet is already overflowing with shit I never wear.

It's been a long week since family dinner last Friday, and I need to get out of here. Being stuck in an apartment with Rose is shitty at the best of times. Being stuck here while we're learning to navigate our new situation? So much worse.

When we initially agreed to stay married, I didn't think anything would change at home. I figured that we'd only notice it when we were around others, lying our asses off. But there have been constant reminders, and, just like at breakfast with Jazz, the guilt is eating me alive.

First, it was our official marriage certificate. It arrived the Monday after family dinner and I didn't want to lose it, so I stuck it to the fridge with the purple poker chip magnet, assuming Rose would file it away wherever she keeps all her important shit. But she didn't. Five days later, and it's still stuck up there, a glaring reminder every time I want a snack.

Then, the gifts started arriving. Rose's parents clearly feel guilty about how they acted at family dinner, because they've sent thousands of dollars worth of gifts: gift cards, kitchen shit, fancy towels, bedding, and, weirdly, a personalized welcome mat. Rose still isn't speaking to them, but she wrote out a thank-you card and mailed it to them.

They must have told their friends about us, too, because packages have been arriving daily from people I haven't heard of. I felt guilty at first until Rose pointed out that most of them probably outsource gift-sending to their personal assistants and wouldn't notice the dent in their bank accounts.

The gift that bothered me most, though, was the drawing Kami's daughter, Lexi, drew for us. It's mostly scribbles, but it's two clearly defined people, one with black hair, one with yellow, and a giant purple heart. She even painted a frame for us. Every time I look at it, displayed by the TV, I wonder how many asshole points Rose and I gained for lying to a four-year-old. Probably more than I want to know.

But tonight, I'm putting all of that out of my brain. I'm going to my favorite lesbian bar to have a drink, meet a woman, go home with her, and have so many orgasms that I don't spend a second thinking about—

Shit. We never talked about this. I should probably ask Rose if she's cool with me hooking up with other women while we're married. Knowing her, she'll probably say no just to spite me. I grab my purse and heels and head out into the living room.

Rose is lying on the couch with her feet up, a barely cracked paperback in her hand (god forbid she breaks the spine). I perch on the arm of the couch, and she doesn't bother hiding her sigh as she puts the book down.

"What?"

"I'm going out tonight," I say, and she raises an eyebrow that clearly says, "and why would I care?" I count to three in my head. "I wanted to make sure you were okay with me sleeping with other women."

Rose furrows her brow. "Why wouldn't I be?"

"Because we *are* technically married."

"Legally, yes. But that's it. Personally, we still hate each other's guts, and I don't care what you do."

Succinct and a little mean: the Rose Cannon specialty.

"Great. In that case..." I stand and head toward the door.

"Where are you going?"

"I thought you didn't care," I say, looking back over my shoulder.

"I don't, but if something happens and I can't tell the police where my wife is, they're going to think that's pretty suspicious. Actually, maybe we should just share our phone locations with each other. Spouses do that, right?"

It's not the worst idea. Jazz often sits and watches Liam's location dot when she's feeling clingy at work (and, when she's not watching his, she's showing Cal Maggie's, since he can never find the right app on his phone).

I quickly share my location, and a notification pops up to say Rose has shared hers.

"Great. I'm going now."

"Sierra," she calls the second I have my hand on the door handle.

I grit my teeth. "What?"

"You might want to take your wedding ring off."

The bar is dark, the music just loud enough that I have to strain to hear the woman standing beside me, and I can't shake the feeling I'm doing something wrong. I owe Rose nothing, but something about standing here, trying to hook up with some random woman while she's at home, feels wrong.

Not trying to have a repeat of Vegas, I ordered a single glass of white wine, but it tastes sour on my tongue. There's a gorgeous brunette flirting with me, but every time I look into her piercing blue eyes, I think of hazel instead.

She ruins everything.

"Anyway, I feel like I've been talking about myself for hours. What do you do?" April asks, leaning in closer. Her perfume is pretty—vanilla with floral undertones. Roses, probably. Fuck.

"I'm an assistant at a law firm downtown," I say, leaning back and breathing in my wine instead.

"Nice. So, do you live nearby?" April asks through fluttery lashes and, as out of sorts as I am, I recognize the cue.

"I'm like ten minutes away. You?"

Her eyes twinkle. "I'm just around the corner. My place is much quieter than this if you'd like to..." She trails off, her gaze falling to my glass. Fuck. I didn't take my ring off.

April raises a brow. "Is that an engagement ring?"

"It's a wedding ring, technically," I answer without thinking. I flinch. "Shit. No, I mean... It's complicated. I'm—"

"Wait." April holds up a hand. "Don't tell me. I won't feel as guilty if I don't know the details. You want to come back to my place?"

The knowledge that she's not put off by the ring on my finger zaps any of the attraction I feel for her. She has no idea my marriage isn't real, and she doesn't give a shit.

But it's also just another reminder in a long line that, even though she might not feel guilty, I do. It doesn't matter that Rose okayed me coming out tonight. My stomach is in fucking knots.

I drain my glass and set it on the bar top. "Actually, I think I'm going to head home. It was nice talking to you."

I turn to leave, but April grasps my shoulder. "Hey, she doesn't have to know. I won't tell if you won't."

The urge to laugh, because she wouldn't care if she did know, rolls over me, but I just pull out of April's grip. "Goodnight," I say, heading for the door and wishing I'd brought a jacket as I step out into the cool night.

I consider calling a cab, but it's only a ten-minute walk, and I could use the fresh air. Two weeks married to Rose, and I haven't really let myself think about it. We talked about when to tell our families, how to approach Rose's colleagues, and made sure we were both aware of the end date, but neither of us brought up what this would look like day to day.

Maybe it's me. Rose doesn't seem nearly as cut up about it all as I do. The guilt is eating me alive. I can barely sleep, and she doesn't seem to give a shit. It's so fucking typical of her—icy and aloof.

Is this what life is going to be like for the next three months? I'm already exhausted. And all I wanted was a goddamn orgasm or two.

I stop outside our apartment building. How the hell did I get home so fast? It's like the closer I got to home, the closer I got to *her*, the more pissed off I got. It was Rose's idea for us to stay married—how dare she be so calm about it all?

The front door bangs behind me as I storm into the building and up the stairs, forgoing the elevator. My keys shake in my fingers as I force them into the lock and push open our apartment door. I drop my keys on the entryway table and kick my shoes off messily—fuck Rose's shoe organization.

It doesn't look like she's moved since I left. She's still lying on the couch, her book in one hand and a blanket covering her body. She looks up, confused. "That was... fast." She picks up her phone and frowns at the time. "You've only been gone for forty minutes. How did you meet someone—"

"I didn't," I interrupt, sounding as pissed off as I feel.

"Okay..."

"Well, I did, actually. Her name was April, and she didn't care that I'm married."

"And the problem is?"

"I care!" I shout without meaning to, and Rose's eyes widen. "Fuck," I mutter, rubbing my face.

"This seems like a bigger conversation than I thought," Rose says, sitting up and putting her bookmark inside her book. She sets it down on the table and looks back at me. "Okay. What's going on here?"

I suck in a long breath, trying to get my thoughts together. "Marriage means something to me, Rose. I grew up watching my parents so happy and in love, and all I ever wanted was a marriage like that. And I know it's just a legal contract, and it doesn't really matter, but I never expected to be thirty and married to someone who hates me, with the intention of getting divorced in three months."

I can tell from her expression that she doesn't get it, and of course she doesn't. "And this stopped you hooking up with this April person because…?"

"Because *you* are my wife." I'm shouting again. "Sure, it's not real, but I already feel so fucking guilty for lying to everyone we know about this marriage. I can't handle the guilt of feeling like I'm cheating on you."

"It's not cheating. We're not in a relationship. None of this makes any sense."

"I know that! Logically, I know that. God knows I don't fucking want to be in a relationship with you, but it doesn't matter. Look, you're free to sleep with whoever you want, but I can't do it. This is all too much." I turn on my heel, heading toward my bedroom.

"Where are you going?" Rose asks, sounding completely baffled by my outburst.

I take a steadying breath. "Since I'm apparently going to be celibate for the next three months, I'm going to give myself an orgasm. Put some music on or something if you don't want to hear it."

CHAPTER FOURTEEN

Rose

You realize you're my wife (ew) not
my mother, right? - S
P.S. Still 81 days. Boo.

Sierra is usually so laid back she's practically horizontal. Seeing her this rattled is... something else.

I have to force my jaw closed as I watch her go, her black hair streaming behind her. What the fuck was that?

Not that she was particularly clear with all the shouting, but I can't wrap my head around the problem. Marriage is nothing more than a legal document—it's not a big deal. It's not like a marriage makes a relationship. Well, not an emotional one anyway. I can't imagine Jazz and Liam's feelings for each other changed just because they signed a piece of paper, or Maggie and Cal, or Eliza and Danisha. Or Sierra's parents. Marriage has nothing to do with how strong their relationships are.

If it meant anything, my parents would have some kind of affection for each other, surely. And if a little piece of paper had any bearing on feelings, Sierra and I wouldn't hate each other the same way we always have. We've spent more time together in the past two weeks than we have in a year of living together, and, while I have a newfound appreciation for the ease with which she lies, I still can't stand her.

It's not like she's had a personality transplant since she put the ring on her finger. Or since I did, I suppose. I eye her heels, kicked off by the door, and sigh. She still has no regard for our shared space.

I throw off my blanket and walk toward the door, picking up her heels to put them back neatly. They're nice shoes, and her legs did look amazing in them. And the pants... God, the pants. Tight burgundy leather that accentuated every curve. Then there was the semi-sheer lace shirt. Knowing about the snake inked on her sternum has admittedly been a little problematic for me. It's not like I think about it *all* the time, but it pops into my head at the most inconvenient moments.

She really was onto something tonight, going out and trying to meet someone. I didn't exactly check that off my list in Vegas, thanks to her. It's been a while. But the thought of finding someone on an app, getting all dressed up, going out, and trying to impress them sounds exhausting.

I look toward Sierra's bedroom door. I can't hear anything, but I am on the other side of the apartment. My mind wanders to a place it shouldn't, wondering about things I have no business wondering about. Like how she touches herself; how she likes to be touched; what she looks like writhing in the covers; what she sounds like when she—

Shit, no. I shouldn't go there. Because once I think it, I can't unthink it. And as tempting as it is to drag my feet across the floor and knock on her bedroom door, if I open that door, I can't close it. And casual sex between room-mates is a bad enough idea, let alone casual sex between roommates who hate each other and are also kind of married.

Things are already complicated—I shouldn't complicate them further.

But...

Things *are* already complicated. What's the worst that could happen? We already don't like each other, we already wish we weren't living together, so there's no danger of us fucking up a civil living arrangement.

And while I don't think I'd have the same hang-ups about sleeping with other people as she does, there's always a worry I'd run into a colleague or a friend of a friend while out flirting with someone. I don't want to go three months without sex, and I bet Sierra doesn't either.

This has all gotten so out of hand.

My feet take me across the apartment before I can stop them, but I pause before raising my fist. I can't take this back, and Sierra's already spiraling about things. But maybe she just needs an outlet. And I could be that outlet.

I knock—three short taps on the door.

There's a rustling noise before Sierra answers, sounding

just as pissed off as she was before she disappeared. "What do you want?"

"Can I come in?"

"I'd rather you didn't. Do you have to?"

"I want to talk."

I hear her huff. "Fine."

The hinges creak as I force open the door—force, because Sierra has clearly just dropped her leather pants where she was standing. Jesus, it's a mess in here.

I'm pretty sure if you looked up maximalist on Pinterest, Sierra's room would pop up. There are bright splashes of color everywhere, from the pink quilted headboard to the yellow and blue floral comforter. The walls are covered in shelves with little trinkets, frames with completely mismatched art prints, and there's a giant lesbian flag hanging above her bed with a smudged Sharpie autograph I've never been able to make out. And then there's the plants. There have to be three dozen, if not more, dotted around the room. I have no idea how she sleeps in here—it's so chaotic.

She's lying in bed, the comforter pulled up to her chin.

"I'm kind of busy," she says. "Did you miss that I was clearly planning on spending some alone time with my vibrator?"

"I've seen your vibrator—you leave it in the bathroom after cleaning it sometimes—and, if you're planning on staying celibate for the next three months, you really should upgrade."

She gasps as I perch on the edge of her bed. As messy as

her room is, it smells amazing. Like a less overwhelming Bath & Body Works.

"Don't offend Olivia Newton-John like that!"

"You... named your vibrator after Olivia Newton-John?"

Sierra shrugs and sits up, pulling the covers with her. "I was going through a Grease phase when I bought it. And I would very much like to be using her right now, so can you get whatever you want to say out of the way so I can carry on?"

"Patience is a virtue, you know."

"I swear to god, Rose, I—"

I hold up a hand. "Okay, okay. I wanted to say that I don't understand why marriage is so important to you—"

"Yeah, I got that," she interrupts, and I take a deep breath.

"This is going to take a lot longer if you keep interrupting."

Sierra mimes zipping her lips and gestures for me to continue.

"As I was saying, I don't understand, but I do recognize that you probably have a different outlook on marriage, considering how different our upbringings were. Look, I don't like you. You don't like me. I get that this isn't what you dreamed about as a kid, and if you want to call this now, we can get a lawyer and figure out the divorce stuff tomorrow."

She narrows her eyes at me, clearly suspicious. "Why are you being so nice to me?"

"I'm not being nice, I'm being pragmatic. If you're

going to keep having meltdowns like you did earlier, this isn't maintainable."

"Right," she scoffs. "The damage is done now. We might as well see it through."

"Alright. Well, on that note, if you want me to stay celibate while we're married, I can do that," I offer.

Sierra raises a brow. "You don't need to do that."

"Good. Because I don't want to." I take a deep breath. Here goes nothing. "What if you didn't sleep with anyone else? What if you slept with me?"

Sierra stares at me like I've grown a second head. "I—what?"

"You don't want to sleep with anyone else and, honestly, this whole fake marriage thing is taking up most of the energy I reserve for meeting new people, so why don't we just kill two birds with one stone?"

She just about manages to close her mouth before dissolving into a fit of gasping laughter. "Oh my god. Are you serious? We hate each other, Rose. What makes you think either of us would enjoy sleeping together?"

I shrug, my eyes snagging on the crumpled leather pants. "Personality-wise, I don't like you. Physically... I do. And apparently you think I'm hot, too, according to my sister."

"I mean, duh. I have eyes. But a lot could go wrong here."

"Like what?"

"What if you fall in love with me?"

I snort. "Yeah, that's not going to happen."

"What if *I* fall in love with you?"

"Even less likely. I'm pretty mean."

"True." Sierra looks like she's racking her brain, searching for reasons this is a bad idea. "I bet we wouldn't even be compatible sexually."

"What are you into?"

Sierra's cheeks turn pink, and she clears her throat before answering. "I'm pretty submissive. In bed," she adds, as if I don't live with her and know all about how *not* submissive she is the rest of the time.

Of course she's submissive in bed. Why wouldn't the universe make the one person I don't want to want exactly my type?

"Well, I'm not submissive. Like, at all," I say, trying not to sound pissed off about it.

"Oh." With one word, her entire demeanor changes. Sierra's uncertainty morphs into intrigue, and it tells me a lot about her. "How dominant are we talking?"

"Not like *'collar you and make you crawl for me'* levels, but I'm pretty dominant. I mean, if that's what you're into, I could…" I trail off because I can picture it clearly. And I like it. A lot.

"I could be into that," Sierra says, so quietly it's practically a whisper. "We would have to have rules, though. Boundaries, you know."

"Obviously. Like not falling in love with each other."

"Exactly. And it would just be as long as we're married. As soon as we sign the divorce papers, we go our separate ways, as planned."

"Agreed. Any other rules?"

Sierra draws her lip between her teeth, chewing the skin. "Is kissing okay? Or is it too intimate?"

All of this is too intimate. But it was my idea. "I like kissing. But we should keep it to a minimum. Only during sex or when we're in public around other people."

Sierra nods. "Yeah, that makes sense. Also, I'm not really into people being mean to me during sex, so maybe we could keep fighting to a minimum when we're, you know."

"I'm not into that, either. No fighting during sex. I make no promises for the rest of the time, though."

"I'd expect nothing less. Okay, so, we're doing this?"

"I'm in if you are."

Sierra considers me for a moment, her dark eyes searching my face. Whatever she sees seems to reassure her, because she nods. "I'm in."

I clap my hands together, internally cringing at how awkward I am. "Great. We should probably talk everything over and make sure we're fully on the same page about what we're okay with and what we're not. Do you have a safe word?"

Sierra's cheeks turn scarlet. "I do. But I'm going to pick a new one."

"Why? What do you usually use?"

She sucks her breath in through her teeth. "Your name."

"Oh."

"Yeah, well, you know how I feel about flowers, and… Anyway, I don't think that's going to work here."

"Definitely not. I'm going to take a lot of pleasure in making you say my name over and over."

CHAPTER FIFTEEN

Sierra

There's something in her voice that makes my mouth go dry. This is a terrible idea. Not the worst idea we've ever had—I'd say moving in together, drunkenly getting married, and then choosing to stay married take bronze, silver, and gold for bad ideas. This is up there, though.

But I said yes anyway. With little convincing. Because I know, without a doubt, that Rose absolutely will have me saying her name over and over. I don't know anyone who sticks to their word quite like Rose Cannon.

"Take off the blanket."

My eyes widen. I'm no stranger to Rose demanding shit, but this is... different. Her voice is low, melting into my skin and heating me from within. "N-now? Like this?" I stammer, looking around the room. Nerves flutter in my chest. She's so intense, but it doesn't usually faze me. I guess there's something different about it when she's about to see me naked.

Rose follows my gaze, her lips pinched. "I mean, if you

want to clean up in here first, you know I'd never say no. But that might take a while."

It's incredible, really, how quickly she can take me from turned on to pissed off. "That's not what I meant," I say through gritted teeth. "I'm pretty much naked under here."

"I'm sorry, did you want to get dressed before we have sex?"

"Can you turn out the lights?"

Rose tilts her head, narrowing her eyes and surveying me. God, I've never felt more like prey in my life.

She crosses her arms. "Why?"

I blink, surprised by the question. It's not like I expected her to listen and do as I asked—though it would've been nice. I know her better than that at this point. My lungs feel tight as I suck in a breath. "I prefer keeping the lights off. It means I don't have to feel self-conscious, you know."

Rose sighs and shakes her head. "I'd tell you there's nothing to feel self-conscious about, but I don't know why I think you'd listen. So I suppose I'll just have to show you."

"I—what?" I splutter, but Rose has already turned away.

She looks over my dresser, and I can practically feel her wrinkling her nose at the clutter. Or what she perceives as clutter, anyway. Everything is actually placed intentionally, laid out so I can see all my favorite things.

Rose looks over her shoulder at me. "Lighter."

It's a demand, not a question, but I bite down the retort tickling my tongue. My nightstand drawer is no less chaotic than my dresser, but it only takes a couple of seconds to find the lighter and toss it to her. It might be chaos, but it's *my* chaos.

She catches it with ease—I bet she played some fancy-ass sport like lacrosse or tennis growing up—and turns her back on me again.

I listen to the click of the lighter and the crackle as she lights one of my many candles, but I stare up at the ceiling, steadying myself.

It's not too late to call this off—any of it. All I have to do is say the word, and we can pretend we didn't agree to sleep together. It would be easy. Getting out of the rest of it would be a little trickier—I don't even know if we can annul this thing anymore—but we could figure it out. I just have to open my mouth and say I'm done.

But I don't. I force air into my lungs as Rose lights more candles, and, when she flicks the light switch and plunges the room into shadows, I force myself out of my head and back into the moment.

"Better?" Rose asks, and I meet her gaze, curious but not judgmental.

"I guess."

She returns to the end of the bed and holds a hand out for the blanket. I start to take it off, but hesitate.

"Why are you nervous?" Rose asks.

"You're not?"

She shakes her head, her lips lifting at the edges. "No. You know why?"

"Why?"

"Because I know you don't like me. And you know I don't like you. We have nothing to lose here."

Well, when you put it like that...

I sit up enough to push the blanket off, and Rose tugs it

away. I shouldn't be surprised that she stops to fold it before placing it on a chair, but I am. The anticipation is painful, waiting for her to look at me. But once the blanket is safely stowed away, she still doesn't.

Rose takes her time, standing with her back to me as she pulls her college sweatshirt over her head. Her blonde hair tumbles down her bare back as she folds it and drops it on top of the blanket.

I draw my knees up to my chest as I watch her twisted little power play. The candlelight illuminates freckles on her back I've never seen before, dotted around like a constellation. Without a word, she shucks her slippers off and tucks them under the chair, then shimmies out of her cycling shorts, leaving her in nothing but a black lace thong.

Pink satin. Black lace. What the hell is up with her lingerie collection, and how have I never seen any of these in our laundry room? Probably because she washes, dries, and puts everything away without waiting three to five business days.

I open my mouth to snark about her surprisingly spicy lingerie, but the words die on my tongue when she nonchalantly turns around.

My cheeks burn, but I can't help but drag my eyes over her, drinking in every inch. I regret asking her to turn the light off, though the candles light her enough for me to take in the lines and details of her body I've never been privy to.

Rose's body is the kind you'd see in a swimsuit magazine—long and lithe, model perfect with curves everywhere society claims is acceptable. Her skin is unmarred other than a surprising belly button piercing and a few scars on her upper thighs.

Even from my spot over here, I can tell her breasts are a perfect handful, with pretty pink nipples the exact shade of her lips. God, I need to get my hands on her.

I raise my eyes to her face and find her watching me, an eyebrow raised and a smirk on her mouth. "Are you done ogling?"

I shrug. "I didn't expect the piercing."

"I got it in high school and was too scared to take it out in case it left a scar."

She kneels on the end of the bed, and the proximity of her makes me a little lightheaded. "Are you going to hide away like that all night?" The words are sarcastic, but she sounds softer than she usually does.

"No," I reply, gulping down a breath but making no move.

Rose screws up her lips. "Okay. Don't be alarmed, but I'm going to be nice to you for a second—"

"Someone call the news."

"Ignoring that... You know I don't like you—"

"Is this your idea of nice?" Sounds about right.

"You know, I was planning on keeping things nice and light tonight, but if you're going to interrupt everything I say, your ass is going to become well acquainted with the palm of my hand. Are we clear?"

My mouth pops open, and I swear my legs part ever so slightly of their own accord. It's simultaneously sexy and terrifying how her expression doesn't change, how she says something so threateningly filthy without batting an eye.

"Crystal clear," I answer, but my voice sounds a million miles away to my own ears.

"Great. As I was saying, I may not like your personality, but your body? Fuck, Sierra. That little glimpse I got when we woke up in Vegas has been haunting me. You're infuriating, but you're beautiful. I get the feeling people haven't always made you feel that way. Am I right?"

I hesitate before finally nodding. I half expect pity, but fire flashes in Rose's hazel eyes and she huffs, her nostrils flaring like a pissed off bull.

When I lived in Canada, we lived near a lot of other Asian-Canadian families. It was a diverse neighborhood, and I never felt out of place. Until we moved back to Washington, and I realized I didn't fit the average American stereotype of an Asian woman.

My first week at my new school, I overheard a group of girls in my grade whispering about me: "I thought all Japanese girls were skinny," one of them said, and the rest just laughed. Teenage girls aren't known for their kindness.

I was sixteen, so it wasn't the first time someone had made a shitty comment about my appearance or my race. And god knows it wasn't the last. But it was the first time it had happened without the community I was used to having around me, and sixteen is a formative age.

I'm thirty years old now, and I've had a long time to come to terms with my body looking like it does. I don't hate it, not like I did when I was a teenager, but I don't love it either. It's just skin and bone, designed to hold all the things that make me *me* in place. If anyone asked me, I'd swear I was completely neutral about the curve of my stomach, the wobble of my thighs, the way my breasts droop, and the stretch marks painted across my skin. And sometimes I am neutral. But sometimes I remember hiding in the school bathroom and fighting back tears. Sometimes, I look at bodies like Rose's and wonder *what if?* How would the world look at me if I was a size four instead of a size fourteen? How would I look if I fit the stereotype?

"Sierra," Rose says, her expression gentler. "When we first moved in together, you used to have this lime green tank top. Do you remember?"

My brows draw together. "Yeah." I tossed it after I accidentally spilled paint on it at one of Jazz and Liam's paint and sip nights.

"It rode up whenever you stretched, and I remember sitting on the couch watching you reach into the cabinet for a wineglass. It slipped up and showed off your midriff. It was my first time seeing that part of you, and do you know what I thought when I saw your stretch marks?" I shake my head, and Rose continues, "I wanted to trace them with my tongue. I've never once looked at your body and thought anything but gorgeous. Your body is beautiful. You are beautiful. Okay?"

She emphasizes every word, her eyes shining with conviction. It's a little scary, honestly, but somehow reassuring at the same time. I nod, quickly.

"I want to hear you say it. Tell me you're beautiful, Sierra."

Jesus Christ. This is a whole new side of Rose, one I find it hard to argue with. I really can't let her figure out how easy it would be for her to win this stupid battle of wills we've been fighting for the past year, if only she spoke like this on a regular basis.

"I…"

"Say it."

"I'm beautiful," I whisper. The words sound foreign and weak from my tongue, and Rose raises a brow that clearly says, "not good enough." I clear my throat. "I'm beautiful." Better. I sound stronger, like I might actually believe myself.

A sensual smile lights Rose's face. "Yes, you are. Now here's how this is going to go." She crawls closer. "If at any point you want to stop, say 'red' and we stop. No questions asked. If you need a breather or to slow down, 'yellow.'"

"And 'green' if I like it?"

Rose licks her lips. I follow the motion of her tongue and wish it was on me instead. "I'll know if you like it."

She places a cool hand on my knee, and I jump, my heart racing. She looks over my face, waiting for me to nod before she holds my other knee. Her palms are smooth against my skin as she drags them along my thighs.

"Drop your arms," she commands, and my body listens before my brain catches up. I let my arms fall, clenching the sheets in my fists.

Rose lets loose a ragged breath, but her gaze doesn't stray from my face. She's the pinnacle of control as she parts my knees and kneels between them.

Slowly, like time means nothing, she lowers her gaze. I swear her hands tighten on my thighs, her pupils swallowing her golden-hazel irises.

"Fuck," she whispers, blinking like she's as surprised as I am by the word slipping from her lips.

She leans forward, dragging a single finger over my skin, skimming my stomach. "What does it mean?" she asks as she traces the black snake and rose tattoo on my sternum.

"Nothing. I just thought it was pretty," I lie, because I'm already vulnerable and she doesn't care, not really. This is all foreplay, getting me comfortable and supplicant beneath her touch.

"Of course you did. It is pretty. I'll give you that," she replies with a short, humorless laugh.

For the first time, I realize she's as affected by this as I am. She wants me, and she hates it.

The thought emboldens me, and I loosen my grip on the sheets. This version of Rose might be sensual, intense, and, frankly, intimidating, but she's still the stuck-up, bossy Rose who thinks she's better than everyone else. I can want to come apart at the seams under her touch and hate her guts at the same time. She can say pretty things and get me to do as I'm told while the lights are off and still be completely insufferable the rest of the time. She's just Rose.

It's like she watches everything click into place behind my eyes, and the last of her hesitation melts away as I breathe out the tension.

"We'll have a proper conversation at some point about boundaries and shit, but for now... How are you with praise?"

"Giving or receiving?" I ask, though I know she means receiving. And she knows I know it, which is why she doesn't answer, just quirks a perfect blonde brow. "I like praise."

"Pain?"

"Nothing crazy, but I like a little."

"Do you like being talked through it, or quiet?"

"Um…" I trail off, unsure how to answer. I'm not big on talking, usually, but I like how Rose has talked to me tonight. "I'm not sure, actually. Can we try talking and see how it goes?"

"We can do that."

"And you? What do you like?"

Rose continues the ascent of her finger, tipping my chin up. "We can talk about me tomorrow."

"But—" I'm cut off when Rose pushes her fingers and fists them in my hair, tugging my head back. It isn't painful, but it's on the edge. I gasp, groaning as she pushes me back against the pillows and threads my right hand with hers.

"Don't answer back," she chastises, and I'm so fucked. I think I could actually get off from her scolding me alone. This is such a problem. "You're going to do as you're told for me, aren't you?" I nod, but she tuts. "Use your words."

Christ, she's so condescending. And I really, *really* like it. I'm fucking soaked.

"I'm going to do as I'm told," I whimper as her grip on my hair tightens.

"For…"

I grit my teeth. "For you. I'm going to do as I'm told for you."

A wicked smile falls across Rose's lips and she bends

her head, her mouth hovering an inch from mine. "See? You can be a good girl when you want to be. And good girls get rewarded, Sierra."

CHAPTER SIXTEEN

Sierra

I expect her to kiss me, to close the gap, and press her lips to mine. But this is Rose, so of course she doesn't do that. She catches my lower lip between her teeth and bites down. I cry out, my hips lifting from the mattress. I desperately need her hands on me, but it's not like I'm going to say that.

Rose pulls back a hairsbreadth and runs her tongue along my lip. She captures my left hand with hers, bracketing my head and holding me against the pillows. My eyes flutter closed as she brushes my ring with her thumb, a shiver rushing down my spine. Why the fuck is that so hot?

"I'm going to kiss you now," she whispers, and I don't have time to process before her lips are on mine and my mind goes blank. For a moment, I feel nothing, and then all I feel is *her.* She consumes me, flooding my senses until there's no space for anything else. Rose smells like the world after a thunderstorm, but she tastes sweet. Like Earl Grey and vanilla, warm and cozy.

Her lips are velvet moving over mine, soft to the touch

but claiming and demanding. Like she might suck the soul out of me, just for fun.

And then she moans, the sound vibrating through me and instantly taking the top spot for my new favorite sound. I've spent so much time with Rose, not necessarily will-ingly, and I could've sworn I'd seen every side of her. If I had to, I could describe her with ease: a little shy, a lot awkward, sharp and blunt like a steel axe, biting cold like a January frost.

But her moan is anything but shy, and her fingers are anything but awkward as they snake between our bodies, teasing and toying with me. She drags her warm lips down my jaw, soft and intentional. Her breath tickles my skin, and I squirm beneath her as she moves over my throat, nipping at my shoulder, and sliding down my body.

She pinches my nipple between her finger and her thumb, and I push my head back into the pillows, a ragged curse spilling from me. As she grips my sensitive skin harder, I squeeze my eyes closed, and my thighs try to close around her, like dominoes falling in a line. My body searches for friction, but Rose uses her free hand to spread my legs. She tugs on my nipple once more, well into pain territory, then closes her lips around the hard tip.

The switch-up of sensation is almost too much to bear. I don't realize I've knotted my fingers in her hair until she carefully untangles them and stretches them over my head.

"Hold on to the headboard," she says, her breath blowing warm across my nipple. I whimper and she grins, her chest and cheeks flushed maroon.

She sits back on her knees, brushing her thumb over my

nipple once more before drawing her finger down the center of my torso.

Her finger stops right at the edge of my underwear. "I like you a lot more when you're lying here all soft, your body begging for me."

Her condescending tone breaks through my haze, grounding me. I glare at her, because it's about as much as I can manage without combusting. "I hate you."

Rose smirks. "Oh, really?" She hooks her fingers in my underwear. Instead of pulling them off, she tugs them roughly to the side, and her eyes flame when she takes me in.

With a featherlight touch, she drags a finger through my lips, stopping just short of my clit.

Holy fucking shit. It hasn't been that long since I've been touched by someone. Why the hell does it feel so good?

"Hmm, you're pretty wet for me, considering how much you claim to hate me, *wife*."

Wife. Oh god, this is really going to fuck me up.

I try to hold on to a shred of some kind of control, but my body fights me, straining to get closer and closer to Rose. I can feel her watching me, her gaze burning my skin, her finger painfully still.

"Rose." I grind my teeth together, wrapping my legs around her. She holds steady, though.

"You want more?" she asks, her voice smooth and cool like marble. I nod and she hums, leaning over me until her body is pressed against mine. Her hand is trapped between us, still a fraction of an inch away from where I want her.

Warm air tickles my nose, and I open my eyes, sucking in a breath when I realize her face is hovering right above mine. My eyes fall to her lips, pink and a little swollen. I lick mine, missing the taste of her.

"Be a good girl and say please, wife," she murmurs, increasing the pressure of her finger. If she was just a little bit higher up, I'd already be coming.

"Seriously?"

She smirks, nodding, and brushing her lips over my cheek. I groan, trying to move my hips, but she has me trapped. Rose has the upper hand here, and she knows it. This is more than her being dominant and me being submissive; this is the same fight to the death we've been in for a year. And it's about time I took back a little control.

"Please, honey," I say, lifting a hand to cup her face. I'm both happy and surprised I don't sound like I'm begging, because I'm damn close to doing just that. "You feel so good. Please give me more."

Rose pulls back, her eyebrows lifting in surprise before she narrows them. I didn't miss the bob of her throat when I called her "honey" at the picnic, or the way her pupils dilated.

She chuckles, humorless. "You're playing with fire, Sierra," she says against my lips.

I slide my fingers into her hair, dragging my nails over her scalp until she lets loose a soft sigh. "Then light me up, Rosie."

"Fuck," she mutters, then presses her tongue between my lips at the same time she drags her finger up, finally grazing my clit.

Lights sparkle behind my eyelids, lighting up the darkness like fireworks. Rose circles my clit slowly, soft and gentle, but her mouth is anything but. Her tongue battles with mine. With her free hand, she grips my face, her fingertips pressing hard against my temple.

I twist beneath her, my body ablaze as she drinks down every whimper, every cry, every curse trying to escape my lips. She pulls back, giving herself more room, and pinches my clit lightly between her fingers.

"Oh fuck. *Rose.*"

"There it is," she replies, sounding smug as fuck, but it's hard to care when she moves back and teases my pussy with two fingers. "Is this oka—"

"Yes, yes. Fuck, please." I'm officially into begging territory.

"Listen to you begging for me." Of course she noticed. "You sound so good," she says, pressing her fingers inside me and curling. I clench around her, my head spinning. "But you look even better. Falling apart for me suits you."

I want to argue, to talk back, to prove her wrong. But she's not. Falling apart for her is exactly what I'm doing, and I couldn't stop even if I tried.

Her thumb brushes back and forth across my clit as her fingers curl inside me, hitting something fucking magical. Pressure builds to a boiling point at the center of my chest, and I gasp for air because I've forgotten how to breathe properly.

She pulls her fingers out of me, and I cry out at the loss of her. Her ponytail tickles my thigh, and I open my eyes, my vision hazy. I look down just in time to watch her spread my thighs and duck her head between them.

Her lips close around my clit, and I think I leave my body for a second. Her name is ripped from my throat, my fists clenched so tight I can feel my nails pressing into my palms. Rose lavishes me with her tongue, bringing me to the edge of a cliff. She groans, the vibration almost enough to tip me off. Just as I'm sure I might fall, she pulls away.

She stares up at me, framed by my thighs, her lips soaked. With me.

Oh god.

"Do you want to come now, or do you want me to drag it out?" she asks, and fuck me, she's panting.

"I get a choice?" My voice is like gravel, hoarse from crying out.

"This time," she says. "This time you get to choose. Don't get used to it, though."

This time. This isn't a one-time thing. We live together, we can do this whenever we want. It's not like I have to hold back now, because this is all we have.

"I want to come."

She raises a brow, expectantly.

"Please may I come?"

"Good girl." And she fucking winks. Rose Cannon. Winking. Have we stumbled into Wonderland or something? "As you wish, wife."

And then her tongue is on my clit, her fingers are inside me, and for a brief moment, I forget that I'm supposed to hate her. I soar, pleasure hitting me full force as I plummet into the depths of the strongest orgasm I've had in... ever, possibly. Heat ripples over my skin, so hot I feel like I could burn up. It's the kind of heat that steals the air from your lungs, punishing and exhausting, but I never want it to end.

Rose rolls her fingers inside of me and grazes my clit with her teeth, pulling me deeper into the orgasm. Every time I think I've hit the peak, I somehow soar higher. And when I finally crest, my scream dies on my lips, as every shred of energy I have is stolen by pleasure.

I float back into my body slowly, Rose bringing me down at a snail's pace by pressing soft kisses on and around my clit until I stop shaking.

She sits up, presses her palm flat against my thigh, and squeezes. I try to raise up on my arms to look at her, but I just flop down.

"Are you okay?" she asks in a soothing tone I've never heard from her. She rubs gentle, tentative circles on my thigh, like you might pet a cat if you've never met a cat before.

"I'm... fuck. Yeah, I'm fine," I manage, gulping in breaths.

Rose crawls up to sit beside me and reaches for my cup on the nightstand. "Drink," she orders, a soft command I'm all too happy to oblige. I chug the water, but she pulls the cup back. "Slowly. Don't choke, please."

I roll my eyes but do as I'm told—I might as well get the last of it out of my system, because as soon as we're done here, I'm done listening to her. When I've had enough water, I hand the cup over, and she sets it on the nightstand.

"Just give me a second to catch my breath and I—"

"No," she interrupts, shaking her head. "Not tonight."

I frown, wondering if I'm misunderstanding, or if she really means... "Are you seriously going to make me come that hard and not let me reciprocate?"

Her lips quirk up. "Next time."

She stands up and turns her back on me, walking out of the room and leaving me goddamn speechless. I suppose I shouldn't be surprised—this is Rose we're talking about. I'd probably be more surprised if she was the hang-around-after-sex type. She made sure I was okay, made sure I had water—it's more aftercare than some of my previous partners have provided.

I blow out a breath and close my eyes, swallowing down the post-orgasm crash of serotonin. I rub my face, and my cheeks are burning to the touch. What a strange turn this night took. I can't believe she didn't let me touch her. I thought for sure she'd—

"Come on."

Rose's voice jolts me out of my brain and I turn my head, cracking a lid to find her standing in the doorway. She's still wearing nothing but that fucking thong, but her skin is flushed pink. I may not have touched her, but she clearly enjoyed this.

"Come where?"

"I'm running you a bath. I'll order food while you're in there." She holds out a hand, beckoning me closer.

My body protests as I sit up and swing my legs over the side of the bed. I swear my bones creak with every step I take toward her.

"Why?" I ask suspiciously.

She rolls her eyes, her ponytail swinging behind her and

almost hitting me in the face as I follow her to the bathroom.

"Because I'm not the kind of asshole who doesn't take care of their partner after sex."

She might not be *that* kind of asshole, I'll give her that. Especially when I see the tower of bubbles in the tub. I recognize the sweet scent of the lemon snowdrop bubble bath Maggie gave me last Christmas. It's my favorite.

"That explains the bath," I say, testing the water with my pinky. It's not too hot, so I drop my underwear—how the hell did she make me come so hard without even getting me out of my underwear?—and climb in. I sigh as the water rushes over me, soothing my muscles.

I settle back against the tub and skim the top of the water with my fingers. "It doesn't explain the food, though. You're going to eat dinner with me?"

Rose immediately wrinkles her nose. "Oh. No, I wasn't planning on it. I just figured I should probably feed you. I mean, I will, if you really want me to."

I almost say yes, just because she looks like she can't imagine anything worse. But as nice as this has been, I'm not all that interested in spending time with her when we have our clothes on. "I really don't want you to."

"Great." She sounds relieved. "I'm ordering pizza."

"Pizza sounds good," I reply, but she's already on her way out.

"I wasn't asking. Enjoy your bath," she says, closing the door behind her just a little harder than necessary.

And just like that, everything is back to normal.

CHAPTER SEVENTEEN

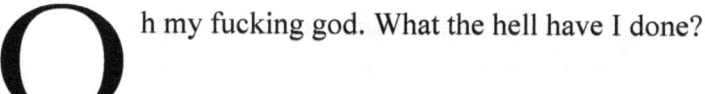

O h my fucking god. What the hell have I done?

CHAPTER EIGHTEEN

Rose

*Is there a reason you need to have such a loud
alarm at the ass crack of dawn? - S
P.S. One day down, 80 to go*

Sierra always sleeps in on Sunday mornings, but she sleeps in longer than usual the morning after. I guess I tired her out. It's pretty inconvenient, considering I'm waiting to talk to her.

I sit at the kitchen island, bouncing my knee and watching condensation gather on the oat milk iced lavender latte I picked up for Sierra. The only reason I know her coffee order is because Jazz drinks the same thing. Why anyone wants to drink flower-flavored coffee is beyond me.

I usually drink my cold brew unsweetened with just a splash of almond milk, not because I like it, but because that's what I'm used to. The first time I ordered my favorite hazelnut mocha in front of my mom was the last time I ever ordered it. She didn't even have to say anything. She just looked between the drink and my waist with pursed lips.

I'm self-aware enough to know that my parents only have power over me if I let them, but it's not that I really care what they think anymore. Over the years, it's become second nature to make decisions based on how I expect my parents would react. It's not that I don't want to choose the things *I* want, I just don't remember to.

That's not to say I haven't done anything for myself. I'm trying. There was the whole dropping out of med school thing, not to mention impulsively marrying my roommate, and even more impulsively suggesting we consummate said marriage.

The Rose of a few years ago would be scandalized.

Truthfully, the Rose of this morning is a little scandalized. I'm trying.

I take a sip of my plain-ass coffee and scrunch up my nose. Squaring my shoulders, I push back from the island, hop down from my stool, and brave Sierra's kitchen cabinet.

We never intended to have separate cabinets when we moved in together, but just a few days living in the same apartment as Sierra was enough to make me separate everything. We each have two and a half kitchen cabinets (though her stuff often creeps into my half of our shared cabinet). We have half a fridge each, half a freezer each, and a small section of shared spices and condiments.

I tried to implement the same system in the rest of the apartment, but she has so much fucking stuff. It was a complete failure in the bathroom, so I just keep my stuff in a caddy in my room and take it with me when I need it like I'm in a goddamn college dorm.

I'm breaking a sacred roommate rule by rummaging around in Sierra's stuff, inspecting the dozen half-empty bottles of coffee syrup, but what's hers is mine and whatever the fuck else we probably said while legally tying ourselves to each other.

Everything is very… sticky. My skin crawls, and I grab the least sticky bottle I can see: s'mores. Could be worse, I suppose. I take the lid off my cold brew and pour a little of the syrup in, watching it swirl through the clear cup.

Our fridge is pretty bare, but I crouch down, looking through the bottles and jars at the back.

"What are you looking for?"

I sit up, banging my head on the glass. "Ouch. Fu—" I glare over my shoulder at Sierra, but the curse falls off my lips when I see her standing, sleepy, in nothing but a baggy sweatshirt and fluffy pink socks. "Could you not sneak up on me next time? Be a little louder."

"What are you looking for?" she shouts sarcastically, and I wince.

"Coffee creamer."

Sierra drops onto the stool opposite mine with a yawn. "We're out. You don't usually like creamer in your coffee."

I stand up and close the fridge. "I wanted something sweeter today."

"Is that for me?" Sierra asks, eyeing the latte, her brow furrowed.

"Yeah."

She pulls it toward herself and sniffs, surprise flashing

in her eyes, before turning to look at me. "There's brown sugar ice cream in the freezer. Put a spoonful of that in your coffee. Trust me."

Who the hell puts ice cream in coffee? I suppose it's just frozen creamer, but still. I'm curious enough to try it, so I grab the ice cream and spoon a dollop on top of my coffee, using my straw to break it up and mix it in as much as possible.

Sierra watches me take a sip, and I can't even pretend it's not good. I really have to stop putting myself through plain coffee.

"It's alright," I say with a shrug, and Sierra snorts, seeing right through me.

"You bought me coffee."

"Clearly. There's a pistachio croissant in the box for you, too," I say, and Sierra narrows her eyes at me.

"Dinner *and* breakfast? Careful, Cannon, people might start to think you like me."

"It was supposed to be breakfast, but considering it's"— I make a show of checking the time on my phone—"11:48, I think lunch would be more fitting. And I don't like you. Quite the opposite."

"Sundays are for sleeping in." Sierra bites into the croissant and moans. I look away, pretending the sound doesn't go right to my head. "So, what's the occasion?"

I pick at the sticky label on my coffee cup as I answer. "We have shit to talk about today, and you're more reasonable when you're sugared and caffeinated."

"I'm freshly fucked, and I just slept for eleven hours. I'm in a great mood." She stretches out like a cat in the sun.

"But the sugar and caffeine are nice. Have you just been sitting around all morning waiting for me to wake up so we could talk?"

"No." *Yes.* "I went for a run." *And couldn't focus, so I came home after a half mile.* "Then I finished my book and picked up the coffee and pastries." *I only had one chapter left, and I DoorDashed them.*

Sierra attempts to hide a smile behind her coffee cup. "I'm sure. Okay, I'm listening. Talk."

I take a long drag of the beautiful, sugary coffee before speaking. "Last night was a mistake."

"Oh, wow. Who could've seen this coming? Not me. I'm so surprised," Sierra replies, sarcasm dripping from her tongue.

"Can't you take—"

"Can't you take anything seriously, Sierra?" she interrupts, trying to imitate me in a singsong voice that sounds nothing like me. "Or is it *wife* now?"

I scowl because, actually, yes, that's exactly what I was going to say. Minus the wife part.

"This *is* serious. I don't think we should do this." Even to my own ears, I sound exhausted. Understandably so, considering I was awake all night, my mind whirring.

Sierra must hear it, because the smirk slides off her face in favor of a pinched expression. "Okay, I'll hear you out. Did you not enjoy it? Because I sure as hell did. And I bet you'd have enjoyed it more if you'd have let me touch you."

"I enjoyed it plenty. That's not the problem."

"So what's the—oh." Sierra crosses her arms. "You don't like that you enjoyed it. Is that it?"

I say nothing, and she rolls her eyes, laughing without a lick of humor.

"Are you fucking kidding me, Rose? This was your idea! Did you think sleeping together was just going to reaffirm how much you hate me? Sorry for exceeding your impossible expectations, I guess."

If she's trying to make me feel bad, it's not working. "Are you done throwing a fit?"

"Are you done letting your own self-importance get in the way of you enjoying yourself?"

I gape at her. The audacity. "I... How dare... What the fuck?"

She snorts. "Eloquent. Okay, look, do I like that someone I despise made me come harder than anyone else ever has? Fuck no. Am I willing to look past that since we're already in a shitty situation and I like orgasms? Sure. What's the risk here, Rose? We're tied together for three months, anyway."

I know I'm fucked when Sierra, of all people, starts making sense.

"Okay, okay." I hold up a hand. "I see your points. I don't like that I see them, but I see them. If we are going to keep doing this, we should have a more thorough conversation about likes and dislikes. Honestly, I should've talked to you more before we started last night. I'm sorry." It's not like me to go ahead without having those kinds of discussions, and I hate to think anything I did made her uncomfortable.

Sierra shrugs, catching her coffee straw with her tongue and taking a long sip before replying. "Maybe, but

I liked everything you did last night, so no complaints here."

That's something. I don't love that we're clearly so sexually compatible—I'd much rather we were roommate compatible.

"In addition to what we talked about last night... Penetration? Toys? Other than Olivia Newton-John," I say, sarcastically.

She gives me the middle finger before answering. "I'm good with both. Penetration-wise, I like fingers and toys, but I'm not a big strap person—giving or receiving. I can make it work if you're into it, but it's not my preference."

"So you're cool with dildos, just not the strap?" I could take or leave the strap element personally. I've been with plenty of people who liked them, and plenty who didn't.

"Yeah. Something about it just feels... impersonal."

I can see that. "Cool. Bondage? Impact?"

"I haven't dabbled much in either, but I'm interested. Nothing too crazy impact-wise—spanking, sure, but maybe not like a whip or anything like that. Bondage... I don't like the idea of cuffs, but ropes or chains or something like that, I could be into. I..." She trails off, blushing.

"What?"

She swallows. "There's something about the possessiveness of bondage that appeals to me. Like, I've always been intrigued by the idea of a collar, maybe a leash."

My eyes immediately zero in on the ring on her finger. I'd be lying if I said seeing it there, knowing that—real or not—she's claimed by me, wasn't unbelievably hot. I had to stop myself from drawing attention to it last night, because bringing up this sham marriage when she's clearly cut up about it seemed unnecessarily cruel. Calling her "wife" was already pushing it. But if she likes possessiveness, and she's interested in a collar… My mind whirs with ideas.

"Anything else you like or don't?" I ask, and Sierra thinks about it for a second but shakes her head.

"I'm open to most things, and I'll tell you if I don't like something."

"Good."

"What about you? I could tell you were into what you were doing to me last night, but you didn't let me touch you. Did I do something wrong?" She draws her lip between her teeth, looking concerned.

"Definitely not," I assure her. "I just don't always like to be touched. Kind of. It's more like I don't always like to be the focus of touch. Like, if you hold on to me or whatever, it's cool, but if I feel like all the focus is on me, I can get overstimulated easily. But that doesn't mean I didn't enjoy last night. I can be perfectly content, even if I'm not being touched."

Sierra's shoulders slump, as if she's relieved. "That makes sense. Will you tell me if you're feeling over-stimulated?"

"Of course. If we're going to do this—and just so we're clear, I still think it's a terrible idea—then we have to communicate."

"Your pessimism is noted," Sierra replies, waving her hand dismissively. "But we're doing it anyway, right?"

Right. Because one night, and I'm already craving the taste of her again.

What could possibly go wrong?

CHAPTER NINETEEN

Rose

Maybe try glaring a little less if you want to make friends at work. - S
P.S. 70 days until we can get divorced!!!!

SIERRA

Did you throw my flowers out?

Yes.

What the fuck?

Care to elaborate?

You had four vases. No one needs four vases of flowers. I only threw out the roses because they looked like they were dying, anyway.

They're antique roses. They're supposed to look like that 🙄

Well, they're ugly. Why are you even home? Shouldn't you be at work?

I have a ton of data entry to do and it's quieter here. Is that okay with you, Mom???

Don't call me that.

Sorry, honey

Have you socialized with your colleagues today?

I said good morning.

Oh, wow. I'm surprised they didn't promote you on the spot. You'll be CEO before you know it.

I'm going to stop replying now.

Not an airport, Cannon. No need to announce your departure.

Rose.

Seriously, go hang out with your colleagues at lunch. You can thank me later.

Thank you how?

I'm not fucking sexting you.

I roll my eyes as I lock my phone and drop it on my workspace. Why would anyone want roses that looked half-rotted?

"I'm starving," Minah, the lab tech who's working beside me today, says, peeling off her gloves. It's the same every day: one person says it, and everyone else falls in

line, like they were just waiting for an excuse to go for lunch.

I don't get it. If you're hungry, eat. Why wait for a dozen other people? This isn't kindergarten. We're allowed to eat unsupervised.

"Do you want to come for lunch, Rose?"

I open my mouth to decline, like I do every day, in favor of eating at my workstation, or in my car, but Sierra's text niggles at me. Since the team picnic at Lisa's place, I haven't made any effort to integrate myself into the team. It was easier with Sierra around, socializing on my behalf.

Forcing my face into a somewhat eager expression, I take my gloves off and grab my phone. "Lunch sounds good."

I pretend not to notice the surprised expressions exchanged between my colleagues as I follow them to the elevators. I can't blame them, I suppose.

The idea of squeezing myself into a metal box with other people is painful enough that I almost always take the stairs, but two elevators arrive at the same time, and I don't get the chance to volunteer to save space before I'm ushered in. I press myself against the back wall of the elevator, holding my breath and trying to tune into the conversation so I'm not totally out of the loop.

"So she shows up at my cousin's wedding with a date, and you'll never guess who it was," Minah says, and everyone leans in, as if we might be overheard in here.

"Who did she bring?" Imogen asks, bouncing on her toes.

"Her sister's high school ex-boyfriend!"

"No way."

I raise my eyebrows in a way I hope looks suitably scandalized, though I can't really see the big deal unless they're not long out of high school or the ex did something shitty.

The conversation continues as we stand in line waiting for food, with everyone debating whether they would date a sibling's ex after so many years.

"What about you, Rose? You have a sister, right? Would you date any of her exes?" Imogen asks, through a mouthful of romaine.

"A brother and a sister, yeah," I confirm. "But my brother is perpetually single because he's been in love with his best friend since they were kids, and my sister's dating history is... questionable, so definitely not."

"How questionable are we talking?"

I tear my pita bread into strips and shrug. "I'm pretty sure her dating criteria was whoever would piss our parents off most. But she's married now, and her husband is great. Though they started out pretty questionable, I guess..." I trail off, talking mostly to myself, but every eye is trained on me, and no one is eating anymore.

"You can't leave us hanging, Rose! Tell us everything."

My skin crawls under their attention, but I'm socializing, at least. "Um, okay. Well, I guess it all started when my sister's best friend started hooking up with her boss..."

When we head back to the lab, fifteen minutes and a hundred questions later, my colleagues seem much more endeared to me. Gossip works wonders.

Lisa is standing near my workspace, chatting with one of her bosses, and she lifts a hand, waving as we all filter back in. I sit in my spinny chair and tuck my stuff under the desk.

"Hey, Rose."

I jump as Imogen's head appears over the divider between our spaces. She laughs. "Whoops, sorry. Didn't mean to scare you. Listen, Minah and I are going on a hike this Saturday with our partners. I remember Sierra mentioning she liked hiking at Lisa's. You guys should come."

Fuck. I was so looking forward to a weekend at home. I make myself smile. "That sounds amazing. Sierra loves hiking." I've literally never heard her mention hiking. "I don't think we have anything happening this Saturday, but I'll check with her tonight and let you know."

"Amazing. Hey, what's your number, and I'll call you so you have mine?"

I recite my number and a second later, my phone buzzes with Imogen's number. I'm adding her to my contacts when Minah pipes up.

"You should add Rose to the group chat."

My thumbs still. "The group chat?"

"Yeah, a lot of the team's in it. It's mostly just Mike sending memes and everyone sharing pet pictures, but it's good to keep in touch with everyone."

"Added!"

I watch as a new chat pops up on my phone:

Imogen Weisz added you to The Lab Rats.

This promotion better be worth it.

The apartment is suspiciously empty when I get home. Empty and tidy, considering Sierra has been home for most of the day. Tidy by Sierra's standards, anyway. The kitchen cabinets are all open, there's a coffee cup on the island, and a sweatshirt on the floor by the couch. I've seen much worse.

"Sierra?" I shout, straightening the shoes by the door and hanging my bag on the dedicated hook.

"Through here!" Her voice is muffled and entirely too cheery. Suspicion fades into outright panic. What the hell has she done?

"Through here" isn't exactly a place, but our apartment isn't big. Her bedroom door is open, but she's not inside, and I'm not sure she ever willingly goes into the laundry room, so that leaves the bathroom. The door is cracked, and the light is on. I knock lightly.

"You can come in," she says, in that same overly happy voice. And as soon as I push the door open, I know why.

My gaze falls to her lap, and I immediately close my eyes. I take a steadying breath and pinch the spot between my brows.

I grit my teeth before looking at her. "What is that?"

Sierra screws up her face, like she doesn't understand the question. "It's a rabbit."

Deep breath. One, two, three… "I know it's a fucking rabbit, Sierra."

"Well, you ask—"

"Why is there a rabbit in my bathroom?"

"Our bathroom, honey," she chides in a sarcastic, singsong voice.

"Why is it in *our* bathroom?"

"*His* name is Thorne. And that's Dibbles." She points to a second, bigger ball of fluff, sitting perfectly still in our towel basket. She blends in so well with the gray towels that I didn't notice her.

I must be losing it. There's no way even Sierra is such an awful roommate that she brought home two rabbits without asking me. "Okay." I press my lips together, trying not to shout. Fuck Sierra, quite frankly, but I don't want to scare the rabbits. I'm not *that* much of an asshole. "Why are there *two* rabbits in *our* bathroom?"

Sierra runs her fingers lightly over the rabbit's back, and his eyes half-close, like he's relaxing into her touch. "It's actually really interesting, but rabbits need to live in pairs or they get lonely. Apparently, they form super close bonds, like mating bonds, and when their mate dies, they can actually die from a broken heart."

How morbid. And completely beside the point.

"Right. I just feel like I've missed a vital part of the story here. Like, perhaps, the part where there are rabbits in our apartment, and what the reason for that might be?"

Sierra's shoulders droop, as if she's realized she can't dodge the question forever. She looks up at me and shrugs. "I mean… look at them."

"I don't want to look at them! I want to know why they're here and when you're getting rid of them." I can't stop my voice from climbing.

Sierra rears back, narrowing her eyes. "Don't shout at them."

"I'm shouting at you, not them!"

"I'd prefer if you didn't do that either. The shelter was desperate. They needed parents."

I ball my fists, taking out my frustration on my palms as my barely there nails bite into skin. The pros really outweigh the cons of having short nails, but sometimes I wish I kept them longer. "Two things. One, you didn't think that asking your roommate before bringing living things into the apartment you share was the polite thing to do? And two, you think *you're* the right person to parent them?"

"I knew you'd say no. And I don't see why I can't be a good mom for them," she replies, indignant.

I flick my eyes toward the rabbit in the basket. "That one's eating a towel."

"Shit. Dibbles, no! Gimme." She sets the smaller rabbit down and speed-crawls toward the basket.

The little one hops over to me, and I crouch down, kneeling on the tile. When I'm settled, he sits up and rests one paw on my knee, looking up at me. He has shaggy brown and gray hair, like a lion's mane. One of his ears points straight up, but the other flops a little, twitching, like it's supposed to be straight up too, but it's being lazy.

I offer my hand and he sniffs it, his tiny nose moving a mile a minute. After he's sniffed my hand, he moves to sniff my pants before rubbing his chin on my knee.

"He's marking you with his scent," Sierra explains, and I look over to find her sitting against the wall with the gray rabbit in her arms.

"I know nothing about taking care of rabbits. Do you?"

"Technically, no, but we're intelligent people. You went to med school, and I went to law school. We can figure it out."

"I quit med school, and you flunked out of law school," I remind her, but she just scoffs.

"We got in, though."

The little rabbit rests his other paw on my leg and uses his back feet to push up until he's more or less on my lap. I lift him the rest of the way and sit back against the side of the tub while he nuzzles into me, sniffing everywhere he can. "Are they going to live in the bathroom?"

"Just until we bunny-proof the living room." Ah, they've been upgraded from rabbits to bunnies. Somehow cuter. "They'll be free to roam the living room and kitchen for the most part, but I've ordered stuff to make them a big open plan enclosure if we need to shut them away at all. Well, actually, I'm probably going to rope Maggie into making it for us."

She continues on, chattering away about her plans for their setup, but I tune her out, looking down into the sweet, brown eyes of the little rabbit on my lap.

"You know, if you really don't want them here, we can take them back to the shelter..." Sierra says, the words cutting through me.

Over my dead body is anyone taking this rabbit away from me. But I can't let her know how much I love him already. "*If* we keep them," I begin, "you're going to have to stop leaving shit all over the place. Otherwise, one of them might eat something that makes them sick. Speaking of, you need to research the plants you have and any flowers you want before bringing them into the house. And we're going to learn how to take care of them properly."

Sierra sits forward, her eyes lighting up. "Of course. Yeah. All of the above. So… we can keep them?"

I nod jerkily, and she grins.

"What are their names again?"

"That's Thorne," she says, nodding to the rabbit on my lap. "And this is Dibbles."

"Dibbles? Jesus. I don't suppose you're open to changing that?"

"Nope. They're both around two and a half, and that would just confuse them."

"Great." Thorne and… Dibbles. "I guess we're moms now."

CHAPTER TWENTY

Sierra

Did you seriously replace the flowers I threw out?
One. Vase. It's a rule, not a suggestion. - R
P.S. 66 days

I'm never telling anyone I like hiking again. What kind of person agrees to a 9 a.m. hike on a Saturday? Rose, that's who. Being awake before ten on a weekend is criminal.

I mean, would I have been awake anyway, since Dibbles and Thorne demand food at seven on the dot every morning? Sure, but I *could* be snuggled up in bed watching them eat their breakfast greens. Instead, I'm sitting cross-legged on the floor beside the new enclosure Maggie made them, wearing a bra and pants at *this* godforsaken hour, hand feeding them long pieces of kale with my eyes closed.

Their happy little crunches have quickly become one of my favorite sounds. Unlike the soft footsteps that approach.

"Morning, babies," Rose coos, and I force my eyes open

to watch her crouching down to scratch them both between their ears. Considering how pissed off she was when I brought them home, she sure has come around. I swear she's like a different person with them.

I didn't realize she could be so nice with her clothes on. Who knew?

Her happy expression disappears when she looks at me. "Do you want to pick up coffee on—"

"Yes."

"Alright, grumpy. Let's go."

I bite my tongue, trying not to snap at her as I trail her to the front door, well aware that I agreed to this trip when she asked. Did I agree only because I'd just brought home the bunnies and she was already mad? Maybe, but a deal's a deal. And I do like hiking—at a more civilized hour.

Rose is wearing black leggings she usually wears for running, a cream tank, and an oversized plaid shirt, the color of fall leaves, that makes the gold in her eyes pop. It's a cute outfit, but she ruins it completely when she sits down on the bench by the door and pulls a pair of boots out of a bag.

"What the fuck are those?"

She furrows her brow at me, pausing with one boot halfway up her calf. "They're boots. For hiking."

"No. They're metallic pink cowboy boots. Where the hell did they come from?" I'm not a cowboy boot fan at the best of times, but these are... hideous. Shiny and garish, in a shade of pink that's somewhere between Pepto-Bismol and shrimp.

"I borrowed them from Jazz. I don't have hiking boots,

and she wore these when she went hiking on her honeymoon."

Of course they're Jazz's. I have a vague memory of her claiming to be in her *cowboy boot era* for a couple of weeks last year, when she started wearing black boots to work, and I'm not surprised she bought multiple pairs. Naturally, I haven't seen her in a single pair of boots in months.

"You can't wear those. They're not hiking boots." It's too fucking early for this.

"Jazz said they were comfy!" Rose protests, and I palm my face. Jesus.

"Jazz didn't go hiking on her honeymoon. Yes, they went to see a mountain with the intention of climbing it, but they just took pictures from the ground, then went back to the hotel and... climbed each other."

Disgust contorts her face, and she drops the boots. "Oh my god. *In* the boots?"

"I don't have that much detail, and I don't want it. But you can't wear those. What shoe size are you?"

"An eight."

"I'm a nine. Go put on some thicker socks and I'll grab my spare pair."

The only reason I find my spares quickly is because I pulled everything out of my closet looking for the sweatshirt I'm wearing this morning. I make a feeble attempt to push some of the mess back into the closet before giving up and heading into Rose's room.

She's perched on the edge of the bed, tugging fluffy off-white socks over her feet. I kneel down and pull her foot toward me, but she pulls it back.

"What are you doing?"

"Putting the hiking boots on you."

"Why?" She sounds more disgusted than she did when I told her about Jazz and Liam's honeymoon activities.

"We're about to spend hours pretending to be newly-weds. I'm reminding myself to act couple-y."

She huffs, but doesn't complain as I slide her feet into the boots and set them on my thighs to tie the laces in tight knots.

Standing and brushing my jeans off, I offer my hand. She grumbles when I tug her to her feet, but she still lets me.

"In the interest of acting couple-y, I have a present for you. I was going to give it to you tonight, but you might want to wear it."

She hands me a small, thin black box I hadn't noticed sitting on her nightstand. It's clearly jewelry. Why the hell is my semi-fake wife buying me jewelry?

I flip open the box and gasp, my heart racing and my blood warming. The gold chain glitters in the glow of the sunlight creeping through Rose's blinds, and I run my finger across the dainty links.

"Is this... a collar?"

"Yes," Rose replies, watching me curiously. "You said you were intrigued by the concept and I..." She trails off, toying with her ring as if it's subconscious at this point. "I like the ring. Seeing you in the ring, I mean. The claiming, *mine* kind of thing really does it for me. But I know you're struggling with the marriage side of things, so I haven't been focusing on it. I don't want to take you out of your head, but I thought this could be a good alternative."

It's surprisingly thoughtful, and really, really fucking hot. I've always liked being marked by my partners—a bite, a bruise, a handprint here or there. And like Rose, I find our rings such a turn-on. Just a... conflicting one.

I've imagined being collared before, but I've never been with someone long enough to bring it up. Collaring means different things to different people—for some, it's a bigger commitment than marriage. For others, it's purely sexual. But it feels fitting for the weird little situation Rose and I have crashed into.

"You picked this?" I ask, and she nods. "It's so me." It's gorgeous, a gold chain and two beautiful roses that meet in the middle, connected by a gold ring.

"I know your taste. You leave your shit all over the place." She sounds almost defensive, like it's embarrassing to know anything about me. Which is fucking stupid, considering we've lived together for a year and we kind of share family, albeit her by blood and me by employment. You don't have to like someone to pay attention.

I pull it from the box and hold it up to the light. There's a small gold clasp-type thing joining the chain at the back, but not any kind I recognize.

"It's a lock," Rose says, holding her hand out for the box. When I pass it over, she pulls out the velvet lining and dangles a tiny key. "It's designed to break if someone tugs it, or if you need to take it off in an emergency, but other-wise, you need the key to open it. The locking is optional, and you can keep the key yourself if you want. You don't have to wear it all the time like some people do. Hell, you don't have to wear it at all. I just thought..." Her nervous rambles fade off into nothing. "Shit, this was a stupid idea. Forget about it."

"I want to wear it," I say, holding the collar out of her reach when she grabs for it. "And I want you to keep the key. Will you put it on me?"

Her eyebrows rise a fraction, like she didn't expect I'd say yes, but she nods. I turn my back on her and start to move my hair out of the way, but Rose stops me. She gathers my hair in her hand, her fingers brushing the nape of my neck softly and deliberately. I pass her the collar, and she moves my hair over my shoulder before taking it and looping it around my neck.

The metal is cool against my skin, but Rose's fingers are anything but. My skin burns everywhere she touches as she settles the collar around my throat. She clips the clasp together, and I feel a tiny click as she locks it in place. Her fingers linger on the lock, and I watch her eyes flame in the full-length mirror on the back of her closet door. She likes that I'm locked into this, and she likes that she was the one to do it.

And fuck, I do too. My heart is beating so hard, I'm surprised I can't hear it. Part of me wants to forgo the hike, to stay home and walk backward until we're both a tangle of limbs in her bed. The other part of me wants to take the collar out and show it off, a mere necklace to the untrained eye.

If I know Rose, and, at this point, I reckon I do, she hates that she likes this so much. Which explains the thin set of her mouth, despite her blown pupils, as she pulls my hair back over my shoulder and rests her hand flat on my throat, right below the collar, her eyes glued to our reflections. She brushes the chain with her thumb and blows out a long breath that teeters somewhere between resigned and pissed off.

Her gaze flicks up, meeting mine in the mirror. "It looks good on you."

I hum in agreement, raising my hand to rest it on top of hers. Of course, she can't have that. She lifts her hand and traps mine below it, both of us lightly holding my throat.

"Maybe we should stay home," she murmurs, her other hand creeping around my body. She slips her fingers beneath the waistband of my pants, and my breath catches in my throat, my mind hazy with lust.

The hike. Rose befriending her colleagues. Her promotion. My inheritance. Our... divorce.

The thought is like a slap to the face, dousing me in ice water. I pull out of her grip.

"Later. Let's go show your colleagues how sickeningly in love we are."

CHAPTER TWENTY-ONE

Sierra

Trying to focus on the conversation with Rose's colleagues while she's walking in front of me, her hips swaying with every step, is torture. This one's on me—she suggested staying home. I'm the one who had to be sensible for a change, and now all I want to do is let her drag me through the woods and fuck me against a tree.

Who the hell gave her ass the right to look like that in leggings? It's cruel.

Before the picnic at her boss's place, I expected Rose's colleagues to either be like her—intense and a little stuck up—or complete nerds. I can't speak for what they're like at work, but they seem fairly normal. I'd almost go as far as to say they seem fun, and Rose seems surprisingly at ease socializing with them.

I've heard her refer to herself as antisocial and not good with people more times than I can count, like she equates being introverted with being unlikable. But her being unlikable has nothing to do with her introvertedness—she's just really fucking hard to live with. Part of me wonders if it's easier for her to assume people won't like her than to put the energy into trying to make friends, and I certainly can't begrudge her that. Her colleagues and their partners seem to like her, though.

She's spent most of the hike chatting with Imogen's partner, Kai, who grew up near her and seems just as awkward and quiet as Rose is—the opposite of Imogen. They work in marine biology which, apparently, Rose is interested in. News to me.

Minah's partner, Annie, a photographer, and Imogen stop along the trail every few feet to take pictures of interesting plants and bugs, leaving me with Minah. I like her. She reminds me of Cal—friendly, a little cheeky, and absolutely feral for any kind of gossip. She's also insanely curious and wants to know all about me and Rose.

"So, you work with Rose's sister, right? Jazz?"

"I'm her assistant, yeah. But we're friends, too."

Minah raises a brow. "How did she take you dating her little sister? You're older than Rose, aren't you?"

"Only by a couple of years. Rose is twenty-six, I'm thirty." Which, by our little family's age gap standards, is practically the same age. "Jazz wasn't thrilled at first. She's pretty protective, and she can be scary when she wants to be, but I think it has less to do with me being me and more to do with no one being good enough for Rose, you know?"

"Oh, I get that. My little sister's only sixteen, and I'm dreading the day she starts dating," Minah answers with a laugh. "Do you have siblings?"

"A big brother, Kyo. We're only eighteen months apart,

though. He and his partners moved down to Sacramento at the start of the year, and my parents moved a couple of months ago to be closer to them."

Minah gives me a sympathetic smile. Even I can hear how wistful I sound. I try my best not to think about how much I miss my family, but it's hard. For so long, they were the only people I allowed close to me. And now I have Jazz and Cal and their family, and I love them, but I still wish my parents and Kyo were around. They would slot in with the Michaelsons so well.

"It's good you have Rose's parents since yours are so far away," Minah says, and I swear I try not to screw my face up, but I fail miserably. "Damn, you don't get along?"

"Rose's parents are..." I search around for a word to describe them that's not simply "the fucking worst" but come up empty, and those three words slip out of my mouth before I can stop them.

Minah bursts out laughing, covering her hand with her mouth. "You should see your face. God, are they really that bad?"

"Yes," I answer, with no hesitation. Honestly, I don't understand why Rose and Xan still talk to them. Jazz, I'm pretty sure, only speaks to her parents because she doesn't want to lose her siblings. When Maggie went no contact with her parents, after they used her as free labor and a walking ATM for most of her life, her three younger siblings stopped speaking to her too, and, while I know she doesn't regret it, she definitely misses them.

Given her gossipy nature, I refrain from giving Minah too many details about Rose's parents. I can't imagine she'd want the nitty gritty of her family drama spread around the lab. But I give her a brief rundown, and, when I'm finished, she whistles.

"Shit. No wonder Rose is so..." she trails off, her cheeks flushing.

"I promise I've probably thought whatever you're thinking. We hated each other when we met," I reply with a laugh. "But yeah, after growing up like she did, she's not the most personable. Once you get to know her, though, she's..." Rose looks at me over her shoulder, the corner of her mouth lifted slightly. Golden sunlight filters through the trees, lighting her hair up and casting pretty shadows on her face. She drops my gaze, looking at the ground, her brow furrowed.

"She's pretty great," I finish, turning back to Minah. I don't mean it. Obviously. She's still Rose, even if we have matching rings and I have her collar around my throat. Even if she looks like a goddamn angel in the sunshine.

We stop at a cute little picnic spot with benches, a covered shelter, and a couple of fire pits for lunch. When I was a kid, my parents were big on camping. It was, for all intents and purposes, a cheap vacation, but Kyo and I never felt like we were missing out when our school friends talked about their trips overseas or to the big, flashy cities we rarely visited. Even now, I'd take a tent in Manitoba over a penthouse in Manhattan any day. It's one of the reasons I love filling my space with plants. It feels like home.

The trail is quiet today—we haven't seen another soul while hiking. Sure, it's raining on and off, but the sky is a brilliant, sunny blue and the air isn't too chilly. I'm not complaining, though. I like the peace.

I mostly let everyone else do the talking while we eat, chiming in only when someone addresses me directly, letting Rose take the lead. She does well, laughing and joking in a way I'm not entirely convinced is feigned, while I toy with her hair, trying to make it look absentminded.

Rose looks over at me and wipes a smudge of something from the corner of my mouth, her hazel eyes twinkling, and it takes everything in me not to sink my hands into her hair and—

"Shall we get moving?"

I jump as Kai stands up, brushing crumbs from their pants and shouldering their backpack. I didn't even notice everyone packing up.

Rose and I stand up, and I gather our trash into a pile, dropping it in the garbage cans and recycling bins.

I watch as Rose says something to Kai and then turns, walking back toward me. She wraps her arm around my waist with an impressive familiarity, and heat spreads over me from the spot where her fingers clasp my hip.

"I think we're going to hang out here for a bit," Rose says, and I swear she struggles to drag her eyes away from me. "You guys go ahead. We'll catch up with you."

"You sure?" Imogen asks, and Rose nods, waving goodbye as they traipse back onto the trail.

I look up and find her watching me, her eyes blazing. "What are—"

I don't get the chance to finish, because she fists her hand in my hair and pulls me in close, capturing my lips with hers. She groans into my mouth, the sweet taste of strawberry and peanut butter flooding my tongue. God, I could just drown in her—in the *taste* of her. Not her.

She nudges me until the backs of my legs hit a bench, but I don't sit down. I spin us so she's pressed against the bench and break away from her, dropping to my knees at her feet.

It's been two weeks since we first slept together, and though she's touched me plenty, she's barely let me lay a finger on her. It's killing me.

"Please," I beg, looking up at her flushed, rosy cheeks and dark eyes, my heart pounding. "Please let me taste you."

Rose doesn't take her eyes off mine as she kicks off her shoes and pushes her leggings down. It's bold, bordering on stupid, considering her colleagues could double-back at any second, but I can't think about that. Not when she sits down and spreads her legs. Her underwear is white and sleek, with a wet spot that would have me on my knees if I wasn't already here.

I place my hands on her knees, shuffling closer, but she stops me.

"Uh-uh," she tuts, and I sit back on my knees, suitably scolded.

Rose slowly moves her hands down her body, and I follow them like a dog with their favorite toy. A whimper spills from my lips as she slips her hand inside her underwear. I can't see anything but the outline of her fingers through the white fabric, but I hear the moment she brushes her clit. She lets out a soft sigh, her head falling back a fraction. I watch her fingers move beneath the fabric in slow, torturous circles, exactly where I want to be.

"Rose, please." My voice is nothing more than a desperate whisper. "I want to taste you. I *need* to taste you."

She runs her tongue along her lower lip and pulls her hand out of her underwear, holding her fingers out to me. They're fucking glistening. "Then taste me, wife."

I lean forward and take her fingers between my lips, groaning as I finally taste her. My eyes flutter closed, my tongue lavishing her fingers, savoring the sweet, salty, *Rose-y* taste of her. I could get hooked on this if I'm not careful. Not on her. Never on her. But this? The feel of her pressing her fingers deep in my mouth, towering above me, commanding me with nothing more than the two digits... this I like.

She pulls her fingers out of my mouth, wet with my saliva. In another world, I might be grossed out by the sight of my spit practically dripping from her hand. But in this world, Rose uses her other hand to tug her underwear to the side and I finally get my eyes on her perfect pussy. I watch, transfixed, as she parts her lips and circles her entrance with her fingers—fingers coated in *me*. And when she presses them inside herself, and her body falls back against the picnic table, I can't stop myself from leaning closer.

I don't touch, as tempted as I am, just stare with my mouth open like I've never seen something as hot as the sight of her fucking herself with her fingers. And maybe I haven't. Maybe I'll never see something this hot again.

"You can touch," she says, her voice curling around me like scalding smoke.

"Where? How? Tell me how you want me. Tell me what to do." She wants control, and I'll hand over the reins any day of the week if it means I get to touch her. *Reel it in*, I remind myself. *You're into sex, not Rose.*

Rose leans down and places a finger under my chin, tilting my head up to look at her. "So eager to please me," she murmurs, her eyes twinkling. "I could get used to this." She brushes her thumb across my lip, then presses it into my mouth. My lips close around it automatically, obliging a command she didn't even have to give.

"Put your mouth on me," she says, leaning back and spreading her legs again. "Make your wife come before anyone comes by and catches us."

I whimper at the reminder that we're out here where anyone could see. This isn't like me. I'm strictly a *behind-closed-doors* kind of girl. But I'm not usually the kind of girl who wears a collar, or fucks the roommate she hates, or gets drunkenly married in Vegas. Who said you can't evolve in your thirties?

My heart is trying to burst out of my rib cage as I shift closer to Rose and run my hands up her legs. I look up, her hair falling back, glimmering golden, the sun-streaked foliage casting soft shadows across her skin. For someone who hates the outdoors, she sure does look heavenly out here. She tastes heavenly too, and I'm so fucking ready for more.

I take a deep breath and dip my head between her legs. Rose sinks her fingers into my hair, and I peer up at her. She's watching me, her chest rising and falling.

"I want you to make me. Please, honey." The nickname

slips out, less sarcastic than it usually is. And I just know she's going to give me shit for it later, but for now...

Rose's eyes flare, and her grip on my hair tightens. She clasps my face with her other hand, her touch gentle, almost ticklish for a split second, until she releases me and presses my face against her.

I run my tongue over her and groan. *Gorgeous.* Maybe she has the right to act like a stuck up asshole ninety-nine percent of the time, considering she tastes so fucking good. I swirl my tongue over her before closing my lips around her clit, and Rose moans, wrapping her legs around me and pulling me closer to her. Every breath is a struggle, but I don't care, because Rose is shaking and whimpering and grinding against my face, and it's bliss.

"Fuck, fuck, *fuck*," she cries, her free hand slamming down on the wood. "You're doing so good, so fucking good, I—*oh*." I graze her clit lightly with my teeth, and she melts.

In my experience, most people tense when they come. They clench their fists, tighten their legs, every muscle tensing so much it might snap. But not Rose. Perhaps it's because she's so damn tense the rest of the time, but she softens. Her hand falls away from my hair, her legs part, slipping down my back, and her body loosens. It's like she's boneless, floating on a wave and riding it out.

I pull her through it, licking and sucking and devouring every last drop of her I can get until I feel her hand smoothing over my hair. Sitting back on my knees, I let my gaze rake over her. Her body is limp, her skin flushed pink.

"Thank you," I say, whispering without meaning to. Without the sounds of her breathy cries, the rustling leaves and fluttering wings of the birds flying around the forest feel too loud, too close.

Rose chuckles, her voice hoarse. *"Thank you?* Shit, I don't know what to do with you."

"You could take me home and fuck me," I suggest boldly, and Rose just shakes her head, a sleepy smile on her face.

We're quiet for a moment—Rose with her neck extended, her eyes closed, facing the sun, and me on my knees, like she's a goddamn altar. Finally, she clears her throat and sits up, grabbing her phone from the picnic table.

She squints at it and sighs. "Do you have service?"

I pull my phone out of my pocket and nod. "Yeah. Why?"

"Because we should probably let the others know that we're leaving before I take you home and fuck you, don't you think?"

CHAPTER TWENTY-TWO

Rose

*God forbid we add a little color to our living room
with some flowers. Not everyone likes living
in a showroom. - S*
P.S. 66? This is the longest three months.

The second Sierra steps over the threshold into the
apartment, I kick the door closed and press her up
against it. I had to fight the urge to get her to pull
over no less than a dozen times on the drive home.

Being eaten out on a public trail wasn't on my radar for
the day, but holy shit, I'm pretty sure it's the hottest thing
that's ever happened to me. And then she *thanked me*. I
never expected this side of Sierra, but I like it. Well, I like
what it does for me, anyway. I don't like Sierra.

Her eyes are wide as I press my forehead against hers,
my lips brushing the tip of her nose.

"You're driving me crazy." I don't mean to say it, and I
don't sound happy about it. I'm *not* happy about it.

For two weeks, all I've been able to think about is touching her. Kissing her. Making her come. For two weeks, I've successfully avoided letting her touch me because I know it's going to wreck the modicum of self-control I've been clinging to.

Well, goodbye, self-control.

"I'd say I'm sorry, but I'm really not," she replies, her warm breath tickling my face.

"You like driving me crazy, huh?"

I lift her sweatshirt, and she gasps as my fingers graze her waist. They're ice cold, but they warm up quickly with the heat of her skin.

"It's what I'm good at, isn't it? Driving you crazy, honey."

There's that word again. *Honey.* I thought she was saying it to deliberately piss me off, but I'm not sure. Her eyes flash, for a split second, like she's pissed off at herself because she didn't mean to say it.

I catch her lip between my teeth and she groans, her eyes fluttering closed. At normal times, I couldn't pay Sierra to do what I want her to, but when I have her like this? She's putty in my hands.

"Shoes off," I tell her as I pull her away from the door and kick mine off with difficulty. Sierra tied my laces before we left the hike, and she must have been a Girl Scout or something, because they're the most secure knots I've ever seen.

With both of our shoes off, I make her sweatshirt my next priority. As I pull her through the apartment toward my room, I leave a trail of her clothes all over the floor like breadcrumbs. Thank god the bunnies are tucked up safely in their gated area of the living room.

I push her onto my bed and lean down, making quick work of the button and zipper on her jeans. "Lift," I say, hooking my thumbs in the waistband and pulling them off.

"In a rush, Cannon? You're awfully demanding today."

Demanding, desperate... What's the difference?

"Do you want me to slow down?" I ask, hoping like hell she's going to say no. The hour I've been waiting to get my hands on her already feels like an age, but I don't want her to be uncomfortable.

"I didn't say that," she replies, and I breathe a sigh of relief.

Her underwear has to go. It's in my way, and if she doesn't want me to slow down, I'm done with waiting. I pull it down her legs and throw it away, spreading her thighs and sighing happily as I kneel between them.

If her surprised yelp is anything to go by, she doesn't expect me to dive right in, but it quickly turns to a moan as I run my tongue through her folds. Already, I feel a little drunk on her.

If I'd known she tasted like this, if I'd known how high I could get on the little sighs and whimpers she sings, we could have gotten along better earlier. I'm not above casual sex, and, sure, sleeping with your roommate isn't known for working out well, but it's not like we would've been risking a friendship. What a waste of a year, when I could've been making her come over and over and over and—

"Rose," she cries, as I press my tongue inside her. I need

her closer. My face is pressed right against her pussy, but it's not enough. I need more.

She protests when I pull back, sitting up and spluttering. "Where are you going?"

I don't answer right away, instead stripping my clothes off, piece by piece, as she watches me hungrily. I climb up onto the bed and lie down with my head on the pillows. "Get up here."

"What?"

"Sit," I order, pointing to my face, and Sierra's eyes go comically wide.

"Absolutely not. I'll crush you!"

"Fuck, that sounds amazing." Yet another inside thought slips out, but I don't mind, because Sierra's lips part and her cheeks flush scarlet.

"I don't want to hurt you," she says softly.

One thing I didn't expect about Sierra was her lack of confidence in her own body. I should have. *I'm* obsessed with her body, and since when do Sierra and I ever see eye to eye on anything? I'm going to make her see it, though.

"Do you trust me?" I ask.

Sierra tilts her head, chewing her lip. "Somehow, against my better judgment, yes."

"Good. Because this"—I point between us—"is only going to work if we trust each other. I trust you to use your safe words if you need to stop or slow down, or if you just don't like something. And I need you to trust me to do the same."

"Ugh. When you say it like that..." Sierra pouts as she

kneels on the bed, crawling over to me. She hesitates, so I reach up and grab her chin, gently.

"Do you want me to beg? Do you want me to tell you how I've been thinking about this for hours, weeks, hell, *a year*? Because I will, if that's what you need. I'll describe in detail all the dreams I've had about you sitting on my face, falling to pieces on top of me, since the second I laid eyes on you. I can tell you just how many times I got myself off thinking of this exact moment, if it'll make you realize how badly I want this."

Sierra sucks in a breath, still as a statue, before sitting up on her knees and sidling closer to me. She pauses. "Do you actually keep a record of the things you think about when you're getting off? Because it seems like the kind of thing you'd do, so I can't tell if you actually know the number or if that's just a line."

I roll my eyes. "I have a journal. It's not an exhaustive list, but I write about it sometimes."

"Interesting... Can I read it?"

I furrow my brow. "No. Now, are you going to get up here and ride my face, or what?"

Nerves flicker across Sierra's features, but she nods. "Okay. Do you want me facing the headboard, or away?"

"Away." I have no preference, but I suspect facing away from me will be easier for her.

Sierra takes a deep breath and swings her leg over me until she's straddling my face. My mouth waters, desperate to get all over her, but she hovers above me.

"Sit," I say, grasping her hips. I don't pull her down. I want her to feel comfortable enough to do it herself.

"But I—"

"Trust, remember?"

She releases an anxious whinny. "But what if you can't tell me to stop because I'm on top of you?"

"If I need you to stop and can't talk, I'll slap your thigh twice. But it's not going to happen, okay?"

"Okay," she whispers.

I squeeze her hips. "Now be a good wife and soak my face."

Sierra curses and lowers herself. She stops just shy of touching my mouth, but it's close enough. I pull her down the last half inch and moan in relief when my tongue finally touches her pussy.

All it takes is a few strokes of my tongue, a few brushes of my finger over her clit, for her nerves to disappear. She rocks against me, rolling and grinding her pussy over my mouth. It's everything I've ever imagined and so much more.

She leans over slightly, and I use the new angle to run my tongue around the rim of her ass.

"Oh fuck," Sierra cries, her thighs tightening around my head.

I'm in heaven.

She seems to like me playing with her ass if the increase in volume is anything to go by. I drag my tongue from her ass to her clit and back again, and she falls forward further, holding on to my thighs to brace herself.

"Rose," she moans, reminding me of my name right before she zaps it from my head when she drags her hand up my thigh and presses her thumb against my clit.

"Is this… *fuck*, is this okay?" she asks, testing me with soft, gentle circles.

I'm unwilling to take my mouth off her long enough to answer, so I moan against her pussy and spread my legs for her.

She takes the invitation immediately, rubbing my clit with two fingers as she works her pussy all over my face. I drink her in, savoring the taste of her, trying to focus on how she tastes and not on the not-so-gentle attention she's showing my clit. She wrenches a cry from my throat, but it mingles in the air somewhere with hers until I can't tell who's making what noise.

Her thighs are twitching as she gets close, and I want to taste her coming on my tongue. Apparently, we're more in sync than I thought, because Sierra pinches my clit at the same moment I close my teeth around hers, and we both spiral into oblivion together.

I'm not a multiple-orgasms-a-day kind of girl—I'm too easily overstimulated—but for the second time today, I feel myself go limp under Sierra's touch. I feel her everywhere, like an assault on each one of my nerve endings, but it doesn't feel too much like it usually does. It's a soft rippling pleasure, like a stone skipping across the water that keeps going into the horizon.

When we're like this, a beautiful mess of moans and cries, trembling bodies, and heavy breaths, it's all too easy to forget the reasons we dislike each other.

CHAPTER TWENTY-THREE

Sierra

Can you try to be ready for 4 like you promised so
we can be on time for a change? - R
P.S. How is it STILL 38 days?

I'm not sure I've ever seen Rose look as disgusted as she does when the bored-looking teenager hands her a pair of worn bowling shoes.

"Are these mandatory?" she asks, sighing when the attendant tells her they are.

It's not *not* funny, but I stop myself from laughing at her.

When Jazz told us she wanted to go bowling for her birthday, I half expected Rose to say no. I think I would've been surprised if she seemed excited about the idea of spending her Saturday in a loud, sticky bowling alley, but she's here, and she's not complaining—much.

Jazz is in her element. Apparently, Liam in a bowling shirt has been high on her "to-do" list—and by that, she literally means do. I really don't want to think about it, but Liam, being Liam, is wearing a custom bowling shirt in Jazz's favorite color, with MICHAELSON embroidered on the back. And Jazz, being Jazz, can't keep her eyes off her husband. I may not understand the bowling shirt hype, but they're cute.

And maybe I would understand if it was Rose wearing the shirt. Instead, she's wearing a lilac skort and tight white tank, and she's driving me crazy.

We all pile into our lane, and I can tell she's over-whelmed right away. She perches on the edge of the bench, toying with the hem of her skirt and staring at the floor. I can't say I blame her. The room is dark, save for the fluores-cent-lit lanes, a few spotlights on the ceiling, and the flashing neon lights emanating from the arcade section. And, though I'm not usually bothered by loud noises, even I can recognize how loud it is.

It's putting me on edge—not the bowling alley, but how it's impacting Rose. I can't shake the urge to comfort her, even though I know that's probably the last thing she wants. But it's normal—expected even—for spouses to comfort each other, and we are in public…

"Hey. You okay?" I ask softly, nudging her with my hip, preparing for her to snap at me.

"I'm fine."

There's no heat in the words, though she says them too quickly. And I don't believe her at all.

Rose and I are last up in the lineup of bowlers: Jazz, Liam, Maggie, Cal, Xan, and Kami all go before us. I like Kami, but she's god-awful at bowling. She struggles to pick a ball, then drops her choice before making it to the end of the lane. It does nothing to diminish her enjoyment, though —she laughs it off, joking with Xan that she hasn't improved since they were kids. And Xan takes full advantage, grabbing the ball before it rolls away and standing behind her as she bowls, his hand against the small of her back, giving her tips on her form.

I watch as his thumb brushes the edges of her burgundy braids, a wide smile stretching over his face when she knocks down half the pins. He raises his hand for a high five, but Kami hugs him instead, and it's like a lightbulb goes off in my head.

"I've never done this before," I say, and Rose turns to me, frowning.

"You've never bowled?"

"Nope. Anything I need to know? I just throw the ball, right?"

Her eyes widen. "Please don't throw the ball. You *bowl* the ball."

I do my best impression of clueless.

Of course I've bowled before—my dad was obsessed with our local bowling alley's nachos growing up, and we were there pretty much every weekend until they changed the salsa they used.

"What does that mean?"

"You want to build up momentum when you swing back, then push it through the air."

I continue my confused facade. "That sounds a lot like throwing it."

"No, no, it's like... Okay, watch me."

There are a few things about Rose Cannon that no one could ever dispute: she loves to be the best at things, and she loves telling people (mostly me) what to do. And both are enough to distract her from how overstimulating this place is.

The most surprising thing is that she's not a bad teacher —when I'm not being too stubborn to let her teach me, that is. Rose patiently explains what she's doing as she picks up her ball and takes her position at the end of the lane.

She bowls a perfect strike. Of course she does.

When it's my turn, she hovers by my side while I look through the balls. I already know I'm going to pick the shiny orange one Maggie used, but I weigh up a couple before asking her which one I should choose.

"Put your fingers there—don't," she warns when I open my mouth to make a joke. "Okay, how does that feel?"

"It feels a little loose. Like it could slip."

"Not that one." She takes it and glances over the other balls. Her eyes zero in on the orange, and she checks the weight before handing it over. "Try that."

I slide my fingers into the ball—the jokes really do write themselves. "That feels good. Tight, but not too tight. I feel like I have good control," I say, rotating my wrist.

Rose follows me to the end of the lane, talking a mile a minute about velocity and angles and a bunch of other stuff that makes no sense to me, but she no longer seems stressed, so it's working.

I plant my feet, and she adjusts my stance. I do a test swing, and she wraps her arms around me from behind, directing me like we're in an early 2000s rom-com and she's teaching me how to play pool.

She smells so good, feels so good wrapped around me, that I don't want her to let go. But she does, reminding me to aim for the gap between the pins, and I let the ball fly.

Badly. Very, very badly. It rolls along the gutter and doesn't take down a single pin, because years of bowling practice as a kid didn't prepare me for how to aim when Rose clasps the back of my neck, her thumb pressing into the clasp of my collar, and murmurs, "You've got this."

I expect her to laugh at my attempt, but she shocks the hell out of me. "Don't worry. You'll get them on the next one."

She squeezes my neck before heading off to retrieve my ball, and I suck in a deep breath. I was supposed to be calming her down, not riling myself up. Fuck. I don't like how easy it's become for her to distract me.

"Let's try again," she says, her voice soothing.

I swear I've unlocked a side of Rose I only ever see in bed—a patient side. Since she mentioned the promotion, I've had a few doubts about her in a leadership role at work, but I can see it. She's a good teacher.

Her hand is glued to my back as I swing the ball.

"Rose?"

"Yeah?"

"You're distracting me," I admit, begrudgingly.

"What do you—oh." She pulls her hand away, and I look back at her to see her eyebrow raised and her lips in a smirk.

"Shut up."

"I didn't say anything!" she argues, but she's smiling, and she doesn't seem to notice the lights and sounds and greasy deep-fryer smells surrounding us.

It's a problem how relieved I am.

I throw the ball—*bowl* the ball—and take down seven pins. Before I can blink, Rose wraps her arms around me from behind, hugging me tightly.

"Look at you go," she says, before pressing her lips to my cheek. "Well done."

"Thanks." My voice comes out breathier than I'd like, like she's stolen half the air from my lungs with one kiss on the cheek. I pull out of her arms and turn around, clearing my throat. "You're a good teacher."

"I know." She flashes me a smug smile and a shrug as she walks back to the bench. There she is. I watch her go, wondering when that smug smile stopped bothering me so much.

Jazz skips up beside me, her ball precariously balanced in her arm. "You know," she begins, her voice low enough that I have to strain to hear her over the crash of pins from the next lane, "I stalked your Facebook page before we hired you."

"I wish I could say that surprised me, but why do you bring it up?"

Jazz takes her time, bowling straight down the center of the lane and somehow knocking down only one pin. Liam still cheers for her, and she blows him a kiss before turning back to me. "You don't post a lot, but your parents tag you all the time. I know this isn't your first time bowling."

It's been years since I went bowling with my parents. How far back did she go?

"Okay, it's not my first time. So what?"

"Nothing. Just…" Jazz trails off, looking past me to where Rose is talking to Kami, looking a lot happier than she did ten minutes ago. "It was a good idea. You really understand her in a way I'm not sure anyone else ever has."

The relief I felt at seeing Rose less overwhelmed is replaced with guilt. This constant emotional whiplash is becoming far too common. I haven't known peace since the second I woke up half-naked in Rose's hotel room.

CHAPTER TWENTY-FOUR

Rose

Heading to work early. Try not to miss me. - S
P.S. 19 days until freedom!!!!!

My alarm is splitting my head, but I can't bring myself to turn it off. I squeeze my eyes together like it might dampen the sound, and when it doesn't, I force myself to sit up. My body moves like I'm dragging my limbs through mud, a heavy, fuzzy weight pressing down on me.

The room is pitch black, save for the light of my phone screen.

7:03

It's already an hour later than I usually get up, but I snoozed the previous six alarms, and I can't afford to snooze another and still make it to work. So I switch off my alarm and lay my phone face down on the nightstand, plunging the room into darkness.

My own breath feels heavy and thick in my lungs, my

thoughts just a little out of reach. *Get up. Shower. Coffee. Car. Drive. Work.*

Get up.

Get. Up.

But the distance between my bed and the floor feels a mile long. My body rebels against the thought of putting so much as a toe down on the hardwood floor, my lungs screaming because I can't seem to force air into them.

I'm semi-aware of my brain screaming, "Not today," trying to remind me about things like promotions, paychecks, and never-ending to-do lists. But right now, I can't remember why I ever cared about those things.

It's not a conscious decision to text Lisa and let her know I won't be in, to lie back down and tug the covers over my head, to close my eyes and sink into oblivion. It's just all my body, all my brain, will let me do.

CHAPTER TWENTY-FIVE

Sierra

"Honey, I'm home!"

I kick off my shoes and drop my bag on the bench by the door, yawning. Being woken up by a ringing phone at 5:30 a.m. isn't my idea of a good time, even when it's Jazz on the other end of the call. She and Cal were scheduled for a 6:30 a.m. call with a client in the UK, but she'd been up all morning throwing up and begged me to go instead. It was an easy "yes"—Jazz would do it for me in a heartbeat.

Most of our clients at Michaelson and Hicks live *and* work in Washington, but Cal keeps a select few clients that operate businesses here and live elsewhere. Jazz never called him to tell him she was sick, probably trying not to worry him, but that only worried him more, and I've spent all day trying to figure out Jazz's chaotic calendar and keep her father-in-law calm. By the time 2 p.m. rolled around and we finished our last meeting, I told him to go home and finished out the day on my own.

What a fucking day.

I didn't see Rose before I ran out the door this morning, but I left her a note, the last cranberry white chocolate muffin (that, admittedly, I hid from her yesterday morning because she pissed me off before I had coffee), and an iced latte in the fridge.

It's been two months since we added sex to our arrangement, and I'm not sure when eating together became part of our routine, but it's a regular occurrence. It started with dinner. We never talk or debrief our days, just sit in relative silence while we eat—sometimes with the TV on, or watching the bunnies play—either before or after sex. After sex, we tend to be a little nicer to each other. Before, all bets are off.

And then there were a couple of morning hookups, and the breakfasts that followed. Now, we eat breakfast together most mornings, and dinner almost every night. It's fine, I suppose.

I walk into the apartment and stop short when I see the Post-it and muffin still sitting on the kitchen island. Even if she didn't want the muffin—and it's her favorite, so that's unlikely—Rose would never leave anything on the counter, cluttering it. They haven't moved at all. Is she not home?

The lights are on, but that doesn't mean anything. Rose installed smart lights on a timer not long after we moved in together, because she complained that I always forgot to turn them off. I still think she just wanted an excuse for smart lights.

A scuffle commands my attention, and I spin around to see Dibbles sitting on top of the little wooden house I ordered for them. She and Thorne are still in their fenced-in area of the living room, but the gate's open, which means Rose did at least open that at some point today.

Her bedroom door is closed, but I knock softly and open it when there's no response. The room is pitch black, but I can see a shape under the covers thanks to the light from the living room.

"Rose?" I whisper.

There's nothing but silence for a moment, and my heart stills until I see a small movement beneath the covers.

"Yeah?" Her voice is weak and scratchy, like she hasn't spoken all day.

I'm across the room in a heartbeat, perching on the edge of her bed. I can't see her face since she's turned toward the wall, but I can see the yellow collar of the T-shirt she went to sleep in last night.

"What's wrong? Are you sick?" Maybe she has whatever Jazz has. I reach for her forehead.

"I'm not sick."

I snatch my hand back. Huh. "Okay... Did you go to work today?"

"No." She sounds so fucking small, and it's making my stomach flip-flop uncomfortably.

"Did you eat?"

"No. I fed the bunnies, though."

I'm somewhat at a loss for what to say. She's not giving me much to work with. "Can I do anything?"

Rose is quiet for a moment before tugging the covers higher up toward her chin. "I just want to be alone."

My breath catches in my throat, and I stand up like she

physically pushed me away, my stomach twisting. "Oh. Okay. Well... yeah. Okay."

I leave the room and close the door, dragging my feet toward the couch. I pluck Thorne out of the enclosure before I sit down, placing him on my lap and running my hand over his soft little ears. Ever the jealous type, Dibbles hops over, jumping up on the couch to join us.

"At least you want to spend time with me," I grumble, even though I definitely forced Thorne to be here, and I'm pretty sure Dibbles just wants to see if I have snacks. I shouldn't care that Rose doesn't want me around. It's not like we're friends. Sure, things have been a little more civil and a little more orgasm-y around here, but she still hates me, and I... Well, we're not friends. We're temporary wives and roommates who happen to be sleeping together.

And even though we're just that, it's normal for me to be worried that she appears not to have functioned today. It's not like her—she barely naps, and spending a whole day in bed is almost unheard of. In the time we've lived together, I could count on one hand the number of times she's done this. Every few months, I guess. It's not like I ever paid much attention before.

I wrack my brain, trying to connect the scattered dots. The start of May, when she bailed on a girls' night with Jazz, and I was just happy she wasn't there. February, at Maggie and Cal's anniversary party, when her mom kept asking if she was sick because her dark circles were so bad. Just after Thanksgiving last year, when she barely ate for a few days.

Sometimes, she's down for a day, sometimes longer. At

the time, I think I just chalked it up to her being on her period. She always gets a little out of sorts a few days before. Jazz has PCOS, and though Rose's periods aren't nearly as bad, they're still worse than most people's.

Admittedly, Rose often seems a little out of sorts—a little sad. For a while, I've suspected there was something going on with her—that there has been for a long time, if the long-faded scars on her thighs are anything to go by. But sad or sick, she shouldn't be on her own. And right now, I'm the only one around. She can push me away all she wants, but that doesn't mean I have to let her.

I sigh and gather the bunnies in my arms before standing up. Dibbles buries her face in the crook of my neck, tickling my skin. "Come on, you two. Let's go make your mama mad by forcing our—*your* love on her," I correct, shaking my head and starting for Rose's bedroom. She has my brain so fucking fried.

The bunnies make opening her door tricky, but after a little finagling, I push it open with my knee. I'm not being quiet, but I don't believe Rose is really sleeping, anyway. She hasn't moved since I left the room, but I see her body tensing when the light floods through the door. I close it and cross the room, kneeling on the bed and leaning over her to place Thorne and Dibbles in front of her. Thorne immediately hops up to her pillow to nuzzle into her face, while Dibbles snuffles around the covers, probably still looking for snacks.

"What's going on?" Rose asks, sounding groggy.

I lift the blankets and slide in beside her. It's toasty. I

grab Rose's phone from the nightstand. "What's your passcode?"

"1723," she answers, and it's a testament to how out of sorts she is that she doesn't refuse to give it to me.

I punch in the numbers and pause. 1723. January 17th and October 23rd are Xan and Jazz's birthdays. That's... surprisingly sentimental of her. I file it away for later.

"Here's what we're going to do," I say, setting an alarm and putting the phone down. "You can rot for one more hour, but you're going to have to put up with me and the bunnies cuddling you while you do it. When the hour's up, you don't have to get out of bed, but you do have to come back to life, okay? We're ordering food, and you're going to eat, hydrate, and talk. Deal?"

Rose turns her head a fraction toward me, but not enough that I can see her face. "Why?" she asks, her voice small.

I lie down and sling my arm over her, snuggling against her back. "Because like it or not, temporary or not, we're family. And it's about time someone showed you that family is supposed to take care of you."

Rose sucks in a breath that pushes her closer to me, and I hold her tighter. After a moment, she lifts her hand and lays it atop mine, threading our fingers together.

And my heart does something... unexpected. It calms.

I didn't realize how panicked I was, how worried about Rose I was, until she showed a sign of life again.

Oh *shit*.

I care about her. And not in a "she's my friend's sister, so of course I'm concerned about her well-being," kind of way. Not even in a "she's my roommate and temporary wife and I'm legally invested in her health and safety," kind of way.

I care about her in an "I want to keep her" kind of way. And that's a massive fucking problem.

This is bad. This is so, *so* bad. So much for being calm. How the hell did I get myself into this mess?

My heart beats so fast I'm surprised I can't hear it ricocheting against my ribcage like it might jump straight out of my chest.

Because, for once, my three-month deadline isn't optional. It's a mutual agreement, and even if *my* heart is acting up, there's not a chance in the world that Rose will want anything to do with me when our three months are over. Which means I have a month to get my act together and get over this stupid little crush.

That's all this is—a crush. It's natural, considering how much time we're spending together and the sheer number of orgasms we've been trading. I'm only human.

But for now… now she strokes her thumb over my ring and leans her head back, like she wants to get as close to me as possible. And I soak it all in.

CHAPTER TWENTY-SIX

Rose

I force myself to bite down on the egg roll, but it tastes like sawdust. Sierra didn't ask me what I wanted, just ordered all my favorite things from my favorite Chinese takeout place, and even though I have zero appetite, I don't have the heart to push it away.

Not that I think she'd let me. Sierra seems determined to feed and hydrate me—if the protein bar and mini Gatorade she forced into my hand while we waited for the food to be delivered are anything to go by.

She's right that I'm not used to being taken care of like this. I started getting these "foggy spells," as I call them, when I was sixteen. By that point, my brother and sister had long moved out, and my parents had never been the kind of parents to comfort us when we were sick. So, I just learned to get on with it. There's never been an alternative.

I know it's not normal, that not everyone has days, weeks, months where just the thought of basic tasks like showering or brushing their teeth feels like climbing a mountain. Just like I know it's not normal to struggle to enjoy anything, to not get excited about anything, to dread the thought of speaking to people.

But knowing that doesn't give me the motivation to do anything about it. I've gotten used to the world being dull and desaturated, and now anything bright and shiny is just overwhelming.

"Drink." Ice clinks against the plastic cup as Sierra presses the iced jasmine tea into my hand.

I sigh and take a sip, wincing when all I taste is the paper straw. I hand it back to Sierra and she takes a long sip, sighing happily.

"God, that's good. Here, try this. It's a little spicier than the chili garlic sauce."

I open my mouth to decline, but Sierra just uses it as an opportunity to pop a cube of her Szechuan tofu in my mouth. The force-feeding is a little much, but I dutifully chew and swallow. It's fine. I can tell it's spicier, but it still doesn't taste of much.

"I've had enough for now," I say, setting down my chopsticks and wiping my mouth with a napkin. Sierra flicks her gaze over my face before nodding.

"Okay."

She piles the containers back into the bag and sets it on the floor beside the bed before standing up and leaving the room. Disappointment settles over me. She said she wanted to take care of me, and feeding and hydrating me is that, I guess, but part of me wanted her to stay. Bright and shiny things might overwhelm me, but I've become somewhat desensitized to Sierra. It's not like she's under any obligation to stay, I suppose. And I'm used to—

She walks back in, a bunny in each arm, and drops them gently on the bed. They had their dinner in their enclosure when our takeout arrived. Rabbits, we quickly learned, are surprisingly speedy and good at stealing human food, so they're no longer allowed to eat with us.

Sierra climbs back under the covers beside me and tosses a shiny red package my way. "You have to open your fortune cookie. I don't make the rules."

She tears into her own cookie and snaps it open. Her eyes widen as she reads the fortune, a laugh that sounds somewhere between amused and pained falling from her lips.

"What does it say?"

"Sometimes the rose is true love's prize," she reads out, shaking her head.

I frown. "What does that even mean?"

"No idea." Sierra folds the paper and sets it on the night-stand. "Open yours."

I crack open the cookie, flinching at the crumbs that fall over my blankets. I'm not an eating-in-bed kind of person. The waxy paper is rolled up, so I smooth it out and read aloud. "Pain loses its potency when we share it with others." Well, shit.

Sierra snorts. "Thank you for that segue, little fortune cookie." She sits back against the headboard and pats my pillows.

I sigh, tearing off tiny pieces of the cookie and giving them to the bunnies before placing the rest on the nightstand out of their reach and sitting back. Sierra slings an arm around my shoulders, twirling her fingers through the knotted ends of my hair. I can feel how tense I am, every muscle on edge like I'm about to be attacked.

"Hey," Sierra says, tugging me in closer to her so I'm basically lying on her chest. From this angle, she can't see my face, and it's easier. "We don't have to talk about what has you feeling like this. Don't get me wrong, I think we should, because I agree with your fortune cookie. But if you're not ready, I'm not going to push you."

"I don't know if I want to talk about it. I don't even know where I'd start," I admit, and Sierra runs a soothing hand down my back.

"Those are two different things, honey."

Honey. It no longer sounds sarcastic when she says it. Maybe it's just that I'm getting used to it, but I don't mind it so much anymore.

"If you don't want to talk about it because you don't want to talk about it, that's a fair reason. But not knowing how to do something isn't a reason not to try."

In theory, she makes sense. In practice, I've never been good at doing anything less than perfect.

"But what if I do a bad job?" My voice cracks, and Sierra tightens her hold on me.

"A bad job of talking? That seems unlikely. And even if you do, you have nothing to lose. Because you don't care what I think, right?"

"Right," I confirm, though the word tastes bitter as I force it out. "Um. Okay, well... Where should I start?"

"Start with this morning," Sierra prompts.

I tell her about struggling to wake up, struggling to turn off my alarm, or put my feet on the ground. I tell her about forcing myself out of bed to feed the bunnies and practically running back to my room, because every second out of the covers felt like my body was in attack mode. I stumble over the words at first, but once I start talking, it's hard to stop. Everything just spills out.

Sierra listens, silently, as I tell her about almost failing my eleventh-grade English class because my brain was too foggy to understand the book I was supposed to be writing my final report on. I cried and begged my English teacher not to fail me, to give me more time, and she just gave me an A, promising me I'd shown her enough great work to pass the class. At the time, I wondered what I'd done to deserve her kindness, but I later remembered she'd had both Xan and Jazz in her class, and she probably knew how my parents were.

I tell her about how my girlfriend in my freshman year of college broke up with me because I went radio silent for a whole week, and refused to tell her why—my parents were out of town and there was nothing to incentivize me to get out of bed when I woke up feeling like death.

I tell her about the constant fear of judgment, the panic that someone would see through me and tell my parents, and the picture of me they had would crumble.

My only job was to be the perfect sibling, the easy sibling. Xan was the leader, set to take over my dad's company. Jazz was the fun one, always meant to break away and spread her wings. But I was the perfect one. The youngest, the brightest, the most likely to elevate the Cannon family name to new heights.

Until I cracked. Until I woke up one day and realized

that no amount of begging and crying to my med school professors was going to get me through. I didn't have it in me, and it was easier to tell everyone I was dropping out because I didn't like it than it was to admit there was something wrong with me.

I don't regret dropping out. I just wish it wasn't because of that.

There's no judgment on Sierra's face when I finally stop spilling my heart out and risk looking up at her, but her expression is heavy, and guilt instantly floods me. I don't want her to worry about me. I don't want anyone to worry about me. This is my cross to bear, and it's not anyone else's problem.

"Thank you," Sierra says, running her fingers through my hair.

I squint at her, confused. "Thank you?"

"For telling me that. I know talking about shit like that isn't easy." The way she says it, it sounds like she's talking from experience. "Can I ask you one more thing?"

"Yeah."

Sierra hesitates, worrying her lip with her teeth, before speaking. "The scars on your thighs—"

"They're stretch marks," I say, on autopilot.

"They're not, and that's okay. No judgment. I'm only asking to make sure you're safe. That it's not something you're still doing or want to do."

Fuck. The stretch mark answer has been serving me for almost a decade, and no one has ever called me out on it. Not that I show my upper thighs off to just anyone.

I rub my face, taking a moment to shield myself from

Sierra's gaze. How the hell does this woman, who doesn't even like me, see right through me, time and time again?

"It's been a long time," I say, finally. "I was seventeen, and you know what seventeen's like."

"That I do," she replies wryly. "So, you haven't wanted to since?"

I shake my head. It's not like I haven't found other ways of self-harming over the years, intentionally or not. Pushing myself through med school for so long, skipping meals, canceling on my friends one by one, just waiting for them to cut me out of their lives altogether, working too much, drinking too much, taking pills I was offered at parties without asking what they were, running.

Running was the one that really stuck—pushing myself past the point of comfort at the gym or on a track until I could barely walk. Now, I force myself to stick to a strict routine on my home treadmill because the second I deviate, I slip back into hurting myself. I know how I come across— controlling, immovable, rigid—but I'm just trying to stay sane.

"I'm guessing you've never spoken to your doctor about any of this?" Sierra asks.

"No," I answer quickly. "They'll just throw medication at me, and I don't want that."

"Why?"

I blink at the question. "It makes you spacey. And…" I sigh. "It feels like admitting I'm a failure. Like I can't get through the day without help. I know it's not rational."

Sierra laughs, soft and twinkly. "You're right, it's not

rational. Did you know I've been on antidepressants since I was eighteen?"

My eyes widen. I had no idea. As disorganized and frustrating as she is, Sierra has always seemed so happy to me.

"Not the first time I've gotten that reaction," she says, tapping me on the nose. "But I do need them to help me get through the day. Not every day, but they keep me level. You know we moved back from Canada when I was sixteen, right?" I nod. "Well, that's a shitty time to leave behind everything you've ever known. My friends made promises to keep in touch, but we were sixteen, and that was easier in theory than in practice. Within a few weeks, they'd pretty much all stopped talking to me. I didn't make any friends at my new school. Hell, I haven't really made any close friends since, except for Jazz and Maggie now, because it fucked me up so much."

My heart cracks at the thought of teenage Sierra being scared to make friends in case they left her. How have I never noticed that, like me, she doesn't really have anyone? She dated in the year we were living together before our accidental wedding, and she even had a couple of girlfriends in that time, but the only time she went out with friends was with Jazz and Maggie.

"My parents begged me to take a gap year before college, to try medication and therapy. I didn't like therapy, but the medication helped a lot. It's not a cure-all, don't get me wrong, it just gives me a little breathing space to work through things when I need to. I started spending a lot more time outside, too, which made a big difference."

"Is that why you love plants and flowers so much?"

"It's part of the reason," she says with a soft smile. "How come you hate them so much?"

"I don't hate plants. I find them messy, and I hate mess, but plants are fine. And it's not that I hate flowers, I just hate the intent behind them," I answer.

"What do you mean?"

"People give them just for show. My parents, for example. They barely tolerate each other, but my dad always bought my mom extravagant floral arrangements so she could show them off to her friends and brag about how thoughtful he was. I'm pretty sure he just has a card on file with our local florist and tells them to do whatever they want."

Sierra frowns. "That is… a very jaded view of flowers. Understandable, but you know it's not like that for everyone, right?" I shrug, and she blows out a long breath. "Okay. Well, my family isn't like that. We love flowers. For as long as I can remember, we've all gotten flowers for each other for every occasion. Or even just because we spotted someone's favorite flowers at the store and picked them up. It was a way of showing our love."

The difference in how we grew up really is staggering sometimes. "Your family is a real family, though. My family isn't like that. We barely like each other, let alone flowers."

A surprised laugh bursts from Sierra's mouth. "What are you talking about? I don't know your parents that well—thank god—but even I know your mom loves flowers. She literally named her daughters Jasmine and Rose. And Jazz loves flowers—and you, for the record. She has your birth flower tattooed on her ribs. Xan's too, alongside everyone else she loves."

"That's what her tattoos are? I had no idea. I assumed she just got them because she thought they were pretty, like your snake tattoo."

"I lied about my reason for getting that," Sierra says with a guilty expression. "When he was a baby, Kyo had a toy snake called Sierra. My parents used to hiss whenever they said it—*Sssiera*. It was Kyo's first word, when my mom was pregnant with me, so they named me after the snake. And roses have always been my favorite flowers."

She lights up whenever she talks about her family, and I wish I wasn't so jealous.

"You must miss them now that they're so far away."

"So much," she says, with a wistful sigh.

"Why didn't you move with them? I know you have a good job here, but you could find something else." It's not the first time I've wondered, but it's not like I could ask her when we are at each other's throats all the time.

"I love being my parents' daughter and Kyo's sister, but I thought it was important that I practiced just being Sierra for a while. I miss them, but I know I can survive it now."

"Can I be honest about something?" I ask, and she holds her hands up as if to say, "What have you been doing this whole time?"

I ignore her and clear my throat. "I get jealous whenever I hear you on the phone with Kyo. I've always wished Xan, Jazz, and I could be so close."

"So talk to them, honey. About that, about your parents, about you being depressed. All of it. I know Jazz wants to be closer, too, and I don't know Xan as well as I know the two of you, but I'd bet money he does too. You just need to let each other in."

Just the thought of it makes me want to build my walls back up and hide under the covers, but Sierra's arms anchor me. "I'll think about it. And I'll think about talking to my doctor. No promises, though."

"It's something," Sierra says, surprising me by bending down and pressing a kiss to the top of my head.

"I know it doesn't mean anything coming from me, since you, you know, hate me, but I'm proud of you for opening up about this. Thank you for trusting me with it."

But it does mean something. It means a lot. And that scares the shit out of me.

CHAPTER TWENTY-SEVEN

There's no pressure to do anything today. Just rest and take it easy.

I left a sandwich and cold brew in the fridge. Make sure you eat today. I'll pick up dinner and we can have a quiet night.

I fed the bunnies, so you don't need to worry about it. I bet they'd love to spend the day snuggling with you.

Promise you'll call if you need anything. Even if it's just to talk. I can be home in twenty minutes.

Thank you for opening up to me last night. I'm proud of—

~~I know everything feels awful right now, but you just need to take one minute at a time. And you're not on your own. You've got me. I care~~

The bunnies are fed and there's food in the fridge.
Text if you need anything. - S
~~P.S. 18 days~~

CHAPTER TWENTY-EIGHT

Sierra

Thank you for the coffee. I liked the
pistachio syrup. - R
P.S. The rose cardamom cookie was pretty gross.
We don't need to be eating flowers.

"**T**his is your plan to make me feel better?"

Rose peers up at the storefront with a raised eyebrow. Admittedly, the weathered black and pink sign reading, THE ALTAR, leaves a little to be desired. But it's what's on the inside that counts.

"New toys make everything better," I say, dragging her inside.

A bell chimes over the door, but the adult toy store is otherwise silent. I spy a few other shoppers milling around, but it's not like 10 a.m. on a Saturday is peak shopping time for stores like this.

"And what would you know about new toys, Mrs. Olivia

Newton-John?" Rose asks, looking around, taking in the store.

"That's Mrs. Rose Cannon for now," I reply, and she laughs. It's nothing more than a small bark of laughter, but, after the past few days, it's perfect.

I convinced Rose to take the rest of the week off, but made sure she had a couple of things to do every day while I was at work. Every day, she's been waking up a little more like herself. And it's a real fucking problem how much of a relief that is for me.

She hasn't brought up anything we talked about earlier this week, and I haven't either, but at least she's taking care of herself again. She also hasn't brought up how I'm acting —or maybe she hasn't noticed that I just don't have it in me to fight with her over stupid things anymore.

When I look back at the past year and a half, I can't for the life of me understand what the fuck our problem was. My mind is muddled, my heart is confused, and we're just a couple of weeks away from our appointment with the inheritance lawyer.

A fun morning at a sex toy store and an even more fun evening playing with our purchases is exactly what we need.

Despite it being her first time in the store, Rose takes the lead, and I follow her to a wall of restraints. There's everything from leather cuffs to thick metal chains, but Rose runs her finger over a deep-purple satin ribbon.

"You'd look amazing tied up with this," she says, plucking it off the hanger. "And, for the record, if we were married for real, I'd be taking your last name. Hayashi is undoubtedly the cooler last name."

Not to mention that Sierra Cannon sounds like a cheap, off-brand, ambiguous liquor that gets you wasted in thirty seconds flat. That's what I try to focus on, instead of thinking about Rose with my last name.

"Did you have something particular you wanted in mind?" Rose asks as we head away from the restraints. "Finally ready to move on from Olivia?"

"Never. She's the longest relationship I've ever had."

"Well, yeah. You've had her your entire adult life."

"And she hasn't failed me yet," I say, while Rose shakes her head. "As for anything specific, I was thinking—oh shit, sorry." Not looking where I'm going, I walk back into someone. She drops her bag and a bunch of tissue paper-wrapped packages and boxes spill out.

I crouch down to help her pick them up, apologizing again.

"It's all good, don't worry."

When we stand, coming face-to-face, we both blink in surprised recognition.

"Hallie?" Rose says over my shoulder, and the familiar sapphire eyes Hallie shares with Maggie widen as she looks up.

"Rose. Hi! How are you?" Maggie's sister asks, clearly flustered. Which is fair. A sex toy store is arguably the worst place to run into someone you know.

"I'm good, yeah. How are you?"

"I'm great."

There's an awkward silence before Rose clears her

throat. "Oh, right. This is Sierra. I don't think you guys have met."

"We met at Maggie's bachelorette party," I say softly, and Hallie looks down at her feet. I'm pretty sure that's the last time she saw her sister. She was supposed to be in the wedding, but Maggie's family didn't show up, and she hasn't spoken to any of them since.

"Right, of course." Rose winces. Clearly, she'd been hoping to avoid bringing Maggie up. "So, are you living in the city now?"

"Yeah, I moved out here a couple of years ago," Hallie replies, and she seems relieved by the change of subject. I don't notice I'm toying with the ring of my collar until her gaze pauses on it and her eyebrows lift a fraction. I suppose it's not surprising that she'd recognize it for what it is, considering where we are.

"Congratulations, by the way. I saw online that you got married a little while ago."

We both say thanks, as Hallie's phone chimes. She pulls it out of her pocket and sighs. "Shit, I have to run. It was nice to see you, though. Um…" She hesitates. "Would you mind not telling Maggie that you ran into me?"

"Of course," Rose says, but she's frowning. "It was good to see you, Hal."

Hallie looks like she wants to say more, but she just turns around and leaves the store.

I blow out a breath. "That was…" *Awkward, uncomfortable, painful.*

"Yeah," Rose agrees, before I can finish my sentence. "I

had no idea she was living here. And I don't think Maggie knows, either."

"Were you two friends growing up? You're close in age, right?"

"She's a couple of years younger than me. And we weren't really friends, no. My mom didn't like me hanging around Maggie's siblings, but Hallie was like Maggie's shadow when she was younger, so I saw her more than their brother and sister," Rose answers, toying with the ring on her finger.

"It's sad to think they were so close, and now she doesn't even want Maggie to know we ran into her. I can't imagine not speaking to Kyo." I say it without thinking and immediately regret it when something like regret flashes on Rose's face.

"It's good that you two have each other," she says, and, for a moment, I miss the pissed off, snarky responses she used to give me.

"Honey, I—"

"It's why I could never go no contact with my parents. Even if I wanted to. I don't want to lose Xan and Jazz. We're not half as close as Maggie and Hallie were, and look at them."

She says it all in one breath, like she just needs to get the words out. I'm so taken aback by her opening up that it takes me a second to respond.

"I don't think Xan and Jazz—"

"You said you were thinking of something specific," she interrupts, clearly done with the conversation. Rose steps away, her walls shooting back up.

I'm working on the couch outside Cal's office, my feet tucked under me, enjoying the quiet, when Jazz drops down beside me. She groans, rolling her neck.

"You okay?"

"Hmm? Oh, yeah. I'm fine, just haven't been sleeping great lately. Did you speak to Erik Petterson's assistant about the signatures we need?" she asks, peering at a to-do list on the tablet in her hand.

"I called this morning. Mr. Petterson is out of the country, but he'll be back tomorrow, and she'll have the documents sent over," I answer, and Jazz nods, scribbling out *Petterson* from the middle of her list.

"Thanks." She looks up and narrows her eyes. "I love your necklace. Is it new?"

My fingers immediately fly to my throat, brushing the tiny thorns on the gold rose stems. "Rose gave it to me a little while ago."

Jazz leans in to look closer. "It's really pretty. Do you know where she got it? Maggie would love something in that style."

"What would Maggie love?" Cal asks, peeking his head around his office door. I swear he's like a meerkat, popping up whenever he hears her name.

"Sierra's necklace," Jazz says as he joins us, sitting in the armchair beside the couch. "I was thinking about something similar for Maggie's Christmas."

Cal runs his gaze over my necklace and lifts a brow. Of

course he recognizes it for what it is. He and Maggie are regulars at a literal sex club. "I don't think so."

"You don't like it? I'd get Maggie a silver one, obviously," Jazz says.

He rubs his forehead. "It's lovely. It's just... Christ. It's a collar, Jazz."

Jazz turns to stare at the necklace and balks. "Oh. Shit."

Wonderful. Now that Jazz knows, the whole family will know what it is by Thanksgiving.

"Okay, maybe not for Maggie, then. I don't think she'd even let you put a collar on her," she says to Cal, and he chuckles.

"I wouldn't dare. Speaking of, I'm meeting her at Ethel's for lunch. Want me to bring either of you anything back?"

"Can you get me a chocolate and banana milkshake, French toast sticks, a buffalo falafel sandwich with ranch, cinnamon chip pancakes, Cajun house fries, and whatever fruit plate they have today, please?" Jazz says, and we both stare at her until she shrugs. "I didn't have time to eat breakfast."

"On it. Can you text that to me?" Cal asks, and Jazz pulls out her phone. "Anything for you?"

"I'm good, thanks," I answer, waving him off as he steps into the elevator.

Jazz and I settle into a silence, working through our lists until she drops her tablet on the coffee table and says her eyes need a break. I close my laptop and set it aside. I haven't been nearly as productive as I've wanted to be today. The past week has fucked with my head, and I was hoping the trip to the toy store on Saturday would get me and Rose back on steady ground, but seeing Hallie just unraveled her again.

I know it's not really about Hallie—being faced with her lack of relationship with Maggie made her panic that one day she, Jazz, and Xan would end up the same. And I understand why she'd think that. I know she wants to be closer with them, and I know Jazz does, too, but if I push too much, they'll retreat.

It scares the shit out of me. There's only so long left of our arrangement, and as much as I'm trying not to think about the end date, I can't help but wonder what happens to Rose when I'm not there.

She's never lived alone, and I don't like the idea of her being alone when she's in a depressive episode. Especially considering I seem to be the only one who knows about said depression.

I can't force her to get help, and I can't do anything about our impending deadline, but I can change who knows about what she's dealing with. Even if it does make me the world's worst confidant.

"Hey, can I talk to you about something?"

Jazz looks warily at my collar. "Is it about your sex life with my sister?"

"It's not. Though, for the record, it's fun to see you deal with this after telling Liam more about his dad's sex life than he ever needed to know."

"Touché," Jazz says, holding out her palms. "What's up?"

I spin my ring around my finger. "It's about Rose. She

would be so pissed off if she knew I was talking to you about it, but god knows I'm used to her hating me—"

"Weird thing to say about the woman you married," Jazz points out, but I ignore her.

"Okay, here's the thing. Rose is depressed. And I don't mean recently. She's been depressed since she was a teenager. She seems to manage it okay most of the time, but she's not happy day to day, and she has really bad spells sometimes."

Jazz's face falls, panic filling her hazel eyes. "What? How is that... How could we not have noticed?"

I lean forward and put my hand over hers, squeezing. "It's not you. She's gotten really good at hiding it. We lived together for over a year before I noticed."

"But since she was a teenager? Someone should've noticed. *I* should've noticed."

"I didn't tell you so you'd blame yourself, Jazz," I tell her softly, though I know I'd feel the same if I found out Kyo had been depressed for a decade and I hadn't noticed. "You were dealing with your own shit, too. This is on your parents. Hell, pretty much everything is on your parents."

"Ain't that the truth," Jazz says, and guilt spreads over me as I watch her wipe her eyes. Shit. This wasn't what I was going for.

"Jazz, I'm sorry. I—"

"No, no. I'm glad you told me. I'm just surprised." She takes a deep breath, like she's centering herself. "Okay. When you say depressed, is... is she hurting herself? Do you think she might?"

I shake my head before she finishes talking. "No. I

asked her, and she said no. And I believe her." Mostly. Do I think there's an element of Rose hurting herself in how hard she pushes herself at work? How she doesn't let herself have anything fun? Absolutely, but I don't think she's in any immediate danger.

"I think we need to take it slow in getting her to open up," I continue. "I'm trying to get her to go to the doctor to talk about medication and therapy, and I asked her to consider talking to you and Xan. Not even about this, just in general. I think it would be helpful for her—and the two of you—to process all the shit with your parents together. I know you have Maggie and Liam, and Xan has Kami, but Rose... She doesn't have anyone other than me." *And she only has me for a little while longer,* I think, trying to ignore how much the thought makes me want to shut down completely.

Jazz is never going to forgive me when she finds out we're getting divorced. Especially not after this conversation.

"That all sounds like the best way to handle it," Jazz agrees, sitting back against the couch, her brow pinched. "I won't tell her you've told me, obviously, and I agree with taking it slow, but promise me you'll tell me if it gets worse, Sierra."

"I promise."

And if she hates me forever for it... Well, I guess it won't matter once we sign the papers.

CHAPTER TWENTY-NINE

Rose

*Four whole days off for Thanksgiving!!! However will
we pass the time? - S
P.S. Olivia Newton-John is feeling pretty neglected
these days.*

Sierra hasn't stopped talking since we left home to drive to Maggie and Cal's place for Thanksgiving dinner. For my benefit, I suspect. She knows family dinners are hard for me.

Thanksgiving has never been my favorite holiday, on account of the shitty origin story, and the fact that my parents force us to have a formal meal every year. But last year, Jazz put her foot down and said she wasn't coming, inviting us to the Michaelson Thanksgiving dinner instead. My parents threw a hissy fit and refused to go. I assumed Xan would refuse, too, but when I showed up at their place, the epitome of a dutiful daughter, it was just me. Xan and

Jazz spent the holiday surrounded by laughter, and my parents and I sat in silence.

This year is different. My parents haven't been invited to family dinner since the night Sierra and I announced we were married, and when they texted me a couple of weeks ago to ask about Thanksgiving, Sierra plucked my phone out of my hand and declined their invitation before I could work myself up about it.

"Thanksgiving is for family," she told me, typing out her reply. "And they can be included when they start acting like one. We're going to Maggie and Cal's."

I've never been so grateful to have my phone stolen.

And she's right. Thanksgiving *is* for family. Which is why I stole *her* phone while she was sleeping a couple of weeks ago and got her mom's number.

I was nervous as hell calling, but Andrea Hayashi is not my mom. She was thrilled to hear from me, acting like we'd known each other forever and not like it was the first time she'd ever spoken to her daughter's wife.

Sierra holds open Maggie and Cal's front door as I carry our overnight bags. They insisted we didn't bring any food, because Liam's mom, Danisha, had so much planned and they were already worried about how we were going to eat it all.

I close the door as Sierra chatters away about the new hay she wants to try the bunnies on, corralling her toward the living room. She walks in and stops in her tracks, gasping.

"Oh my god!" Sierra rushes forward, wrapping her arms around her parents, who are standing by the fireplace.

Sierra's dad holds her tightly, pressing a kiss to the top of her head. "We've missed you, sunshine."

Any jealousy I've been feeling about how close she is with her family disappears when I see her step back with a wide smile on her face. My stomach flutters.

"How are you here?" she asks, hugging her mom, Kyo, and both of Kyo's partners in turn.

"Rose invited us," her mom says, turning to smile at me.

Shit. I forgot inviting them here would mean I also had to meet them. I steel myself and cross the room, dropping the bags on an empty chair as I go.

"It's nice to finally meet you," I say, but the words are muffled as I'm pulled into hug after hug, finally ending up, somehow, in Sierra's arms.

"You called my family?" she murmurs in my ear.

"You said you missed them."

She pulls back, and I know her well enough at this point to recognize the surprise and confusion in her eyes as she takes me in. "Thank you," she says, pressing a smiley kiss to my cheek. Blood rushes to my skin, and I barely even notice how nervous I am as she introduces me, officially, to her parents. All I can think about is how much I like making her smile like this.

I force myself to swallow one more bite of Danisha's incredible cinnamon cheesecake and push my plate away. I don't remember the last time I ate so much—or so well.

The Hayashi family fit perfectly with the Michaelsons, though I'm not surprised. It's like everyone has been friends for years. Rylan is obsessed with interior design, and a big fan of Maggie's work, and Sierra's dad, Kento, and Lina are obsessed with the same reality show as Jazz and Cal. Sierra and her mom talk about seemingly everything and nothing, and, though Sierra tries to include me in the conversation, I give her space to catch up with her mom.

From my other side, Xan reaches over me and spears the last bite of cheesecake from my plate. "You, Jazz, and Maggie really hit the jackpot in the in-law department," he says through a mouthful of cheesecake. I wrinkle my nose.

"Don't talk with your mouth full. But yeah, we did." I nudge him with my shoulder. "Kami's dad's pretty great."

"He is, but A, he's not my father-in-law—"

"He might as well be," I mutter.

Xan ignores me. "And B, he hates me."

"And yet, he still treats you better than our dad does," I point out. Xan shrugs. "What's she doing today?" Sometimes, Kami tags along to family dinner with her daughter, Lexi, and her brother, Leon, but I haven't seen them in a while.

"They're spending the day with Evan's family." Xan doesn't bother hiding the distaste in his voice. Unlike Jazz, Maggie, and me, I suppose, Kami did terribly in the in-law department. If you ask me, she also did terribly in the husband department, and she deserves better than any of them. But I always assumed Xan and Kami would end up together, so maybe I'm biased.

I start to suggest Xan invite her family for Christmas,

when Jazz asks for everyone's attention. Xan and I look up, watching across the table as she and Liam exchange a smile.

"We have some news," Liam says, gripping Jazz's hand. "We didn't say anything earlier, because we didn't want to get everyone's hopes up, but we started IUI a few months ago, and…"

Jazz's expression is pure joy when she says, "I'm pregnant!"

There's a beat of silence before noise erupts around the table. People jump up, tears spill, congratulations are shouted, and I push back from the table, processing the sudden noise. Processing the news.

"Holy shit."

I look over at Xan, and he looks as stunned as I feel. "Holy shit," I agree. "Jazz is going to be a parent." Jazz has the chance to be the mom she always needed. And I know in my bones that she will be.

"She and Liam are going to do it right," Xan says, echoing my thoughts so quietly that I wouldn't hear him if we weren't so close.

"Yeah, they are."

I look at the scene before us, watching rather than partaking, because I'm not sure where my place is here. Xan watches too, and I realize this is probably as weird for him as it is for me. Even the Hayashi family, who just met Jazz and Liam today, fit into the celebration with ease.

But the Cannons don't celebrate like this. Hell, the Cannons don't celebrate at all. Is this what it's going to be like for the rest of our lives? Watching, but never experiencing? Unless something changes, it will be. And no one is going to change it but us.

I grab Xan's arm. "Come on."

"Where are we…" His voice is lost to the noise as I tug him into the fray toward Jazz.

"Call me grandma one more time," Maggie warns Liam, with happy tear tracks on her cheeks.

"Congratulations," I say to Liam when he spies our approach.

"Congrats, man. Happy for you," Xan adds, giving Liam an awkward one-armed hug.

He steps aside so we can see Jazz, and she immediately pulls us both into her arms.

"You're going to be the best mom."

"Thanks, Rosie," Jazz says softly.

"Proud of you." Xan sounds as choked up as I feel.

Jazz wipes her eyes, but she's still smiling. "How'd we get so grown up, huh?"

"Hey, listen, can the three of us talk sometime? Not now, obviously, we're celebrating, and there's nothing urgent, I just—"

"Please, now would be perfect. I've had a permanent headache for like two months, and it's very loud in here," Jazz says, looking relieved. She nods to the door leading into Maggie and Cal's kitchen and murmurs something in Liam's ear before leading us through.

They have a small couch in the kitchen, where Maggie likes to sit and work while Cal makes dinner. Their cat, Peach, is lying across the cushions, snoozing. She gives

Jazz an unimpressed look when she moves her, but curls up on her lap and goes back to sleep.

I sit beside them, and Xan pulls a chair over from the little breakfast nook, eyeing me curiously. It's not like I gave him a heads up, and it's not exactly in character for me to suggest we talk.

"Are you okay, Rosie?"

"I'm fine," I say quickly, instinctively. Neither Jazz nor Xan looks convinced. "That's not true. I'm not fine, but I'm working on it. This is me working on it." The words come out in a rush, almost jumbled, and Jazz reaches across Peach —who meows unhappily—to hold my hand.

"Hey, take your time. Whatever you want to talk about, we're here, okay?"

My lungs burn as I take a deep breath. The worst they can say is no. "I want us to be closer. The three of us, I mean. I just feel like we've spent our whole lives with all this distance between us, because that's what our parents wanted, and now I don't know how to fix it. But I want to. I love you both, but I barely know you. And I don't want your kid growing up wondering why their mom barely talks to her siblings. I know you're both really busy, but I'd like to spend more time with you. If you want that, I guess."

"Shit, Rose," Jazz says, tears streaming down her face now. "Of course I want that. And I'm never too busy for you. Either of you."

"You're about to be a lot busier," I remind her, and she laughs, wiping her face.

"And I'll still have time for you. I promise."

"I want that too," Xan agrees, sounding almost relieved.

"Honestly, I've wanted to talk to you about this for a while, but I didn't know where to start. You both have your own lives, and I guess I wasn't really sure where I fit into them."

"That's how I feel about you two," I say.

Jazz shrugs. "I've been trying to force you both into spending more time with me lately, with all the family dinners and the Vegas trip, but I guess I wasn't being obvious enough. I figured you knew and just didn't want to be closer."

The three of us exchange h*ow have we been so fucking stupid* looks before Xan snorts, and we all dissolve into laughter.

"God, our parents really did a number on us," he says, shaking his head.

"That they did," Jazz agrees.

"Do you ever think about going no contact like Maggie did?" I've expected her to do it a hundred times since Maggie stopped talking to her family, but I just can't figure out where her breaking point is.

"Oh, I've thought about it. Only every day," she answers with a laugh. "But I'm not there. Not yet, anyway. I saw the moment Maggie broke, when they didn't come to her wedding, and she realized they were never going to change. She still had a little bit of hope until that moment, and they obliterated it. It's not a feeling I'd wish on my worst enemy, but god, *I've* wished for it a time or two. Wished that I could stop holding onto that hope. That one day they'll be proud of us, stop holding us to impossible standards. You guys know what I mean."

Xan and I echo our agreement.

"But things are different now," Jazz continues, placing her hand flat on her stomach. "This baby isn't going to grow up like we did. They get one chance to be grandparents, but a single disparaging comment about my kid, a single boundary crossed, and I'm done." She looks up from her stomach, worrying her lip with her teeth. "If that happens, though, I don't want to lose you two."

"You won't lose us," I promise, at the same time Xan does.

"It's about time the three of us worked together to heal from all their bullshit, instead of trying to compete for their attention," he says.

Jazz nods, smiling and rubbing her thumb over her stomach. "Then let's do it. A new beginning."

And for the first time, blocking out the voices of my parents in my head doesn't feel so scary.

CHAPTER THIRTY

Sierra

Olivia Newton-John had her time.
It's my turn now. - R
P.S. Did you fold my laundry? Are you okay?

Rose's fingers brush the back of my neck, and I startle as I hear the tiny click of the collar lock. My hand flies to my throat, stopping it from falling.

"What are you doing?" I ask, holding the chain against my skin. The panic in my voice surprises me, but I've become more than a little attached to the collar. I woke up from a nightmare a few nights ago, imagining taking it off alongside my wedding ring, and wanted nothing more than to crawl into bed with Rose. But we don't do that—sleeping together. We sleep together, but we don't *sleep* together.

"Relax," she says, brushing her hand over my bare back. "I'm only taking it off temporarily. I don't want to risk damaging it."

She holds her hand out and I drop the chain in it, feeling somehow more naked, considering there's not a scrap of fabric on me.

Rose sets the chain gently on her nightstand. "Don't move." I hear her shuffling around behind me, then I feel the warmth of her body against my back, her soft fingertips skating up my arms.

I lean back into her touch, my head settling against her chest. Rose bends down to kiss my head, and my eyes flutter closed. I want to memorize every second of this, the comforting, rainy scent of her, the warmth of her skin against mine. For later. For after.

She reaches for something, and a moment later, I feel a thick strap around my throat. The buckle jingles as she fastens it loosely. It's heavy compared to the dainty chain I'm used to.

"It's your choice," she says, spinning the collar around my throat. "Do you want to make me come first? Or do you want to come first?"

"Whatever you prefer," I say, instantly, because she could ask me to suspend myself in thin air and I'd find a way to do as I was told.

"I want you to choose, wife," she murmurs, holding the collar tighter.

"You. I want to make you come first." I expect her to loosen it again. But Rose tightens it.

"Too tight?" she asks as a whimper slips from my lips.

"No. No, it's good."

"Good."

She steps back, and it's killing me not to turn around to see what she's doing. Which is the point, of course. She could easily have laid everything out in my line of sight, or I could easily have stood facing the mirror instead of the door so I could see what she was doing, but where's the fun in that? I like the unknown, the thrill of never knowing what's next. And Rose likes knocking me off my axis. It's a game we're both winning.

I hear soft footsteps and a quiet rattling as Rose crosses the room. Cool metal shocks my skin as she dangles a chain over my shoulder and drags the end up my torso. I groan, goosebumps erupting over every inch of my body.

Rose clips the end of the chain to the ring at the hollow of my throat. "Turn around and get on your knees."

I drop to my knees in the middle of the room, sitting back on my feet with my hands on my lap, the carpet plush beneath me. Rose walks backward, almost lazily, until the back of her legs hit the bed. Her demeanor is cool and collected, but her body is flushed pink, almost as bright as the satin underwear she's wearing because she knows this particular pair makes me feral.

She wraps the chain—the leash, *fuck*—around her fist several times until it's pulled taut and I feel myself tugged forward ever so slightly. "Now be a good girl and crawl for me," Rose says, and I swear I almost fall apart from the dark cadence of her voice alone.

I fall forward, crawling across the floor on my hands and knees, never taking my eyes off her. She draws me in with the leash, her lips parting and her chest rising and falling rapidly. I savor every second as I cross the room, stopping at her feet.

Rose runs her hand over my head, almost like she's petting me, soft and sweet. *Why the hell is that so fucking hot?*

"Take off my underwear."

I tug it down, and Rose steps out of it. She bends and picks it up, dropping the leash. "Stay," she says, and I guess I wasn't imagining the petting, because she does it again, before walking toward the dresser.

It should be degrading; it should piss me off. But I love it.

She didn't tell me not to look, so I watch her set the underwear down, drinking in the sight of her. Rose grabs a bag I didn't notice sitting there, and I can't make out what's in it before she's back in front of me, slowly dragging the chain up my body until it's tight around her fist again.

"Such a good girl," she says, stroking her thumb over my cheek. I almost close my eyes, but I can't look away from her.

Rose sits on the edge of her bed and spreads her legs. She tugs on the collar until I fall forward, bracing myself, one hand on either side of her thighs. My mouth is mere inches from her pussy, but she hasn't given permission yet.

"Please, Rose," I whisper, and she tugs the leash up so I'm looking at her face.

"Please, what?"

"Please let me make you come. I want to make you feel good. I need to."

She leans back, spreading her legs further. "Since you asked so nicely…" She pulls me in closer between her legs by the leash, and I groan as I breathe her in. I've become addicted to the taste of her, and I already know I'm going to have withdrawals in a couple of weeks.

The thought is sobering, but I push it away, focusing on Rose instead.

She holds the leash tight in one hand and sinks her other into my hair with surprising gentleness. "Is this okay?" she asks, tugging on the leash. "It's not too tight? It doesn't hurt?"

"It's perfect," I answer, pressing a kiss to her inner thigh. "You're perfect. I love being entirely under your control like this."

"Show me how much you love it, wife." Rose pulls on the leash until my mouth is pressed against her, and I sigh happily. She's so fucking wet, all for me, and it's dizzying.

I close my lips around her clit, sucking lightly, and she curses, her head falling back.

"Stop a second," she groans, and I pull back, frowning.

"Are you o—"

Rose loosens the leash and reaches back, grabbing a pillow from the bed. "Straddle that. I want you to get yourself off riding my pillow while you make me come. You think you can do that for me?"

I've tried pillows before, but I've never been able to get close to coming by just grinding. I'm so turned on already, though, it's possible I'll fall apart the second the fabric touches my clit. "I can try."

Rose hands me the pillow, murmuring soft words of praise as I fold it and position the firmest part between my legs.

I sit down and roll my hips, moaning at the friction from the silky pillowcase. It's never felt this good before, and I have to remind myself to focus, to lean in and put my mouth back on Rose.

Rocking my hips against the pillow, I lick and suck and nibble through the endless stream of whimpers falling from my mouth. When Rose's thighs start trembling, I press one finger inside her, then two, curling them so I can massage her G-spot.

"Oh fuck," she cries, grinding herself all over my face. "God, Sierra. That feels so good."

Rose curses, tightening her grip on my hair. Her thighs close around my head, and it's instinct to want to push them apart, but I resist. If she wanted me to, she'd tell me.

"Are you close?" she asks, and I don't think she even realizes she's pulling my hair. The tug sends a sharp jolt over my body, pleasure sizzling through me. "I want you to come with me. Can you do that for me?"

I barely pull back enough to groan a quick, "Yes," before my tongue is exploring her again. I'm so fucking close, seconds from splintering, and I can feel Rose's pussy tightening around my fingers already, but I don't want it to end. It's too soon.

It's impossible to hold back, though, when she breathes my name and slips back on the bed, her body falling against the mattress as she comes. She doesn't drop the leash, and the tug pulls me forward with her, stealing the breath from my lungs as I burst into flames.

I squeeze my thighs together as I come, but all it does is push the pillow harder against my clit, and I cry out, another wave coursing through me. Rose soaks my face, and I lick up every drop, paying special attention to her clit until she drops the leash and gently pushes me back.

"Too much. Fuck, too much."

"Sorry," I breathe, pulling back instantly. I already miss the taste of her.

Rose sits up and cups my chin. "Don't apologize. That was perfect. You did so well." She pulls me up until my face is level with hers. "Look at you. So fucking messy for me. Such a good wife."

She brushes a kiss over my jaw before her tongue darts out and she licks around my chin, my jaw, my lips, cleaning me of her. If it wasn't so hot, I'd complain that I wanted that last little taste. I forget all about that, though, when she slips her tongue in my mouth and kisses me so hard my brain goes quiet for a moment.

I cling to her, breathing hard when we break apart.

Rose searches my face. "You tapping out, or can you handle a little more?"

"I can handle whatever you have for me." I mean it, but the challenging glint that appears in her hazel eyes has me doubting myself.

Rose stands and points to the mattress. "Crawl up the bed. Stop by the headboard."

I kneel on the bed as she walks away, and I can tell from

the number of steps she takes that she stops by the dresser, several feet away, with a perfect view as I crawl for her. It's hard to believe I asked her to turn the lights out the first time we were together, and now I'm on full display under her gaze. A few months with Rose, and I've forgotten how it feels to be self-conscious of my body. If she likes my body—and it meets her impossibly high standards—it must be okay, I suppose.

The leash drags along the bed as I crawl, stopping just before I kneel on the pillows. Rose settles behind me, and I gasp as I feel something soft and silky tickling my spine.

"Do you want your hands tied to the headboard, or behind your back?" she asks, tracing the silhouette of my body with the end of the ribbon.

I place my hands behind my back in answer, and Rose wastes no time wrapping the ribbon around my wrists. She loops the thick ribbon several times around each wrist, back and forth, before tying it in a knot.

"Is that okay?"

I test the restraints, and my wrists barely shift. It's not comfortable, but it's not sore. "It's good."

Rose reaches up and pulls the leash up my body. The chain is trapped between me and the mattress, and I cry out as it brushes my clit, the cool metal fucking heavenly. "I want you over my knee."

There's not much space, but I shuffle around and start to bend over her knee before she stops me. "The other way."

I frown, unsure what she means, but she points in the direction she means. Naturally, it's the most tricky position for me to get into and, of course, she does nothing to make it easier. She watches as I maneuver, tied up, orgasm-addled, without a word, but her eyes are dark with lust.

A sigh of relief spills from me when I finally bend over her knee, facing the direction she wants, and she runs her hand over my ass. "Good girl," she murmurs. "You're so good at doing what you're told."

I close my eyes, preening under her praise. She pulls a pillow closer and sets it under my head.

"Thank you." My voice is already hoarse, and she's not done with me.

"Open your eyes, Sierra. Turn your head the other way," she commands, and I immediately do, sucking in a breath. She's angled us so we're framed perfectly by the mirror.

Rose brings her hand down on my ass with a gentle smack.

"Fuck," I curse, squirming in her lap. "Am I being punished?"

She laughs, rubbing her hand over the spot where she smacked me. "Punishment implies you wouldn't enjoy it. And you've been a good girl. This is a reward."

She spanks me again, still softly. Too soft.

"More. Harder," I beg, torn between squeezing my eyes closed because it's too much, and watching in the mirror.

Rose hums. "What do you say if you want to stop?"

"Red."

"If you want to slow down?"

"Yellow."

"And if you like it?"

This time, she doesn't hold back as she smacks me. The

sound reverberates, mingling with the hoarse cry of her name as it escapes my lips.

"Well remembered," is all she says before branding my skin with her palm, over and over, left, then right, until I'm a trembling, sticky mess on her lap.

She nudges my legs apart and, with a softer hand, smacks my pussy. For the first time, I fight against the ribbon tying my wrists together, needing to grab something, hold on to something to see me through the waves of pleasure creeping closer.

Rose rubs between my legs roughly, relentlessly, and I think I black out for a split second, because I blink and our reflections come into focus, and she's pulling the dildo we picked up at the toy store out of the mystery bag. It's like it was waiting there just for us, just for me—a rosebud tip with thorn-shaped ridges winding down the shaft. Rose presses the tip against my entrance, and I whimper.

"Okay?" she asks, and I nod.

"Mhmm. I can take it."

"Of course you can." Her voice is soft and soothing as she presses the rose inside me, slowly, then all at once. My nails bite into my palms as I clench my fists. My body fights to move, not to get away, but for more. More, more, more. Rose obliges, pulling the toy out and sliding it back in, every thrust a little faster, a little harder. The thorny ridges feel like heaven, striking every nerve ending inside me like a match and setting me ablaze.

With her free hand, Rose slaps my clit, and I explode. The orgasm that takes over me is demanding, forcing me to feel it over every inch of my body. My moans turn into cries until I hit a peak, and the sound is stolen from my throat.

Rose slows down, gently circling my clit and drawing the toy out of my pussy, letting me float down from the high, light as a feather. My brain is quiet, my body limp, and, right now, I can't remember what stress feels like.

A gentle hand runs through my hair before Rose leans down to kiss the top of my head. And, for a second, I forget that she doesn't want me like I want her.

CHAPTER THIRTY-ONE

Rose

*I folded your laundry because I was looking for my
blue crewneck. Don't think I haven't noticed you
stealing it. - S
P.S. It smells good after you've worn it.*

I spin around, taking in the wall of brightly colored
bricks and boxes of all shapes and sizes.

"Is this a LEGO café?" Jazz asks, mirroring me.

"Sure is. We each pick out a set and build it. I figured it
wasn't a good idea for us to do anything competitive, given,
well, our personalities."

Xan stands by the door, his hands in his pockets, looking
nervous, like we might not like the activity he planned. He
insisted on being the first one to plan a sibling day out, since
he's the oldest, and Jazz and I gave him free rein.

"Sounds fun," I say, though I can't remember the last
time I built a LEGO set—if ever.

"It does," Jazz agrees. She squints at Xan. "You know,

sometimes, I think if Liam had met you before me, he could've fallen in love with either one of us."

"Um, thank you. I think?" He looks at me, bewildered. Understandably. You never know what's going to come out of Jazz's mouth, but it's always an experience.

"You're not Sierra's type," I tell him with a shrug, and he laughs.

"Can't have them all."

We spend twenty minutes perusing the sets available to build. There are so many. Jazz picks first—a mini typewriter for the nursery Maggie is putting together.

I hover by a bunny holding a carrot, but my eyes keep flicking toward the set that caught my eye when I first walked in.

"We won't judge you for picking them. You know if they had jasmines, Jazz would do the same," Xan says, grabbing the rose bouquet and pressing it into my hands.

I clutch the box against my chest. "They're Sierra's favorite flowers."

"I guess you two were meant to be, huh?" he replies, and I chuckle alongside him, ignoring the way his words hurt a little.

"For Kami?" I ask, nodding to the Polaroid camera set he picks up.

His cheeks flush pink. "Yeah. She and Evan are going through a rough patch right now, and I thought—"

"How rough?" Jazz interrupts, wiggling her eyebrows. "Like breaking up level rough?"

"Jazz! Sound a little less excited about it."

"What? Evan is fucking awful, and Kami deserves better," Jazz says with an unapologetic shrug.

"You're not wrong," I say as we pay for our sets, order coffee, and settle at one of the big tables.

"I don't think they're there, but it's not going well," Xan confirms, as he carefully opens his box and tips the bags out. "Evan hasn't been around much lately."

"Has he ever been around much?" Jazz quips back.

I open my LEGO set and start sorting the bricks by color and size as I watch them volley back and forth. I don't have much to contribute, since I don't know Kami's husband all that well, but I'm just happy to be here. There's no awkwardness between the three of us, and it doesn't feel as unnatural as I thought it might to spend time together like this. It just feels easy.

Doing this together feels like something we might have done as kids, if our parents weren't who they are. Maybe on a rainy Marysville day when we couldn't play outside. I can almost picture it perfectly: the three of us sitting on the floor in the living room, Jazz stealing the TV remote and turning off Xan's playlist in favor of her own.

"I can't believe we never did anything like this when we were kids," I say, clicking the bricks together.

Xan laughs. "I can. Mom and Dad would never have let us hang out like this."

I look up, frowning. "What do you mean?"

"Anytime we started hanging out or getting closer, they always found a way to play us against each other."

I've never noticed it before, but now that Jazz mentions it... "They started making us go around the table to one-up each other with our accomplishments after that summer we went to the music festival together," I say, grateful that Jazz put her foot down on doing that after she and Liam got together.

"Exactly. And when we were kids, and we were all desperate to go see that new Disney movie together, Dad took me and Jazz and told us you didn't want to go anymore, Rose. Then he told you it was my idea to go without you. You didn't talk to me for weeks," Xan adds, sounding more bitter than I think I've ever heard him.

There are countless examples when I think back. For years, I convinced myself that Xan found me annoying and Jazz just didn't care, but how much of that was actually true? I'd be willing to bet that Jazz and Xan both thought similar things about me growing up, all of it carefully crafted by our parents.

"They probably think we're easier to control if we're not talking about shit like this," I say, shaking my head. "And I guess they were right, because it worked. For years, it worked, and we just didn't notice."

"We got there eventually. And this is pretty fun. Good choice, Xan," Jazz says.

I voice my agreement. It's nice to just be around them. They're the only people in the world who know what it was like to grow up with our parents. And the LEGO is fun, too.

I bet Sierra would love this. Maybe I'll need to grab a couple of sets and take them home...

My hands still. Where did that thought come from? Sierra and I don't hang out. We don't build LEGO sets together. We have sex, cuddle for an adequate amount of time to make sure we're both okay, and go to bed in separate beds.

Sure, lately we've crossed paths for breakfast and sat together a few times—most mornings, I guess—and I did help her with her stupid radio quiz yesterday. And we eat dinner together every night, but that's just because it's usually right before or right after sex. We don't hang out. Not really.

But this is the first Sunday in a while that we haven't been together, and I… miss her. Shit. What an inconvenient feeling.

I jolt as Jazz kicks me under the table. "Still with us?"

"Yeah, yeah. Just thinking. Strategy, you know," I answer, holding up the half-formed rosebud in my hand.

"It's LEGO. You don't need a strategy. They do that for you in the instructions," Xan chimes in, already halfway through his camera.

"Right. Sorry." I flip to the next page in my instruction book and grab the correct red piece from my pile, snapping it into place. "I just realized I don't actually know when you're due. I completely missed it in all the excitement on Thursday," I tell Jazz.

"Around the first week of June," she answers, squinting at her bricks. "I'm having a Gemini, which is terrifying, but also probably what I deserve, considering what a menace I am to everyone around me."

"Sierra's a Gemini, and she's not so bad, I suppose," I say, without thinking, and they both turn to stare at me.

Xan raises a brow. "Not so bad?"

"You suppose? That's certainly a way to describe your *wife*," Jazz says, sounding like she's trying not to laugh.

There's no heat in their teasing, but I'm kicking myself internally. Sierra's so much better at this than I am.

"We're just fucking with you," Jazz promises, winking. "We know what you two are like. Half the time, it sounds like you don't even like each other."

"Of course we like each other. We love each other." I jump to defensive so quickly that I don't have time to think about the words before I say them. *We love each other*. They should taste sour on my tongue, but they don't. They taste like sweet maple and cinnamon and chocolate. Like Sierra. Oh shit. Shit. Shit. *Shit*.

"Honestly, if it wasn't for how much you've changed since you got married, I don't know if I'd even believe you," Xan says, smiling as if I'm not in the midst of a fucking crisis over here. Not that he knows, but—wait. *Changed?*

"What do you mean, how much I've changed? I haven't changed."

He blinks in surprise. "Are you kidding? You're like a whole new person. In a good way," he tacks on, quickly. "Look around. We wouldn't be here if you hadn't said something. And I've seen the pictures on Sierra's Instagram of the two of you going on hikes and cuddling with your rabbits. It's nice to see."

"Sierra's changed, too," Jazz says, before I can even begin processing what Xan said. "She just seems lighter, happier, you know? More settled. Like, when we used to hang out, it always felt like she was waiting for the other shoe to drop or something. She feels more present now. You two are good for each other."

They both make it sound so easy, so matter-of-fact. But there's no way I've changed Sierra. For worse, maybe, considering how much she's having to lie about us, but not for better. She probably just seems different because she's overcompensating for the lies so much.

And as for me... maybe there's something to it. I feel like a different person than I was a few months ago, but surely it has more to do with me opening up than the person I opened up to.

Unless it doesn't.

The whole situation feels like a jumble of LEGO bricks, and I'm trying to click them together without a manual. I'm a scientist. I like facts and proof, and things adding up like they're supposed to.

Fact: I've changed for the better.

Fact: Sierra most likely contributed to that.

Fact: I miss her today.

Fact: I can't wait to go home, just to see her.

Fact: Whenever I think about unlocking her collar or taking our rings off, it feels like the world is crashing down around me.

Possible conclusion: I might be in love with my wife.

I click the stem onto the final rose and hold the bouquet in my hand, trying to stop my fingers from trembling.

Because those things might all be true, but I'm missing some key facts. Some painful, unavoidable facts.

Fact: This marriage isn't real.

Fact: Sierra doesn't feel the same way.

Fact: We're meeting with the inheritance lawyer tomorrow, and by this time in a couple of weeks, Sierra and I will be done.

Sierra is on the couch, humming softly to the bunnies when I get home, and my stomach immediately flip-flops at the sight of her.

I sit on the bench to kick my shoes off, taking a deep breath.

"Hey. Did you have fun?" she calls as I tuck my shoes away and slide my feet into slippers.

"We did, yeah. It was nice just to hang out and talk. And Jazz is so excited about the baby." I stand up, clutching the bouquet to my chest. "I made you something."

Sierra sits up as I walk toward the couch, Thorne snuggled against her chest. Her eyes widen as she spies the vase. "Holy shit. You made those?"

"Just the flowers," I say, quickly, setting them on the coffee table and taking a seat on the opposite side of the couch. I spent a half hour in T.J. Maxx deliberating between three vases before spying the white vase with a gold snake painted on the front.

She puts Thorne down, and he bounces over to me to have his nose rubbed. Dibbles is lying in her favorite spot on the back of the couch, half asleep.

Sierra picks up the vase and carefully traces one of the

roses with her finger. "These are amazing. I can't believe you made them for me."

I shrug, my face flushing. "It's no big deal."

"It is," Sierra says, smiling at the flowers. "I love them. Thank you, honey."

"You're welcome." Thorne loses interest in me, hopping up onto the back of the couch to annoy Dibbles. "What did the three of you get up to today?"

Sierra yawns, leaning back against the arm of the couch. "We've had a lazy Sunday. The buns had some treats, we played with their stacking cups, and we all took a nap. Aside from that, we've just snuggled all day."

"That sounds perfect." I'm surprised and a little embarrassed by how wistful I sound. I toy with the frayed edge of a rip in my jeans (another outfit picked by copying a store mannequin).

Sierra nudges me with her foot, and when I look up, I find her holding out her blanket. She nods at the space beside her in a silent invitation.

I shouldn't. Fuck, it's the last thing I should do. But Xan wasn't kidding when he said I'd changed. I'm so over depriving myself of things I want just because I shouldn't want them.

I shuck off my slippers and climb into the spot beside her, wrapping my arms around her middle and listening to her heartbeat as she settles the blanket around both of us.

CHAPTER THIRTY-TWO

Sierra

I'll be home by 12. I'll pick up coffee on the way home. Text me what you want and don't forget your passport and license. - R
P.S. I have our marriage certificate.

The lawyer's office handling my grandparents' estate is a far cry from Michaelson and Hicks. I spend more time around lawyers than most people, but I'm itching to get out of the stuffy office the second I step inside. Even the smell is cloying, like a fancy perfume with a ridiculous price tag that makes you grit your teeth and say, "That's interesting," when someone asks what you think.

I never met my mom's parents, but they lived just outside of Seattle and would have had their pick of firms when setting up their estate. Their choice of lawyer says a lot about them—this whole inheritance situation says a lot about them.

The process is relatively straightforward, at least. It's a lot of listening to the lawyer drone on about terms, a lot of pretending to read documents (that Cal already checked over for me), and a lot of signing. Cal gave me the day off, but it's not all that different from being in the office. Except I do actually read shit there. He offered to come with us, for moral support more than anything, but this felt like something Rose and I should do, just the two of us.

The lawyer hands us off to his assistant after advising that everything looks in order, but they'll be double-checking before making the transfer. By this time next week, I'll have more money to my name than I know what to do with. Half of it will go to Kyo, and Cal helped me set up an appointment with his financial advisor because I have no idea what I'm doing. For the most part, I like my life, and, as far as I'm concerned, nothing has to change alongside my net worth.

Not nothing, I think, as Rose and I step into the elevator with the lawyer's assistant. We still have a couple of weeks until Rose finds out about her promotion, but when she gets the job—and she will get the job—everything is going to change. We'll sign the papers we had drawn up months ago, which have been sitting gathering dust in her desk drawer. I'll move out and stop attending family dinners. Jazz probably won't talk to me outside of work anymore, and I'll have to start over, pretending I want to make new friends and inevitably giving up when people get too close.

And Rose… Rose will move on. She'll meet someone new, get closer to her siblings, and thrive. And I'll be so fucking proud of her, even if I'm not there to see it.

Rose twines her fingers with mine, drawing me back into a conversation I didn't realize was happening. I jump at her touch. She's barely looked at me since we woke up in each other's arms this morning, and she certainly hasn't touched me.

"You have to take yourselves on a honeymoon now," the lawyer's assistant says as we descend.

The elevator is glass-fronted, facing dreary Downtown Seattle. Raindrops stream down the glass, and heavy clouds sit low in the sky, casting everything in blue. "Definitely," I agree. "Maybe somewhere sunny."

The assistant laughs, shaking her head at the view. "It's been endless lately. Sunny sounds nice. Any ideas where you might go?"

"Hmm…" I wrack my brain, but Rose answers before I can think of anywhere.

"Japan. I want to see where Sierra's family came from."

The assistant gushes about a trip her sister took to Tokyo a couple of years ago, but I barely hear her. I want to take Rose to Japan. I want to show her where my family's from and tell her all about my grandparents. I want to take her back to Toronto, show her around my old neighborhood, introduce her to my aunts and uncles, and take her to my grandparents' old furniture store. I want to share my family with her.

I don't want to give any of this up. I don't want to miss seeing her opening up to her siblings. I don't want to miss family dinners. I don't want to miss Rose meeting Jazz and Liam's baby for the first time. I want to see her flourish as an aunt, and I want to be Aunt Sierra.

But those aren't my things to want. That's not what Rose and I agreed on. And even if, by some miracle, she wanted those things with me, I wouldn't know how to let myself have them. I have no idea how to stay.

"Hey." Rose squeezes my hand hard, and I blink. "You okay? You've been staring blankly at me for like two minutes."

I look around, realizing we're standing at the door, and the assistant is already waiting for the elevator again.

"Shit, sorry. I didn't sleep well last night. I think I spent too much time napping with the buns yesterday." It's not a lie, just not the whole truth. Neither Rose nor I made any move toward either of our beds last night. We cuddled before dinner, ordered takeout, then fell asleep wrapped around each other on the couch. Or Rose did, anyway. I stayed awake for hours, just watching her sleep, listening to her breathe, and memorizing every freckle on her skin. Until she woke up and jumped out of my arms, taking off like she couldn't wait to get away from me.

Rose reaches a hand out, as if she's going to touch my face, then lets it fall between us. I look down, watching it dangle by her side, the diamond on her finger twinkling as the overhead lights hit it.

"We should get home so you can have a rest, then," she says, folding her arms across her chest, like she's not quite sure what to do with them suddenly.

"I figured you'd want to go back to the lab for a couple of hours."

Rose shakes her head. "I took a half day. I wasn't sure

how long this would take or how stressed you'd be about it, so I wanted to be there in case..." She trails off, looking outside the glass door before finishing. "In case you needed me."

Fuck, she's making this so hard.

"Let's go out," I say, before I can think about it, and Rose squints at me, like it's a foreign concept to her. It kind of is, I guess.

"Out?"

"Yeah. We have the whole night to ourselves, and we're already here. Let's get dinner and... I don't know, we could see a movie or something?"

It's not a date. Sure, it sounds suspiciously like one, but asking my wife on a date a week or so before we plan on getting divorced would be unhinged behavior.

"Um..." Rose chews her lip, and I brace myself, ready for her to decline the invitation. She's kept me at arm's length all day, so I can't imagine she wants to spend the night out in the city with me. I should've just taken her up on going home and taking a bath, leaving her to do her own thing.

"We're near that Italian place that Liam and Maggie like. You know the one that shows obscure foreign movies with really out-of-sync subtitles? We could go there."

I swear I breathe out all the air in my body, rushing to say yes. "That sounds perfect. Let's do that."

It's an awful idea, spending more time together when I already know how hard it's going to be to walk away, but that doesn't stop me from holding the door open for her.

And when Rose accidentally bumps my shoulder as we walk down the street, it doesn't stop me from threading my fingers through hers and holding her hand.

CHAPTER THIRTY-THREE

Rose

~~1. Twister~~
~~2. Scotland~~
~~3. Katherine Howard~~
~~4. Purple~~
Shit, sorry, honey. I thought it was scrap paper. - S

Things are weird between me and Sierra. I should've been more careful last night. I knew better than to snuggle her on the couch, and I sure as hell knew better than to let myself fall asleep with her. Not only was waking up fucking awkward, but my back is killing me. Admittedly, it might be my fault it's awkward considering how quick I was to pull away from her when we woke up, but it was in both of our best interests.

Part of me thought Sierra would suggest going our separate ways as soon as we finished with the lawyer. Sure, she doesn't actually have the money yet, but it's a done deal, and I figured she'd be jumping at the chance to get away. I might not find out about the promotion for a couple of weeks, but my boss would never know if she moved out. At this point, I'm not sure what Sierra's waiting for.

Dinner was nice, and the movie seemed fine, what little I paid attention to anyway, but I didn't expect Sierra to want to do anything. And I didn't expect her to sit beside me, sling her arm around my waist, and cuddle me while we ate our dinner and stared up at the big screen. She seemed perfectly at ease.

So maybe things aren't weird between me and Sierra. Maybe it's just me.

"Rose?"

I startle, realizing she's been talking to me and I've just been standing against the door, staring blankly into space. "Sorry, what?"

The edges of her lips lift. "I asked if you want to get the wine, and I'll feed the monsters?"

She nods to the rug, where Dibbles and Thorne are sitting right on the edge, waiting expectantly. They don't like the hardwood floor.

"Yeah, sure."

She hands me a bottle of rosé from the fridge, and I rummage in the utensil drawer for the corkscrew while she leads the bunnies back to their enclosure by shaking a bag of mixed leafy greens.

My hands tremble as I uncork the wine and pour two large glasses. I need to get a hold of myself. The last of the bottle sloshes as I carry it back to the fridge. I open the door and take a second. Just breathe. Relax. It'll be okay.

Footsteps sound behind me, and Sierra encloses me in her arms, resting her chin on my shoulder. "Not to sound like my dad, but were you planning on chilling the whole house by keeping the fridge open? It's November."

She surprises a laugh out of me and uses the opportunity to close the fridge and tug me away. She lets go of me, and my body immediately misses the warmth of her.

"Come on." She snags the wine glasses from the island, and leads me toward her bedroom.

I follow her, looking over my shoulder to make sure the bunnies are content. Sierra kicks her bedroom door open, taking a sip of her wine and pressing the other glass into my hand when I'm close enough. I open my mouth, looking for a reason, an excuse, to leave and hide away in my room, but I fall short. I don't want to leave. I want to be here, with her, for whatever time we have left.

"You look like you're thinking pretty hard over there," Sierra says, tilting her head and looking over me with concern.

"It's been a long day."

She plucks the glass from my hand and sets them both on the dresser. "That it has. C'mere."

I let her tug me toward the bed, expecting her to lie down and pull me on top of her, but she doesn't. Sierra spins me so my back is to the bed and lifts my dress over my head. She takes care to lay it on a chair, instead of balling it up on the floor, and it makes my breath catch in my throat. I start to unclip my bra, just for something to do with my hands, but Sierra stops me.

"Let me."

She deftly undoes my bra and pulls it off, crouching to push my underwear down and pressing kisses to my shoulder, my stomach, my thighs, as she goes. Her touch is deliberate, but tender, and I close my eyes, memorizing how her fingers and lips feel on my skin.

"Lie down, honey," she murmurs against my neck, brushing a kiss over my jaw before stepping back.

Her eyes don't stray from me as I lie down, roaming every inch of my body. She quickly strips and climbs onto the bed, kneeling between my legs. She places her hands on either side of my head, leaning over me, raising an eyebrow as if to ask if I'm okay with her being on top.

It's not either of our usual styles, but I nod, desperate to feel her body on mine. She swings one of her legs over my thigh until she's straddling me, then lowers herself so her lips are hovering just above mine. She's holding most of her weight off me, and I don't want that. I want to feel her. I wrap my arms around her and tug her down as much as I can. "I want to feel you. I need to feel you."

She lifts herself only slightly, but I still can feel her body pressed against mine, and it's bliss.

A happy sigh escapes me when our lips touch, and she slips her tongue inside my mouth, meeting mine in a slow dance. It's unhurried and languid—a far cry from the battle of wills our first kiss was. My bones turn more molten beneath her with every brush of her tongue against mine.

She shifts to get close to me and groans as the movement creates friction between my thigh and her bare pussy. I lift my thigh against her in invitation as she breaks our kiss to press her forehead to mine.

"Oh," she gasps as she grinds herself against me. "*Rose.*"

She reaches between us and drags her middle finger slowly through my lips, then finally lands on my clit. I'm already soaking for her, and she draws lazy shapes over my clit as she grinds against my thigh and litters kisses all over my face.

It's tender—soft, and slow, and completely out of my comfort zone. Sierra has a habit of breaking me into pieces and rebuilding me brick by brick, over and over, every time just a little better, a little stronger. And this time, as she tips me over, shattering me into a thousand fractured shards, I feel myself scattering far and wide.

Sierra rolls her hips and catches my lips in a messy kiss as she comes. I swallow down her moans and cries, coming right alongside her when she pinches my clit between two fingers.

We're both fighting for air when we pull apart, my chest burning. Sierra sits up, pulling her fingers out from between us.

"Fuck," she murmurs, barely above a whisper, as she sees how wet they are. She brings them to her mouth and sighs happily, closing her eyes as she licks them off.

It should be filthy—the sight of her straddling my thigh, licking my wetness from her fingers, but it just makes my heart ache.

When she's finished, she collapses onto the bed beside me. As if by instinct, we both roll onto our sides until we're facing each other. Sierra's eyes are half-closed, her cheeks scarlet. I trace the length of the snake tattoo up her body, dragging my finger up her chest, neck, and tucking her hair behind her ear.

"You're so beautiful." I don't mean to say it, but I don't regret it. The words pop into my head every time I look at her, and I don't say it enough.

Sierra covers my hand with hers, pressing it against her flaming cheek. "You've made me feel so beautiful."

Made. Past tense. I look up toward the headboard, blinking and swallowing back the tears that threaten my eyes. This is not the time.

"Will you sleep in here tonight?" Sierra asks, and the "yes" leaves my mouth before she's even finished speaking. Why the hell does this all feel so much like goodbye?

It's masochistic, and later, I'm going to have to find a way to deal with the consequences, but I'm powerless to say no to her. Sierra has no idea how much power she has here.

CHAPTER THIRTY-FOUR

Sierra

Mexican food and a bath tonight? – R
P.S. If I get you a journal, will you stop writing
your quiz answers on my stuff?

The number staring at me from my laptop screen is... staggering. I cross my arms and frown at my bank balance as my heart sinks into my stomach. For the past couple of years, anytime I thought about finally getting my inheritance so I could help Kyo start a family, I imagined being elated. Whatever I'm feeling right now, it's not that.

I snap a picture of my screen and send it off to Kyo.

> Grandma and grandpa came through!!!
> You three are going to be the best
> parents!!!

A second after the message sends, my phone lights up with a video call. I hook my phone grip over my laptop screen—probably bad for my laptop, but I hate holding my phone up for calls—and accept the call.

Kyo's face fills my screen, his initial smile dropping as soon as he sees me. "Whoa. What's this face, SiSi?" He circles the camera with his finger. "I thought this was going to be a celebratory call, but that's not the face of someone who's practically a millionaire."

"You're rounding up pretty generously," I point out, and he rolls his eyes. "But this is a celebratory call. I'm so happy for you guys! You're going to be a dad, and I'm going to be Aunt Sierra!" Not to Jazz and Liam's baby, and that hurts like hell, but I'll be the best aunt I can be to Kyo's.

"Sierra. Come on. Talk to me. What's wrong?"

"Nothing's wrong!" My voice is too high, too squeaky, and Kyo sees right through me. I rub my face, sitting back in the spinny office chair. "I am happy for you, I promise. It's just that this means I have a lot to figure out over the next week. Rose will get her promotion, and we'll have to figure out the logistics of the divorce, telling people. And I have to find a new place, then deal with moving." I *am* a millennial, which means I spend a lot of time scrolling through real estate websites and dreaming. I've seen a ton of nice apartments lately, but I can't picture living in any of them.

Kyo hums. "That is a lot to figure out, I guess. There's also the little matter of you being in love with your wife, of course."

"What?" I hold up my hands. "I have no idea what

you're talking about. Me? In love with Rose? I... Um... Like... No. Just no."

Kyo raises his brows. "Damn. That was very convincing. However... I think the time to tiptoe around it is over. No one believed you two actually loved each other at first."

"Yes, they did! Everyone believed us." Things might have started a little rocky, but even Rose has become a pro at faking it lately.

"No, they didn't. Maybe the people who don't really know you, like your colleagues. And maybe Rose's parents, since they seem to be inclined to believe the worst about her, but everyone else? Not a chance."

"That can't be true. Why would no one say anything?"

Kyo shrugs. "I mean, our family all figured out pretty fast why you'd done it. And as for the Michaelson-Cannon family—from what you've told me, they all started out in relationships that 'weren't real,' so they were probably just waiting for you to fall for each other. I don't know what's in the water with them, but between you and me, I fully expect Xan and his best friend will get together at some point in the next couple of years."

I don't disagree with that, but it doesn't help my point, so I'm not addressing it. "Even if no one believes Rose and I love each other, I don't see what difference that makes. We have the money, and her promotion is more or less a done deal."

"I didn't say no one *believes* you. I said no one *believed* you," Kyo says with a smug smile. "After seeing the two of you together in person? I have no doubts that you have real feelings for each other."

An exasperated growl escapes my throat. "I'm telling you we don—you know what, it doesn't matter. It's a moot point. Because even if I did have feelings for her—and I'm not saying I do"—"You do," Kyo interrupts—"We have an agreement. And that agreement comes to an end this month. Besides, any feelings are entirely one-sided. Rose doesn't have feelings for me."

Kyo crosses his arms. "So you've talked about it."

"Well, no."

"Right. So you know this how?"

"I just know!" I slam my hands down on the desk. "What the hell is with this interrogation?"

"It's not an interrogation. It's a warning. You're running out of time to figure this out. You have to talk to her."

"No. I'm not doing that. I can't do that." I take deep, measured breaths, trying to keep myself calm. And failing spectacularly.

"Seriously?" Kyo groans. "You're going to lose the woman you love over a stupid miscommunication?"

"There's no miscommunication happening here," I protest, not bothering to correct him about my feelings for Rose again. What's the point? "I know exactly what I'm doing. I'm communicating exactly how I always intended to."

"Why? Why can't you just tell her how you feel?"

"Because what if she doesn't feel the same way?" I shout, looking away from the camera. Thank fuck for the soundproof meeting rooms at the office.

"Sierra…"

"I don't want to hear it. I know you're going to say that I

lose her in either scenario. I'm well fucking aware. At least this way, I'm in control. I'm leaving before she gets the chance to this time." I sound like a petulant child, throwing her toys away.

"This time?" Kyo asks, confusion morphing into understanding as he stares at me. "Shit, Sierra. Your friends? That was what, fourteen years ago? It was a lifetime ago."

"It still feels like yesterday to me. I'll never let anyone leave me like that again."

Kyo frowns. "So let me get this straight. You went through something so awful you're still dealing with it fourteen years later, and now you're going to do the exact same thing to Rose?"

"It's not the same. She doesn't have feelings for me, and she won't be alone, anyway." I made sure of that. "She has the Michaelsons, and she's hanging out with her siblings more."

"It is the same. If she does have feelings for you, you're going to break her heart because you're too scared to risk your own. It's a shitty thing to do, Sierra. You knew you were going to do this the whole time?" he asks.

"What? No. Of course not. I mean, it was always the plan to get divorced, but I didn't expect to catch feelings for her. If I had…" I stop short of saying I wouldn't have done it, because I don't know that I wouldn't have.

"You involved people in this, Sierra. Did you not once stop to consider the consequences? You'll almost certainly fuck up the only close friendships you've had in the past decade with Jazz and Maggie. Not to mention the fact that you work with Jazz and Cal."

"I know all of that! I know it's a shitty thing to do. I know it makes me the bad guy. Hell, I've *been* the bad guy in every relationship I've been in over the past decade. Do you think I don't know that?" If I was a better person, I wouldn't date at all. I wouldn't befriend people knowing I was going to drop them in three months. But I'm not a better person. I'm a hopeful person who's spent most of her life living in the delusion that she'd meet someone worth taking a risk for.

Well, I met her. And I still can't make myself do it.

Kyo says nothing, just stares at me, his expression heavy.

"Look, I get it, okay? You're disappointed in me. I'm disappointed in me, too, Kyo."

He drops his head into his hands and sighs. "In what world did you think I'd be okay with you hurting Rose to help me bring a child into the world, Sierra? So yeah, I am fucking disappointed in you. This isn't you."

His words sting more than I'd ever admit. I clear my throat. "Well, it is me, actually. So, I guess I'll add your disappointment to the long, long list of things I'm going to have to learn to live with. I gotta go. Love you. Bye."

I don't give him a chance to respond before hanging up the call and tossing my phone on the desk. Almost immediately, it lights up with a new text. I almost ignore it, not wanting to deal with him again, but it's not Kyo's name on my screen.

I pick my phone up with shaking hands, my heart cracking.

ROSE

Promotion secured!!!!!

I should congratulate her. Send back something, anything, but I'm all out of faux-happy.

A bubble pops up, indicating Rose is typing, and a second later, another message comes through.

Can we talk tonight? Not about the job.
It's important. I just really need to talk
to you.

It's too soon. We were supposed to have a week or two, even a couple more days. But we don't. I'm out of time.

Tears prick my eyes, but I breathe through them. I don't get to cry about this.

I grab my stuff and leave the meeting room, heading out in search of Jazz to let her know I'm taking the rest of the afternoon off. By my calculations, Rose will be home from work in five hours, which gives me approximately four hours and fifty minutes to break my own heart.

CHAPTER THIRTY-FIVE

Rose

I pace outside the apartment door for five whole minutes when I get home. Sierra never texted me back. Granted, it's not unusual for her to type a message out and forget to hit send, but she usually realizes when she doesn't get a reply. Silence isn't Sierra's thing, and now I have no idea what I'm walking into.

What a day.

Lisa pulled me into her office first thing, earlier than I expected. Kayleigh's job, she explained, was going to Imogen, but that's only because she had a different role in mind for me. The company is expanding, converting the fifth-floor offices into a new research lab, and Lisa put me forward for floor manager. I feel wholly unqualified, but she gushed about my drive and organization, and her boss's boss was impressed by my work, so I got the job. I'll be shadowing Lisa for the next month or so before the new research lab opens.

The first thing I did when I left her office was run to the bathroom and lock myself in to text Sierra. Then I stared at myself in the mirror, taking in the glow, the smile that didn't exist until Sierra and I grew closer, and asked myself what the hell I'm doing letting her go without a fight.

Hence my second text. I'm going to tell her how I feel, and I'm going to hope that she doesn't laugh in my face. What we have is far from traditional, and I'm not asking her to stay married to me if that's not what she wants. I'd just like to try and see what's here between us. Because there's something there, and Sierra is too observant not to have noticed it.

It all seemed a lot less scary locked in a bathroom on the other side of the city, though.

I shake out my body and inhale a deep breath of the biting December air, then slide my key into the lock. I'm careful not to jostle the bouquet in my hand too much. God forbid the first time I give someone real flowers, they're all fucked up because I'm too nervous to stand still. I got her purple roses—her favorite flower, and her favorite color—and had the florist wrap them up in brown paper and twine, because Sierra has a picture of her mom holding a bunch of flowers from her dad wrapped like that. It's out of character for me, but I figured I owe my wife a little romance if I'm asking her to take a chance and date me.

Sierra isn't in the living room, so I call her name as I lock the door behind me. There's no answer, but I know she's home because her slippers aren't by the door. She's gotten so much better at putting her shit away that there are no shoes littering the entryway. I'm not the only one who's changed for the better here. She has to see that.

I stop by the bunnies on my way through the living

room, but they're too busy eating to pay attention to me. Sierra must have fed them early.

She's not in the bathroom, and her bedroom door is closed, so I knock before calling her name again. Nothing.

"Sierra?" I try again. "Are you okay?" Worry spreads through me. What if she's sick or hurt? "I'm coming in," I warn, before nudging the door open and stopping in my tracks.

Sierra's not in her room. And not much else is, either. The bed frame and mattress, the dresser, the nightstand, everything that was here when we moved in. All traces of Sierra are gone.

Except... My eyes land on the brown folder on the bed, and the flowers fall from my hand.

It's like someone else is moving my body, pushing me toward the bed until I'm staring directly down at the folder and the neon pink sticky note on top.

Congrats on the promotion.
I've signed everything on my side. You just need to sign your parts and drop them off. - S

That's it? Not even a goodbye?

I sink to the floor, legs shaking. I hug my knees to my chest, staring up at the ceiling, blinking back tears. How could I be so hopeful, so sure she'd seen what I've seen between us, just five minutes ago?

How the hell could I have been so naïve?

I thought the opposite of my foggy spells would be pure joy. I was wrong. Where they feel like a heavy cloud pressing on top of me, weighing me down, life after Sierra feels... hollow. Like my internal organs are doing the bare minimum, taking up as little space as possible inside me, because what's the point in functioning, anyway?

I've spent the past twenty-four hours lying in the bunny enclosure, after dragging a bunch of pillows and blankets in here. The couch and beds remind me too much of Sierra, and I'm well aware of how pathetic that makes me. But the bunnies are good company, and they've barely left my side since I clambered in. I like listening to their feet thudding against the rug as they hop about, their happy little crunches as they chomp away at their hay and greens.

Have they noticed Sierra isn't here? She told me that rabbits bonded so strongly they could die from broken hearts and, right now, I get it.

It's not just that Sierra's gone. I was prepared for that, as much as I could be, anyway. She made her plans to move out once she got her inheritance clear from day one, and I knew convincing her to give us a chance was a shot in the dark. But I don't understand how she could just... go.

Did I mean so little to her? There was no time to ask her to stay, no answers for closure. There's just nothing. I wish she'd just broken my heart instead of leaving it to linger in this hollow purgatory. I wish I'd said something when I first realized I had feelings for her. I wish, I wish, I wish.

I grab my phone and pull up her contact. She hasn't turned her location off yet, and I fell asleep clutching my phone, her little location dot blinking on my screen until the battery died. She stayed at a hotel last night, clearly so desperate to get away from me that she couldn't even wait to find an apartment. Her location dot didn't stray all day, but it's on the move now.

I watch as she walks into The Weather Vane, a bar near her office. I know she, Jazz, and Cal sometimes go there for lunch, or meet Maggie and Liam there after work, but it's Saturday.

Before I know what I'm doing, I'm peeling myself out of the nest I've built, throwing some food at the bunnies, and dressing in a hurry. I throw my hair back in a messy ponytail before jumping in my car and speeding downtown.

I park in the Michaelson and Hicks parking garage, using the key fob Cal gave me, and a few minutes later, I'm standing outside the door to The Weather Vane. I don't have a plan; I haven't considered what to say; I just need to talk to her.

Saturdays are busy in Downtown Seattle, so I don't see her when I first walk in. I hover by the bar until a bartender with bubblegum-pink hair spots me.

"Can I get you a drink?"

"Oh. Um, I'm just looking for someone, actually."

She tilts her head, squinting. "I know you. You're Jazz's sister, right?"

"I am," I say, frowning suspiciously. "Have we met?" I'm sure I've never seen this woman in my life.

"Oh, no. But when Jazz gets tipsy, she tells anyone

who'll listen about everyone she loves—with pictures. It's cute, actually. Besides, you have exactly the same eyes."

Huh. My heart thuds a little, the first sign of life I've felt in a while. "I'm looking for Sierra, who she usually comes in with?"

The bartender's eyes light up in recognition. "If you go around to the right, she's in the booth in the back corner."

I push away from the bar because if I wait too long, I'll lose my nerve, but the bartender keeps talking: "She's on a date. Total smoke show, if you ask me."

Every sound in the bar fades to nothing. All I can hear is the rushing of my own blood as it drains from my face. "She's on a date?"

Realization dawns on the bartender's face. "Oh god. Shit. I didn't... I had no idea. I'm so sorry."

"No, no, it's not... It's okay." It feels like someone else is talking. Like I'm outside of my body, watching as my heart shatters.

The bartender offers me a drink, and she offers to call Jazz for me when I decline, but I'm already halfway out of the door.

I collapse against the wall outside, breathing hard. She's on a date. She left me one day ago, and she's on a date. I can still feel the ghost of her fingers in my hair as she kissed me goodbye before work yesterday, and she's on a fucking date.

The stone wall is freezing against my back, and I suddenly realize I didn't bother with a jacket. I push off the wall and start back toward the parking garage. I don't want to go home, to the silence, and the reminders that Sierra doesn't live there anymore. The bunnies are amazing, but I don't want to spend the rest of the night scrolling through my phone with only them for company. Sierra stormed into my life, changed me until I didn't want to be on my own anymore, and then left.

With shaky fingers, I pull my phone from my pocket and pull up Jazz's contact info. She answers on the second ring.

"Hey. Did you know snails have teeth?"

The greeting is so unexpected, but so perfectly Jazz, that it draws a sound from my throat that might have been a laugh in another life. "What?"

"Yeah, like legit teeth. They can fully chomp things. And they're not as slow as people claim, you know. They make excellent pets."

"We are not getting a pet snail, darling," I hear Liam say in the background, and Jazz huffs.

"We'll see. Anyway, what's up?"

"Um." I have no idea what to say, but I don't have to. Jazz must hear that there's something wrong in that one syllable.

"Rosie? What's wrong? Talk to me."

I take a deep breath. "I don't want to get in the way of your night or anything, but if you're not busy, I was wondering if I could come over, maybe?"

"You're not getting in the way," she says quickly. "Where are you? We'll come pick you up." There's an edge to her voice I've never heard before, somewhere between panic and protectiveness.

"You don't have to do that. I have my car. I'm at your office parking garage."

"Why are you there? What's going on?"

Of course, Sierra wouldn't have told her what happened. We never discussed how to handle the subject of our relationship ending with our families. I thought we'd have time to do it before it was over, but she took that time away.

"When I got home from work yesterday, Sierra had moved out. And now she's on a date with someone else at The Weather Vane. It's over." My voice cracks into nothing on the last word, and I squeeze my car keys in my hand until the metal bites into my palm with a sharp pain.

"Shit. I'm so sorry. We've got you, okay? Just come on over. We've got you. You're not on your own." Her voice is soft, like she's talking to a frightened animal, trying to stop it from running.

But I'm so fucking tired of running from Jazz. From Xan, and the Michaelsons, and my colleagues, and everyone else who's tried to get close to me without success. Maybe if I'd been honest about my feelings for Sierra as soon as I realized them, none of this would have happened. Or maybe it would have, but it's been my choice to carry the weight of all my problems alone for the past twenty-six years. And I don't have it in me anymore.

CHAPTER THIRTY-SIX

Sierra

My camera roll is a shrine to Rose Cannon, and I have no idea how or when it happened. The pictures date back to the picnic, when I guess I must have snapped a picture or two because that's what spouses do, right? At first, the pictures are all from events like that, when other people were around and we were trying to sell a lie. But over the past month, I've taken multiple pictures of her daily. Candid pictures of her making coffee, laughing over a funny video with Liam's moms at family dinner, and scrolling through her laptop looking up LEGO sets since she enjoyed building the roses so much. And there are posed pictures, too. Cuddling the rabbits, looking over her shoulder at me in the shower, half-naked in my bed, with her hair fanned out around her on the pillow. There are thousands of them.

"Are you planning on torturing yourself by scrolling through your pictures all night?"

I jump and drop my phone on the table. "Shit, sorry. I'm not the best company tonight."

Lina reaches for my hand, covering it with her own. "I didn't come here expecting you to be all sunshine and rainbows, SiSi. I came because you're my sister, and no one should have to deal with a broken heart alone."

"I figured you'd be just as mad at me as Kyo."

Lina laughs, soft and melodic. "Oh, I'm plenty mad. But I also get it. And Kyo's a hypocrite, because he broke up with me twice when we were younger, because he was scared of his feelings. Not to mention how hard he fought his feelings for Rylan."

One thing no one prepared me for as a little sibling was how nice it would be once Kyo met someone. He and Lina first got together when they were seventeen, and she's been like my sister ever since. When they met Rylan a few years later, I gained a new brother, and even though I know they're all pissed at me, Lina jumped on a plane to Seattle as soon as Kyo told her what was going on, just in case I needed her. Rylan has sent me no less than twenty animal memes, and, after our call ended so badly, Kyo just texted me a simple *I love you, SiSi. I'm here for you, no matter what.*

My siblings, by blood or not, are worth their weight in gold. And so are Rose's. I hope she's leaning on them. I would've liked a little more time to be sure their day out wasn't a fluke, and she was actually going to let them in, but since when has time been known for its generosity?

"Are we going to talk about it?" Lina asks as I toy with the ring hanging from my neck. I can't take the collar off—I don't have the key, and I'm not willing to break it. So I took my ring off instead, then cried in my hotel room for hours.

But even though I don't deserve any part of the ring anymore, I couldn't separate myself from it completely, so I hung it from a chain like I did before anyone knew we were married. It looks fucking stupid on top of the collar, but my dark circles and bloodshot eyes look stupid too, so at least I'm consistent.

"There's nothing I want to do less than talk about it," I say, taking a swig of my watered-down soda. Alcohol would be preferable, but I can't be trusted with it right now.

My phone lights up on the table, vibrating as Jazz's grinning face smiles up at us. Shit.

"I take it back. I want to answer that less," I groan.

Lina slides the phone closer to me. "Answer it. You have to see her at work in a couple of days, so you have to talk to her."

She's right, but I don't like it. I grab the phone and answer the call. "Hi."

"What the fuck is wrong with you?"

I wince as Jazz shouts down the line. Oh, she's pissed. I knew she would be. I expected this, but it still fucking sucks.

"I can—" I don't get more than two words out before she's ranting.

"I can't believe you, Sierra. What the fuck? You walk out on my sister without so much as a goodbye, with no explanation, and now you're on a date with someone else. I know you have commitment issues, but this is on another level. How could you do this to Rose?"

I sigh, leaning my head on my hand. "It's more complicated than it seems, and—wait, what? What do you mean, I'm on a date with someone else?"

"At The Weather Vane."

How the hell does she know where I am? I bet it was the bartender with the pink hair. She and Jazz are friendly.

"I'm at The Weather Vane, but I'm not on a date. I'm with Lina. She flew up to Seattle to make sure I'm okay."

Jazz is quiet for a moment before saying, "Well, that doesn't change any of the rest of it. Two weeks ago, you were telling me Rose was depressed, and she needed support, and now you're walking out on her and leaving her literally alone. What if she'd hurt herself, Sierra?"

"Do you think I didn't think about that? Of course I did. I knew she wouldn't hurt herself while she had the bunnies to look after, and I was going to call you tomorrow morning and ask you to check on her. I would never do anything to put her in danger. You know that."

"I thought I did, but I never thought you'd do this either. What am I supposed to think?"

I release a shaky breath. "I don't know."

A frustrated growl sounds down the line. "I'm trying to be pissed at you, and you sound like a kicked puppy. You're making it really hard."

"I'm sorry, I guess? Look, Jazz, I know I did a shitty thing. I know I don't have any right to be sad when I pulled the plug. I promise, I get it. But I *am* sad. I know Rose is your sister, so you're on her side—as you should be—so it probably means we're not going to be friends anymore. And yeah, I'm sad about that too. But it is what it is. I knew all of that going into this, and now I'm living with the consequences. That's the choice I made." It all comes out like a stream of consciousness, and it would sound more convincing if my voice didn't crack.

"Hmm."

"What does that mean?"

"Whatever you're doing right now, you're reminding me of myself a little."

That's not what I expected her to say. "Uh, thank you. I think?"

"It wasn't a compliment," Jazz says with a pained laugh. "Fuck. What a mess. I have to go, but we'll talk on Monday. Are you okay? Relatively speaking."

What a loaded question. "I... I'll be fine."

"Is Lina staying with you?"

"Until Monday, yeah," I confirm.

"Good. I know things are complicated, and I can't lie, this puts me in a really shitty position, but if you do need me, I'm here, okay?"

Her being so nice is only making me feel worse. I swallow down the lump in my throat. "Yeah. Thank you."

I want to ask how Rose is, but Jazz is already saying goodbye. She didn't volunteer the information, and it's none of my business, but I think I'll spend the rest of my life wondering how Rose is. Thinking about Rose. Missing Rose.

Every second that passes since I signed those fucking papers, my hand shaking so much my signature was barely legible, feels longer. Every second without Rose in my life feels endless. This was my doing. This was my choice. And I hate it. I hate it, and I hate myself.

It was a mistake, all of it. The getting married, the staying married, the sex, the collar, the lies, the bunnies, the stumbling in love, the leaving. But the only part of it I regret is the leaving.

I regret it so fucking much.

"Why am I like this?" I ask, tears slipping down my cheeks. "Why can't I let myself get close to people? Every time, I willingly fuck it up. Who does that?"

"You're scared, SiSi," Lina says, brushing the tears from my cheeks. "That's all it is. You got hurt so badly once that your heart doesn't know the difference between risk and reward. It just sees the risk."

"I think… I think this hurts more. I think this hurts more than anything has ever hurt before," I admit, and Lina scoots closer so she can hug me.

"It's not too late to fix it."

Maybe it's not. Maybe if I called her up right now and apologized, Rose would take me back. In fact, I'm almost certain she would. Because Rose is inclined to make decisions that hurt her, and that's exactly what I did.

CHAPTER THIRTY-SEVEN

Rose

I t feels good to be back in the lab. Lisa has the day off today, so I'm getting stuck back into lab work instead of shadowing her. It's all hands on deck before we break for Christmas, and having something meticulous to focus on is exactly what I need. They're closing the whole building for a week over the holidays, and everyone is excitedly counting down the days.

Not me—a week off work right now sounds like hell— but I'm glad everyone else is excited. Tomorrow marks two weeks since Sierra walked out, and it doesn't hurt any less.

That's not to say time hasn't done anything. After a couple of days of crying, I forced myself to stop and really think about why she did it. It wasn't about me. I realize that now. She did have feelings for me, because that's the only thing that would scare her enough to make her leave like she did.

But realizing that doesn't make me miss her less, and it doesn't make it easier to sleep at night. All it does is make me worry about her, because if I know Sierra—and I do, even if she blindsided me last week—she's beating herself up about it. All it does is make me think of her more. I'm glad Lina flew up to be with her, and even more glad that she wasn't on a date like I thought.

I can't bring myself to stop wearing my ring. I rub my thumb across the cool metal as I cross the lab to get a new box of pipettes.

I'm halfway across the room, touching my ring, thinking of Sierra, when I hear it. A soft whistle, though I can't pinpoint exactly where it's coming from with all the chatter. I turn to Minah and frown.

"Can you hear—"

The whistling stops.

The room explodes.

I fly through the air. Everything is too loud and silent all at once. Heat licks at my body, smoke filling my mouth. Blinding, deep, excruciating pain ricochets down my left side. Sierra's face fills my mind, the memory of her soft smile, her twinkling laugh, her gentle touch…

And then, nothing.

CHAPTER THIRTY-EIGHT

Sierra

"Stop, Jazz. I'm not picking sides."

Jazz raises an eyebrow at Cal. "The fuck you're not. I'm on Rose's side, and as my father-in-law, you're obligated to also be on Rose's side. No offense," she adds, looking at me and shrugging.

"None taken," I say before shoving a forkful of lettuce in my mouth. Jazz has been a little frosty for the past two weeks, but not unprofessional. Not by our standards, anyway. I'm sure she wouldn't willingly choose to eat lunch with me, but the three of us have had a week full of meetings, and this is the first time we've had a chance to sit down together and review our to-do lists before we close for the holidays.

"I'm on both of your sides," Cal says, ever the diplomat.

"She left Rose without saying goodbye and only left a note!" Jazz protests, but Cal just chuckles.

"Yes, and Maggie did the same to me, remember? And let's not forget that you and Liam would've broken up if he hadn't refused to accept the breakup. Life has a way of working out and giving us the future we're supposed to have." He nods toward Jazz's tummy, where she rests her hand on her tiny bump.

I wish I had that kind of optimism, but right now, I'm just trying to get through the day, and not really thinking about the future. There's nothing worth looking forward to, anyway.

"I'm just saying, if it was—" Jazz stops speaking as the elevator door slides open and a harried-looking Maggie and Liam rush out.

"We've been trying to call you," Maggie says, panting.

Cal jumps to his feet, already halfway across the room to his wife. "We turned our phones off so we'd be productive. What's going on, love?"

"It's Rose," Liam answers, instead, looking between Jazz and me with an expression of dread. "There was an explosion at her lab. They called Xan. She's been rushed to the hospital."

I've never been religious, but I spent every second on the drive to the hospital wishing I had someone to pray to. Someone to beg to make sure Rose is okay.

Imogen met us here. Apparently, she tried to call me after the explosion, and when I didn't pick up, she remembered Xan's name and found him on Facebook. Thank god for his shitty privacy settings, because, for some unknown reason, Rose's employers still keep paper files, and they couldn't get into the building to check her emergency contact. It would've been hours until they'd tracked someone down.

Rose is okay. Better than expected, considering the size of the explosion. She has a broken arm, a concussion, and they're keeping an eye on her lungs because of the smoke, but it could've been so much worse, and she was the only one hurt badly enough for a trip to the ER.

"She was standing closest to the door when it happened," Imogen told us, her face stark with shock. "She should've been the first out, but she refused to leave until she got everyone else out. She was the last one in when the ceiling started coming down."

Thankfully, the firefighters arrived and pulled her out before it fully collapsed, but god... she could've died. She could've been crushed, all alone in the lab. The fact that she wasn't is a goddamn miracle.

"Can you two please stop pacing? Or at least pace together. The constant crossing back and forth is making me nauseous," Xan says with a groan, sitting back in his chair. "I fucking hate hospitals," he grumbles. He does look remarkably pale.

Jazz and I both pause our pacing and stare at each other. I look away first, sighing and dropping into a metal chair across the little waiting room from the rest of the Cannons and Michaelsons. I expect Jazz to take the empty seat beside Liam, but she sits beside me instead.

"She's okay," she says, sounding more like she's trying to reassure herself than me.

"She is," I confirm. "Are you okay?"

"I just need to see her. They'll let us in soon."

Us. I don't fit in here, with Rose's family, who love her and treat her well. Not her parents, mind you. I don't know who the hell called them, but I don't fit with everyone else.

"Who's here for Rose Cannon?" a doctor calls, and half the waiting room stands up: her siblings, parents, the Michaelsons, and a few of her colleagues. Me. The doctor looks just out of med school and seriously overwhelmed by how many people are watching him expectantly. "Um. I don't think you'll all fit, but I can take the family through now."

Rose's parents, Xan, and Jazz all start toward the doctor, but Jazz stops when she realizes I'm not following.

"You're not coming?"

I wring my hands. I want nothing more than to follow them, to push Rose's parents aside and see with my own two eyes that she's okay. But it's not my place. "I don't belong in there, Jazz. Not anymore."

Jazz crosses her arms and takes a deep breath. "Okay. We've all been dancing around this for months, and I'm not doing it anymore. I don't know why you and Rose decided to stay married. We all know it wasn't real, but it doesn't matter. That was then. This is now, and it is real. It's so fucking obvious, Sierra. And I trust you have your reasons for ending things like you did, but whatever reason you think is good enough to lose her over? It's not. I promise. So get your shit together before you lose her for good."

I stare, open-mouthed, at her. "What do you mean you knew it wasn't real? What was with you telling me you knew you could trust me because marriage was so important to me that I'd never do anything to mess with that?"

"I was trying to guilt trip you into quitting while you were ahead, or committing," she replies with a shrug. "Did it work?"

Did it ever. If it wasn't for her getting in my head, I probably wouldn't have gone to the bar that night, and I'd never have left because it felt wrong sleeping with someone who wasn't my wife. Rose and I wouldn't have hooked up, knocking our world off its axis.

"Clearly it didn't work well enough," I say, torn between being furious with her for trying to manipulate me and furious at myself because she saw right through me. They all saw right through me.

"Well, here's another guilt trip," Jazz says. "Rose could've died today thinking you didn't love her. And you would've had to live with that for the rest of your life."

"Jazz," Liam chides softly from his seat.

She holds her hands up. "Hey, once upon a time, I had to hear the hard truths, too. I'm just passing the baton."

She walks away before I can respond, and I fall back into my chair, closing my eyes and squeezing them tight so I don't cry. I hope none of Rose's colleagues heard that. If she lost her promotion after everything, I would never forgive myself. As it is, I don't think I'll ever forgive myself.

I shouldn't be here, but I can't bring myself to leave. I need to be close to her right now.

Maggie sits beside me and takes my hand. Her expression is softer than Jazz's. "Sixty-one days."

"What?" I ask, more confused than ever.

"Sixty-one days. That's how long Cal and I were apart after I walked out on him. And I know it might not seem like much in the grand scheme of a long relationship, but it's my biggest regret, Sierra." Her deep blue eyes are haunted. I didn't know Maggie and Cal then—Cal hired me after he and Maggie got back together, when she decided not to return to Michaelson and Hicks. It's hard to imagine them as anything less than happy together.

"Time is the most precious thing we have," she continues, and it's like I can hear all sixty-one days of regret in her voice. "And I know Rose is a good thirty years younger than Cal, so maybe it doesn't feel as pressing, but the explosion is just proof that there are no guarantees. Trust me, there is never enough time. I would burn the world to the ground to get those sixty-one days back. You have thirteen days you're going to regret for the rest of your life. Don't make it fourteen."

CHAPTER THIRTY-NINE

Rose

"Oh, my poor baby." My mom fluffs my pillow for the hundredth time since she stormed into my room, and I bite my tongue. I don't know who called my parents, but they're officially on my shit list.

My dad is pacing back and forth by the door with a face like thunder. "We're going to sue them, Rose. Just you wait. Cal can help us with that, right, Jazz?"

"We're not suing anyone," I interject before Jazz can respond. "It was an accident. They're paying my hospital bills, and I'm getting as much paid time off as I need to recover." Thank god, considering I'm not sure how I would work with one arm out of commission. I'm left-handed, at least, so I'm not totally useless with my right arm in the cast.

My head is pounding. It's somehow worse than the morning Sierra and I woke up hungover in Vegas. And with that thought, my heart is aching too.

"You okay, Rosie?" Unlike my parents, Xan keeps his voice low.

"Yeah. Just sore. Does Sierra know what happened?" I try not to ask. It's masochism at best, but I have to know.

"She knows," Jazz confirms. "She's here. I tried to convince her to come in, but she didn't think she should."

"Oh." I don't know if it's better or worse, knowing she's here. It means she still cares, but I knew that already.

"She was really worried about you, though," Xan says, like it's supposed to be reassuring. I don't want her to worry. I just want her.

"It's... It's all good, thanks. Did the doctor mention to any of you when I might get to go home? I need to be with the bunnies."

"Don't worry, Liam will check on the bunnies. They want to keep you overnight for observation, but, assuming you're doing okay, you'll be discharged tomorrow," Jazz tells me, and I breathe a sigh of relief. "You can't be on your own for a few days, though. You can stay with me and Liam."

"What? No, I can't. I need to be home with the bunnies." There's an irrational panic in my voice. I know Liam can be trusted with my babies—he's already a dog-dad, and he's about to be a human-dad—but they're all I have left.

"Okay, okay." Jazz holds up her hands. "I'll come and stay with you. It's all good, Rosie."

"Jazz! You can't be away from Liam in your current condition," my mom practically shouts.

"What the hell are you talking about? I'm pregnant, not dying."

My dad frowns at her. "Don't speak to your mother like that."

"I'll speak to her however—"

"Stop," Xan interjects, sounding almost as tired as I feel. "We're not going to fight over this. I'll stay with Rose. Jazz can stay home with Liam."

"You have an important presentation on Tuesday, Xan. You need to be focused," my dad chides, and both Xan and Jazz glare at him.

"Are you seriously implying that the presentation is more important than Rose?"

Oh, how I love to be fought over like I'm not even in the room.

My dad splutters, but he doesn't get the chance to defend himself before my mom cuts in.

"I'll stay with Rose. She's *my* baby, and I'll be taking care of her."

No one says anything for a moment, because my mom has never once taken care of us when we've been sick. And I would really rather she didn't start now.

I wrack my brain, looking for a way to turn her down gently. "Umm…"

"Actually, I'll be taking care of her. If it's okay with you."

My gaze jumps to the doorway, to Sierra standing there, and my heart races. Literally. The monitor beeps, and when I look up, my heart rate has jumped to 128. I draw in a deep, steadying breath to settle it.

Xan snorts. "Oh, I'm going to give you so much shit for that when you're better."

"Shut up."

My mom crosses her arms and glares at Sierra. "I'm not okay with that at all."

"I wasn't talking to you," Sierra replies, sounding genuinely confused why my mom thought she was. "I don't care what you think. I meant if it's okay with Rose."

She turns, and our eyes meet for the first time in two weeks. It's ridiculous how much better I instantly feel. Like the feeling of finally eating after the longest day, when you're starving and the first bite of food is the best thing you've ever tasted.

Sierra is as beautiful as ever, but she looks tired—weary. There are purple bruises and mascara smudges below her eyes, and her radiating sunshine I've become so accustomed to is gone.

The sensible thing would be to ask Sierra to look after the bunnies for a few days while I stay with Jazz. It's the perfect solution, absolving me of any worry for them, allowing Jazz to stay with Liam while she keeps an eye on me, and not prolonging the heartache between me and Sierra. Taking her up on her offer to take care of me, knowing she's probably just going to leave again, is the definition of a bad bet.

But Sierra and I are opposites in so many ways, including this one: I'm willing to risk getting hurt again, even if there's only a minute chance of things working out between us.

So I nod my head—ouch. "Thank you," I say, and try not to put too much stock in the look of relief that crosses Sierra's face.

"Perfect, it's settled," Jazz says, clapping her hands and immediately apologizing when I flinch at the noise. "Between us, this is probably for the best. He'll never admit it, but I think Liam's a little scared of your rabbits ever since the big one grabbed his wallet from his pocket and ran away with it, thinking it was food."

"And yet, you volunteered him to look after them," Xan says, rolling his eyes.

"It's Liam. We all know he would've volunteered himself if he was here instead of trying to give us *family time*. I bet he's hovering around outside, right?" Jazz asks, and Sierra nods.

"Yep."

"You know, that's a great point, Jazz. This is supposed to be *family time*," my dad says, with a pointed look at Sierra. Her face falls.

Absolutely fucking not. As far as I know, they don't even know we're not together anymore. They're probably blaming her for the fact that I haven't been speaking to them lately. But I won't sit by and pretend to be okay with my parents talking down to her.

"I'd like you to leave."

My mom gives Sierra a smug look, and I see red.

"Not Sierra. Mom, Dad—I don't know who called you, but I don't want you here, and I'm not going to let you talk to Sierra like that. All you ever do is make me feel like shit, and I'm usually better at hiding it, but I already feel like shit and—"

"Rose!" They both stare at me in horror.

"No. I'm not arguing. I want you to leave. And please

don't try to reach out to me. I'll be in touch when I'm ready to talk, *if* I'm ready to talk." Once I start, I can't seem to stop myself.

Everyone is silent. My parents and Xan look like I've shocked the hell out of them. Jazz looks impressed. I don't let myself look at Sierra for more than a second, but it's long enough to see that she looks proud.

My mom recovers first. "You don't get to kick us out and decide you're not talking to us. We're your parents, Rose."

"I'm an adult. I can do what I want, actually, and I'm tired of feeling like we've made some kind of progress as a family, just for you to slip back into your usual ways. Go. Please. Or I'll ask someone to escort you out."

Something in my tone must convince them I'm serious, because their chairs scrape as they get up to leave. I wince as the sound sends a sharp pain through my head.

"Shit, Rose," Jazz says, her eyebrows sky-high. "That was... Wow. Amazing. Seriously."

"Are you okay?" Xan asks, his voice softer.

I nod and instantly regret it. Fuck, I'm sore. "I'm fine. I just... God, it's been a day." It's been a week. Hell, a month. At some point, I'm going to have to deal with my parents. I have to decide if they have a place in my life, and, no matter what, I need to make sure Xan and Jazz aren't going anywhere. But not today.

"Of course. You must be exhausted. We'll leave you to sleep."

Jazz reaches over to squeeze my hand, and she and Xan head toward Sierra, who's still hovering in the doorway.

"I'd like Sierra to stay." I brace myself for the blow of her declining, but she doesn't. Her eyes widen, but something like relief flickers on her face.

"Of course." She walks slowly across the room and sits on the edge of the chair Xan was using, right by the bed. Up close, I can see more clearly how rough she looks. Her lips are bitten raw, her eyes bloodshot. She's still wearing her collar. *Fuck.*

"How are you feeling?"

What a loaded question. I know she probably means because of the explosion, but there's something in her expression that makes me think she's talking in general.

"I'm tired, and everything hurts, but I survived."

Sierra bites her lip. "Imogen said you refused to leave until you got everyone else out of the room."

I force my lips into a twisted smile that hurts more than it should. "No one can accuse me of not being a team player now. I definitely earned that promotion."

For all our differences, Sierra and I share the same sense of humor, so I expect at least a little laugh out of her, but horror crosses her face. "Is that why you did it? You risked your life to prove you're a team player?"

"No, no," I assure her, toying with how much to say. "When everything exploded, I blacked out, and when I woke up, I only had a split second to decide how to handle it. I looked around the room at my colleagues, and all I could think was that they were worth saving. I've spent so much time with everyone over the past few months that I know too much about them. And I actually like them." Turns out being social isn't so bad when my parents aren't in my ear telling me everyone is my competition.

"Minah and Annie just got engaged, and they're training a guide dog puppy. Parker's mom is in the hospital, so he's been taking care of his little brother. Angie just applied for her PhD. Joey has a newborn, and Karen, Harry, and Ken all have kids too. Imogen and Kai just booked a cruise for next summer. They're so excited about it. Maren's sewing business is taking off. They all have so much to live for."

The implication is clear, even if I don't say it: they do, I don't.

Sierra's face crumples, and I immediately regret saying anything when tears fill her eyes.

"*Rose*. You can't do that. You're worth saving. You have so much to live for. You're about to be an aunt, and your siblings are finally getting to spend time with you. They've always wanted that. The bunnies would miss you like crazy —we both know they like you more, even though I adopted them. And I…" She trails off, looking away and pressing her lips together like she's trying to physically stop herself from speaking.

"Please think about what we talked about and go to your doctor," she begs, her voice watery. "Your last thought before you might die shouldn't be that everyone else is worth saving more than you."

"That wasn't my last thought."

Sierra looks back at me, and her gaze falls to my hands. I look down, not realizing I'm absentmindedly rubbing the spot on my finger where my ring usually sits. It's become a habit, something to calm me when I need it. Even when I'm not wearing my ring, apparently. No one has told me yet how much I'm allowed to move my fingers on my broken arm, so I force myself to stop.

"I'll make an appointment for the new year," I promise, and Sierra releases a breath. "I'm still on the fence about medication, but therapy worked well for Maggie and Jazz, so I'm going to try it."

"Thank you. I'll go by the apartment and check on the bunnies, and I'll bring you some clean clothes and your contacts and stuff later," she promises, standing up and tugging her sweater down. For the first time, I notice a second chain on top of her collar. Whatever pendant is on the necklace is hidden below the neckline of her thick sweater.

"You don't have to come back all this way today."

"I know, but I'm going to. Is there anything else you want from the apartment? Your book?"

"It's a really heavy hardback, and I don't think I could focus on the tiny text." This is what I get for being a purist and refusing to get a Kindle, even though Jazz, Liam, and Xan all swear by them.

"I gave my keys to Jazz, so I'll get them from her and be back soon."

"Take my keys. They should be in that bag," I say, pointing to the plastic bag in the corner of the room. "They put everything I had on me in there."

She picks the bag up and sets it on the rolling table with her back to me as she rummages through it.

"Got the—" She goes still for a split second before clearing her throat. "Got them." She puts them into her pocket before turning around and placing my phone on the nightstand. I didn't even think to ask for it since I haven't been alone for a second since I got here.

"I'll be back soon. Text me if you need anything."

She's almost at the door when I call her name. Sierra stops and looks back at me.

"The key is in my nightstand drawer, so you can take it off," I say, gesturing toward her neck.

Sierra's hand flies to her throat, toying with the collar and the second chain. "I don't want to take it off," she says, fanning the little flame of hope I should know better than to get attached to.

CHAPTER FORTY

Sierra

My heart feels battered and bruised as I trudge up the stairs to our apartment—Rose's apartment. I could've taken the elevator, but it's the end of the workday and the chances of not running into one of our neighbors are slim to none.

Seeing Rose again was like a punch to the gut. I thought I missed her before, thought I craved her before, but now? I feel it all over me, from the tips of my toes to my stupid fucking brain that thought leaving was the best thing to do.

I should've been there to make her coffee this morning. I should've kissed her goodbye before work and told her I loved her, and I should've been in that hospital room the second I could. Time after time, I've failed her.

I know I have no right to be, but I'm so fucking proud of her for standing up to her parents. If she hates me forever because of how I treated her, it will have been worth it for that—that, and the fact she's going to start therapy.

For the most part, the apartment hasn't changed in the two weeks I've been gone, but there's a vase of dead purple roses on the kitchen island that stops me in my tracks. The leaves are crispy and curled, and there's a puddle of petals around the vase. I reach out to brush a leaf with my pinky, and it disintegrates. I have no idea what to make of them.

Near the bunny enclosure, a blowup mattress is sitting with a neat pile of blankets and pillows on top. Has she been sleeping out here?

When I let the bunnies out, they're more interested in me than food. "I'm sorry I left," I murmur, holding Dibbles to my chest while Thorne snuggles on my lap. "I've missed you—and your mama."

I can't tell Rose, so I tell them: how I know I fucked up, how I've hated myself every day since, how I don't know how to fix things. I tell them how scared I was, not knowing if Rose was okay, how much she loves them, how she'll be home to them soon. I think I'm trying to reassure myself more than them, and it works.

When they start sniffing around my hands and pockets, I feed them, leaving them to eat while I go in search of the book Rose is currently reading. I swung by the store and picked up a Kindle on my way here, but I need to know what to download. For as long as I've known her, she's sworn up and down she'd never switch to an eReader, but she's going to have a long recovery ahead of her, and being able to hold the Kindle in one hand, once she can read again, is going to make a difference.

I find her book on the bottom shelf of the coffee table, and head into the kitchen to grab scissors to open the Kindle. Rose is the second most organized person I know, besides Maggie, but scissors are the one thing that eludes her. We were never able to find them when we needed them. I pull open all the kitchen drawers and pause when I open the junk drawer and spot the brown folder sitting on top. Our divorce papers. She hasn't filed them.

Abandoning my search for the scissors, I pull the folder out and open it with shaking hands, flicking to the last page.

Petitioner: <u>Sierra Kimiko Hayashi</u>
Respondent: _____

She never signed them.

I clutch the papers to my chest and grab my car keys, heading for the door before I can second-guess myself.

It's been three and a half years since Cal hired me, and I still find the office creepy when no one else is around. I bypass the first-floor desks and head straight to the shredder at the back of the open-plan office.

Nothing happens when I press the power button once, twice, three times.

"Oh, come on." Sure, I could just go up to Cal's office and use the shredder there, or go to one of the two dozen other shredders in the building, but why would I do that when I could just kick this one and hope for the best? "Shit," I groan, holding my foot. Why the fuck is that so hard?

"What did that shredder ever do to you?"

I scream and spin around, the folder and all its papers flying out of my hand as I try to hold my heart in my chest. Jazz and Maggie are standing, staring at me with matching bemused expressions.

"Did you teleport in here? How the hell were you so quiet?"

"We really weren't that quiet," Maggie says with a shrug, walking up beside the shredder and crouching. She holds up the power cord. "Did you try plugging it in?"

"I did not," I grumble. "Thanks."

I kneel down and gather up the papers, which Jazz promptly plucks out of my hand.

"What are you shredding? Oh shit, these are divorce papers."

I nod, clearing my throat. "She never signed them. She's had them for two weeks and didn't sign them. And she was wearing her ring during the explosion. I found it with her stuff. That means something, right? That has to mean something." I couldn't believe it when I felt my fingers close around the cool metal of her ring. After I left like a complete asshole, I assumed she'd take it off the second she could.

"Sierra," Jazz says, sounding a little exasperated. "Yes, it means something. It's meant something for months. You're the only one who's convinced she doesn't want you." She passes me the papers. "Shred them."

I clutch them with trembling fingers. "But what if she changes her mind?"

"Then she changes her mind, and it hurts like hell,"

Maggie says, squeezing my shoulder. "But it already hurts like hell, right? So what have you got to lose?"

Well, when you put it like that.

I step forward and feed the papers into the shredder, one at a time. Jazz and Maggie stand behind me, not touching me, but I feel their support, anyway. I've gotten so used to not letting people in and figuring shit out alone that I don't think I realized how much easier it is when you share the burden.

I think back to Rose's fortune: *pain loses its potency when we share it with others.* At the time, it seemed like a message tailored just to her, but everything I've been encouraging her to do is something I could stand to take on board myself.

Open up. Let people in. Get help.

Medication only goes so far, and it's hypocritical of me to ask her to work on her mental health when I'm still stuck at sixteen, abandoned by my friends. She's not the only one who needs to speak to her doctor, and she's not the only one who needs to try therapy. I'm old enough to recognize that I still have a lot of growing up to do, and that starts with no longer avoiding dealing with the things that have left scars on me over the years.

I place the last page in the shredder and step back to watch my signature turn into thin ribbons of paper. Jazz and Maggie wrap their arms around me, and the first tear spills over. Within seconds, I'm sobbing in their arms.

"This wasn't supposed to happen," I say, my voice thick with tears. "I wasn't supposed to fall for her."

Jazz chuckles, but it's watery, and I look up to see her wiping her eyes. "Oh boy, do we know all about that."

"It's worth the risk. We promise," Maggie says. "We're not saying it's going to be easy, but it's going to be easier. Everything's easier when you're with the person you're meant to be with. And you have us, too. Both of you do."

I miss being a "both" with Rose more than I can put into words. "I have to fix this."

"Yeah, you do," Jazz confirms. "Come on, let's get you home so you can make a plan to win my sister back."

CHAPTER FORTY-ONE

Rose

The past thirty-six hours have been the longest of my life. Why do hospitals promise you'll be discharged "soon," then take an entire day to process shit? But Sierra is here, in our apartment—because it's still ours, even if she doesn't live here anymore—and everything feels a little easier.

It was almost 9 p.m. by the time we actually made it home. After the world's longest hospital discharge, all I wanted was greasy fast food, so Sierra drove straight from the hospital to get burritos and Mexican fries, and now I'm so ready for bed.

At some point, before picking me up, Sierra moved the blow-up mattress from the living room, and there's no sign of it. Which is just as well, because I really don't want to explain that I haven't been able to sleep in my bed or on the couch since she left, because they remind me of her.

"I put new sheets on your bed," she says as she carries my bag toward my room. "I thought it might be nice after the hospital sheets."

We haven't talked about her leaving, or the fact that I still haven't filed the divorce paperwork. I haven't even called the lawyer to set up an appointment yet, and I suppose I can probably weasel out of it for a while longer, considering I'm just out of the hospital and it's almost Christmas. That can be a next year problem. For now, I'm pretending it didn't happen. It can't be awkward if we don't address it at all.

I get ready in the bathroom before heading to my room, where I can hear Sierra pottering around.

I pause in the doorway. Someone—Sierra, presumably—has brought the armchair from the living room through and set it up so it's facing my bed directly. It's giving cuck chair.

"What's up with the chair?"

Sierra lifts the blankets on my bed and waits until I climb under them. I close my eyes, and a moan slips from my lips before I can stop it because the sheets feel so nice.

"The chair is so I can watch over you while you sleep."

I crack an eye. "You're going to sit in that all night and watch me sleep? Who are you—Santa?" She stares blankly at me until I elaborate. "He sees you when you're sleeping."

"I think our parents focused on different elements of Santa. But yes, I am. The doctor said I don't have to wake you, but I need to keep an eye through the night. Do you want the light on or off?"

I look between the chair and Sierra, who's waiting by my nightstand to turn the lamp off. "Sierra."

"What?"

"Just get in the bed. You're not sitting in a chair all night."

Sierra hesitates, but nods. "Light?"

"Off, please."

She clicks off the lamp and climbs in on the other side of the bed, keeping a foot between us. "Goodnight, Rose."

"Goodnight."

I close my eyes and try to quiet my mind, but I can't settle. Exhaustion is weighing me down, but every time I've tried to sleep since the explosion, I've been tormented by nightmares: the moment of impact, the choking smoke, the bone-deep panic that I can't get everyone out.

"You okay? You're restless," Sierra asks.

Even with my eyes closed, I can tell she's watching me.

I explain the nightmares, the words slurred with sleepiness, and Sierra shifts closer to me. She slings an arm over my middle, resting her hand on top of mine.

"Sleep, honey. I've got you," she murmurs, and her voice is the last thing I hear before I drift off.

I wake up eight hours later, without having a single nightmare.

It's amazing what a night of good sleep will do. On the one hand, I feel much better physically. My head hurts less, my arm is more annoying than painful, and the room has stopped spinning every time I move.

On the other hand, without the pain and discomfort to distract me, I'm all too aware of Sierra's presence.

She floats around the apartment, cleaning and tidying, bringing me water and snacks (and watching to make sure I eat and drink), and humming away to herself. I don't even think she realizes she's doing it. It's night and day to the gaunt, hollow Sierra who appeared in the doorway of my hospital room on Thursday.

I like it a lot. Love it, even. I want her to be happy and comfortable here. But it's also completely unnerving, because I have no idea what it means.

It could mean she's just happy I'm okay. Or it could mean she's happy to be home. Or it could mean she wants me back—wants me, period, since we were never technically together. Or it could mean nothing at all, and I'm going to end up heartbroken all over again when she leaves. It's all so fucking complicated. But she's here for now, and I've missed her too much to worry about what may or may not happen next.

I get up from the couch and stretch, rolling my shoulders.

"What's wrong? Do you need something? A snack? A drink? Pain killers?" Sierra is at my side in a flash.

"I'm okay," I reassure her. "I know I can't shower, but I was thinking I might have a sink bath and clean up a little."

"Do you want help?" she asks before I can even get all the words out.

"I think I'll manage, but I'll shout if I need you," I promise, and she steps back to let me pass, watching me like a hawk with every step I take toward the bathroom. The overprotectiveness should probably annoy me, but it's Sierra, so I like it.

I struggle through my sink bath, and I have to forgo most of my skincare routine, but I feel better when I smell less like a combination of smoke and the hospital. Putting on a bra one-handed is out of the question—why have I never invested in a front-closing bra?—but I manage to wriggle into one of the sweatshirts Sierra left behind. It's a navy tour crewneck, one of her favorites, and I've been living in it for the past couple of weeks. It's mostly lost the sweet scent of her, but maybe it'll reabsorb it while she's here.

My mirror is not my friend right now, somehow making every bruise and scratch look so much worse than they do when I see them through my own eyes. But I'm alive, and so is everyone else, and Sierra is here. What more could I ask for?

I rub my ring finger with my thumb. I feel so naked without my ring.

The bag they put my stuff in at the hospital is on my dresser. Sierra already took out my clothes, did the laundry, and has put it away. It's a little unnerving, but I tip the rest of it on the bed, rummaging through the sheer amount of shit I had in my pockets. Chapstick, several pens, packaging from lab equipment I hadn't gotten around to trashing, a five-dollar bill, my sunglasses... but no ring.

Panic rises in my chest. Oh god. Did it get lost? Did someone steal it? I'm going to be sick.

I rush back to the dresser, pushing aside pill bottles and information sheets the hospital gave me. My cast catches a candle and it crashes to the ground with a loud thud, the glass cracking into two big chunks.

"Fuck," I say, tears gathering in my eyes. I fall to my knees, my head spinning at the sudden movement, a moment before Sierra rushes in.

Her eyes widen as she spots me, and she instantly drops beside me. "Shit, what happened? Did you fall? Are you okay, honey?"

"I knocked the candle over. I'm sorry. I'm okay, I... I..." I can't get anything else out because I can't get any more oxygen into my lungs.

"Hey, hey. It's okay," Sierra murmurs, picking the candle up and reaching to put it back on the dresser. "Just breathe."

She helps me up as I try to force myself to breathe. My lungs are screaming, my throat is dry as hell, and my eyes are burning as I try to fight back the panicked tears desperate to fall.

Sierra cups my face, running her thumb gently across my cheekbone. "Talk to me, Rosie. What's going on?"

I finally inhale a big gulp of air, and tears spill down my cheeks as I croak, "I can't find my ring. I must have lost it in the explosion, or someone at the hospital took it, but I can't find it. It's gone."

"I have it. I'm sorry, I forgot to tell you. I saw it in your bag when I was getting the keys, and I didn't want it to get lost, so I took it."

The second the words leave Sierra's mouth, I feel my body slump. First in relief, then with exhaustion. I'm so fucking tired. My body is sore, my thoughts are muddled, and my heart doesn't feel like my own anymore. It hasn't felt like mine in a while.

Sierra must see it on my face because she tightens her grasp on me, and her eyes flood with emotion. "Rose—"

"You left me." I don't say it as much as sob it, the words falling out like I've been holding them in for years rather than weeks. I step out of her hold, wobbly on my feet. "I know that was always the plan, but you left without saying goodbye. I told you I wanted to talk, and you just *left*." My voice creeps higher and higher with every word, and I don't know how much she can understand as I cry harder.

She watches me, her mouth parted slightly, completely still. But now that I've started, I'm finding it hard to stop.

"You didn't even give me a chance to ask you to stay. And I know this is what we agreed, and maybe it's my fault for falling for you anyway, but you just left. You made me fucking fall for you and then you left!"

"You were going to ask me to stay? That's why you wanted to talk?" Sierra's voice is the opposite of mine, barely above a whisper.

"Yes. And I know that's not what we planned, but you could've said no. I could've handled it. That would've been better than coming home to an empty apartment and signed divorce papers." My voice cracks, and Sierra looks away, sucking in a breath.

"I'm sorry. I'm so fucking sorry, I should never... It was all too much, and I got scared. It's not an excuse, but I'm so sorry."

I can tell she means it, but her apology does nothing to repair the fissure between the two halves of my heart. But that's not her responsibility to fix, and it never was. This wasn't what we agreed.

Tears pour down my face as I look down at my feet. "I know you were scared. I figured that out. There was just a part of me that thought... that hoped I might be enough to be what you wanted. It's stupid, I know. It's not like this was ever real. I didn't sign the papers—I couldn't—but I will. You don't owe me anything, Sierra. I—"

"I shredded them."

It takes a second for her words to register, and my head snaps up. "What?"

Sierra's eyes are lined with silver. "The divorce papers. I found them when I got here on Thursday night, and I shredded them."

"Why?" I can't stop myself from asking.

"Sit down, Rose. You're shaking." She takes a step closer to me—close enough that I'm wrapped in her soft, comforting scent, but not so close that I can touch her. I hobble backward until I'm perched on the edge of the bed, pissed off at how weak my body feels.

She kneels in front of me. "I left like I did because I was scared. Because I thought there was nothing more terrifying than putting myself out there and telling you how I felt, in case you said no and left me. So I left first, and I know how selfish that makes me.

"But there was something more terrifying. Two things, actually. First, finding out you were involved in an accident and not knowing if you were okay. And second, imagining the rest of my life without you." She draws in a shaky breath. "You have more power over me than anyone else ever has, you know. You could ruin me, Rose. I care more about you than I've ever cared about anything before, and you could destroy me. And god, what a privilege that is. How lucky am I to feel so strongly about you? You are *more* than enough. My leaving wasn't about you, okay? Tell me you know that. I need you to know it wasn't your fault."

I nod one singular, jerky nod. "It wasn't your fault, either. Not really. You have every reason to be scared."

"No, not like that." Sierra shakes her head, a single tear falling down her cheek. "I've spent the past month pushing you to open up and work on yourself, and I didn't give you the respect of doing the same. How I ended things was unforgivable. But I'm going to be a total asshole and ask you to forgive me anyway."

I open my mouth to tell her I've already forgiven her— that I'm still a little mad, but I understand more than anyone how the pain left behind by people treating us poorly causes us to lash out. It's why we work so well—we don't flinch in the face of each other's scars. We saw each other's flaws before anything else.

But Sierra sits back on her knees and unhooks the second chain from around her neck, pulling it out from the neckline of her shirt, and the words catch in my throat when I see both of our rings dangling from the dainty chain. She slides both into her palm and sets her ring and the chain beside me on the bed, but doesn't give me mine back.

She holds it between her thumb and finger and looks up at me. "Rosie. Honey."

My heart damn near stops. "What are you doing?"

"What I should've done weeks ago, instead of running

scared, because I didn't know what I'd do if you didn't want me."

"Sierra, I—"

"No, hear me out. I fucked up here. I ran away, and I'll regret it every day for the rest of my life. I'm so sorry." She takes a deep breath. "I love you, Rose. I love you so much. And I wish I could say it was love at first sight, or that I could pinpoint the exact moment I realized that the most frustrating thing about you is the complete and utter choke-hold you have on me. But I can't. And I'm okay with that. I'm more than okay with that, because the only thing I'd change about us is me walking out two weeks ago."

I swear the room would be spinning if I could see anything beyond Sierra. It's like, with three words, she stitches up the parts of me that have been falling apart for far longer than the two weeks she's been gone. *She loves me.*

"Sierra," I breathe, a smile taking over my face. "I love you, too. And I forgive you."

She holds the ring up to me with shaking hands. I can see how scared she is, but she squares her shoulders. "Marry me, Rosie. Stay married to me. For real this time. We can have a big wedding, or just something small with our fami-lies, but I want to stand up in front of everyone who loves you and promise them, promise you, that I'm going to love you forever. I'm going to take care of you forever."

It's amazing to think that a few months ago, the thought of being tied to Sierra forever was incomprehensible. Now, the thought of anything else is.

"If I say yes, if we're doing this, you don't get to run

again. Not without me. We run away together, or not at all. If I say yes, I'm keeping you."

Sierra nods, wiping tears from her face. "Please keep me. Please let me keep you."

I have to turn my whole body to pick up her ring since it's on my right side, but I finally close my fingers around it and slide off the bed onto my knees before her.

"Sierra. *Wife*."

She releases a watery chuckle, and I cup her face, brushing away her tears.

"I can't promise no one is going to hurt you again. I can't promise you that no one will leave. People will come and go, and sometimes it's going to hurt like hell. But I can promise you that I'm not going anywhere. I'm not going to leave you. We're both going to do better, we're going to get better, and we're going to stay."

"Yeah?" Hope lights her face, and it just might be the most beautiful thing I've ever seen.

"Yeah. Of course I'll stay married to you. It's you and me. Well, and the bunnies."

"I've missed the three of you so much," she says, her face falling a little.

I reach for her hand, sliding her ring onto her finger. "We've missed you, too. But you're home now. We're all home now."

"I'm with you, honey," she says, sliding my ring on my finger. "Of course I'm home."

EPILOGUE

Rose

Sierra groans into my mouth, and I swallow down the sound. Our tongues dance together, fast and unrelenting, and she tastes like chocolate and the room service espresso martini she ordered in lieu of coffee this morning. I ordered a salted caramel latte with Irish cream liqueur, because, although we're not planning to be blackout drunk this time, it only makes sense to have a little buzz to pay homage to the last time we were here.

I drag my lips down Sierra's body, pushing the top of her robe off so she's naked except for her collar and her ring. I'll never get used to the sight of her. I'm as obsessed with her body as I was the first time I saw a sliver of her waist when we first moved in together.

She cries out as I circle her nipple with my tongue, sinking her fingers into my hair.

"We don't have time for this, honey," she whimpers, but she makes no effort to move.

"I can be quick."

"Since when?"

Valid. "They're not going to start without us," I say between licks, and Sierra thrusts her head back into the pillows. "We have time."

"You forget that I know you. You're going to say we have time, get me off, then rush me to get ready so we're not late—oh, fuck."

I nudge her legs apart and press my thigh between them until she's squirming. As if by instinct, she bucks her hips, grinding against my thigh.

She's not wrong. That's exactly what I'm going to do.

"Rosie," she groans. "No fair. I want to play, too."

I make a show of sighing as I rise up over her, tossing my hair over my shoulder. I'm going to regret fucking it up when I need to make it presentable.

"How do you want me, wife?"

Sierra's pupils flood her eyes as I hover above her. She licks her lips, and I chuckle. Message received.

I turn around so I can straddle her face with my back to the headboard. Sierra doesn't even wait for me to settle before she pulls my hips down and runs the flat of her tongue over my clit.

The instant zip of pleasure propels me forward. I lean over and press my middle finger inside her while I take her clit between my lips. Sierra moans against me, and I almost fall apart, but I close my eyes, forcing myself to hold out a little longer.

Making Sierra come is my favorite thing in the world, followed closely by coming at the same time as her. And it feels right today to soar together.

I massage her G-spot with my finger, alternating

between sucking her clit and blowing, until she's twisting in the sheets. She grips my ass so hard that it hurts a little, and the pain just drives me closer and closer to the edge.

My hips move of their own accord, so I'm practically fucking her face, and she meets every grind of my pussy with a stroke of her tongue.

I press a second finger inside her, and she gasps, tightening around me. Over the past few months, I've learned her body by heart, and I know she's close when her legs start to shake. I increase the pressure of my fingers, she pulls me harder against her mouth, and we tumble into bliss together.

She closes her thighs around my head as she comes, but neither of us slows down as we coax each other through it. I would happily stay here, my head trapped between her legs, getting her off again and again, and I'm seriously considering it when an alarm blares.

I sigh and pull my fingers out of Sierra. It's never enough.

Dismounting her face, I lick every drop of her from my fingers as I jump up off the bed and cross the room to turn my alarm off. As soon as I've turned it off, a pillow hits my back.

I turn around, raising an eyebrow at my wife. "What was that for?"

"You liar. You said we had time, but you set an alarm."

"We had time, didn't we?" I crawl up the bed between her thighs and lean in to kiss her. "You requested an hour to get ready, and you have an hour and fifteen minutes. You're welcome."

She tries to glare, but she can't stop smiling enough to do it. "You better let me up to get ready, then. I think showing up to the chapel soaking wet after your wife rode your face is probably frowned upon."

"At the very least, Jazz would kill you," I say, smacking her ass as she gets up.

She shivers. "It's so easy to get on her bad side right now, and I have no interest in making it easier."

Jazz is due in a couple of months, and the closer she's gotten to giving birth to our niece, the more... tense she's become. She just about tolerates people, and she made one of Cal's oldest clients cry a couple of weeks ago. Thankfully, it was a client he didn't like.

We offered to hold off on our vow renewal until after the baby was here, but Jazz has been so excited about this trip that we're forging ahead.

I didn't know how serious Sierra was when she mentioned another wedding, but within an hour of us putting our rings back on, she already had Pinterest open. We weighed the pros and cons of a bigger wedding in Seattle and traveling farther afield for something smaller. We even talked about flying somewhere warm, but decided to stay within driving distance to make things easier for Jazz.

Once we got the idea of returning to Vegas, we couldn't shake it. It just felt like the right place for a do-over—one that we'll remember this time.

We're keeping it small, but it didn't feel right to do it alone this time, considering we wouldn't be here without the people who care about us nudging us in the right direction. Jazz, Liam, Maggie, Cal, Liam's moms, Xan, Kami, and her daughter, Lexi —but not her husband, because they're finally over—Sierra's parents, Kyo, Lina, and Rylan. For the first time in my life, I have a family that lifts me up and supports me unconditionally.

My parents aren't here. I wanted to want them here, but I'm not ready to let them back in yet. Maybe one day I will be, but, as my therapist says, I'm not healing for them. I'm healing for myself, and that means taking things at my own pace. Xan and Jazz have been nothing but respectful of my decision, and we get closer every day.

Like me, Jazz has distanced herself from our parents, not willing to let them stress her with the baby coming so soon. Xan still works with our dad, but he's no longer trying to cling to whatever relationship they had.

The three of us are talking—about the good memories and the bad, the things we never said growing up, and the things we wished we'd done differently. Slowly but surely, we're unpacking the collective trauma of being Alexander and Lilia Cannon's children. Together.

The past few months have involved a lot of work and a lot of healing. Sierra and I both started therapy, and I started medication. It didn't work overnight, but we're both doing better than we were. We've started making more friends, hanging out with Imogen, Minah, and a few others from the lab, and we have a joint therapy session once a month just to give us a chance to talk anything out that we need a little extra help with.

We still fight, and we argue constantly, but it always

ends with us falling asleep in each other's arms—never mad, because I refuse to end up like my parents.

"Are you going to get ready, or just watch me?" Sierra asks, peeking over her shoulder from her seat in front of the mirror as she blends her foundation.

"Shh, I'm trying to watch my favorite show."

Sierra's face lights up like sunshine as she laughs, and it sounds a whole lot like forever.

Sierra

I thought we might remember at least some of the chapel when we came back, but nope. The night Rose and I got married is as much of a blur as it was the morning after.

"You know, we chose pretty well, considering how drunk we were," Rose says, clinging to my hand and looking over the room as the doors open and the music swells. We opted to walk down the aisle together, because neither of us really buys into the being given away thing. We already belong to each other, heart and soul.

The room is gorgeous, with high arched ceilings, and floaty purple curtains lining the walls. At the end of the aisle, there's a giant violet heart with twinkling bulbs that some might consider tacky, but I love it. It's the same heart from the background of our original wedding picture, and I can't wait to hang our new one beside it at home.

There are flowers everywhere, but that was our addition.

Rose's, actually. She planned to surprise me, but stressed herself out so much about picking the right kinds of flowers that she broke down and asked me what I wanted—roses, of course, but she got every other flower from my list of favorites to line the aisle, and there's a spread of petals under our feet as we stand by the officiant.

I may not remember anything about our original wedding, but I know for a fact I didn't feel like I do now. I've never been happier, never felt so fulfilled as I am with Rose. There'll always be a part of me waiting for her to wake up one day and realize she could be with anyone she wanted, but I know her. Even if she did wake up and think that, she wouldn't go anywhere, because she has who she wants. And somehow, that's me.

Standing facing each other, holding hands, the room might as well be empty for all I care. It's just me and Rose, and nothing else matters.

We take a joint deep breath as the officiant clears her throat.

"Dearly beloved, we are gathered here today…"

Thank you for reading Dearly Unbeloved!

I hope you enjoyed Rose and Sierra's love story. If you did, please consider leaving a review and sharing Dearly Unbeloved wherever you like to talk about books!

The next book in the Spicy in Seattle series will be Kami and Xan's book! Sign up for my newsletter and follow along on socials to be kept up to date!

The Spicy Stuff

If you should, for whatever reason, wish to revisit *just* the spicy moments... you'll find no judgment here! But you will find the spicy scenes here:

- Chapter Fifteen
- Chapter Sixteen
- Chapter Twenty-one
- Chapter Twenty-two
- Chapter Thirty
- Chapter Thirty-three
- Epilogue

Enjoy!

Acknowledgments

It's been almost two years since I published my first book, and I've been so lucky to meet and work with so many incredible people on the five (!!!) books I've released (so far!)

First, as always, thank you to my husband Kyle, my sweet Pumpkin, and my best friend Claire for putting up with me while I was writing Dearly Unbeloved. There were less tears this time!!!

Thank you to my amazing PA Danie for all your support. Thank you Katie at Between The Covers Editorial, and Meghan Monarch for your amazing editing and proofreading skills. Thank you to Zo for being an amazing sensitivity reader, Dominique Davis for helping me with the dreaded blurb, and to Ellie at Love Notes PR for helping me get Dearly Unbeloved out in the world. And a huge thank you to Emily Shacklette, all of the amazing people in the Book Marketing by Courtney Discord server for being so lovely and supportive, always.

I'm so grateful for my amazing Street Team—Abigail, Aimee, Allie, Ashley, Caitlin, Charlie, Claire, Danie, Demi, Elena, Hayley, Jenna. Jessica, Karina, Kate, Lil, Molly, Rebecca, Sarah, Sophie D., and Sophie L. I appreciate you all so much!

I was lucky enough to work with some amazing beta

readers for Dearly Unbeloved—Allie, Claire, Danie, Effy, Emily, Erin, Katelyn, Paige, Parker, Rae, and Tiffany. Thank you all so much!

And lastly, to every reader who has taken a chance on me and my books over the past couple of years—thank you. Thanks to you, I'm getting to do the thing I love most in the world. I love you all so much.

Love,
Sophie

Sophie Snow lives in Scotland with her husband and cat, Pumpkin (who she loves dearly, even if he does bite.)

She writes spicy romance books with messy, queer characters and too many Taylor Swift references to count. She has been in love with love stories for as long as she can remember, and writing them as songs and novels since she was twelve.

A forest fairy in a past life, Sophie loves spending time in nature, drinking too much coffee, and trying out more hobbies than she can keep up with.

You can find more from Sophie by visiting her website at www.sophiesnowbooks.com, or scanning this QR code: